Demon Holiday
Torval, Demon Third Class, Layer Four Hundred Twelve of the Eighth
Circle of Hell, has been in the business of chastising sinners longer than he
can remember. Delivering punishment is the only job he's ever known—the
only job he's ever wanted. After Torval witnesses something unexpected,
his demonic Overseer demands that he take time off to resolve this personal
crisis. And so, Torval, the demon, finds himself sent on vacation...to Earth,
the proving ground of souls!

Demon Ascendant
Torval, Demon Third Class, Layer Four Hundred Twelve of the Eighth
Circle of Hell, on vacation to Earth has managed to find another demon,
dated a woman and inadvertently explored some of the sins of humankind:
greed, gluttony, and lust. Through all this, his biggest struggle involves
deciding if he wants his holiday to end or to continue forever.

TANSTAAFL Press
1201 E. Yelm Ave,
Suite 400-199
Yelm, WA 98697

Visit us at www.TANSTAAFLPress.com

Toy Reservations

First printing TANSTAAFL Press
Copyright © 2016 by Thomas Gondolfi
Cover art: Tony Foti, www.tonyfotiart.com

Printed in the United States
ISBN 978-1-938124-36-5

Book layout by Hydra House

Novels by Tom Gondolfi
from TANSTAAFL Press

An Eighty Percent Solution – CorpGov Chronicles: Book One
In a world where corporations suborn governments as a part of good business practice and unregistered humans can be killed without penalty, Tony Sammis, a midlevel corporate functionary, finds himself unwittingly a pawn in a guerilla war between a powerful cabal of business leaders and an elusive but deadly underground movement. His final solution to the biological terror unleashed mirrors Tony's own twisted sense of justice.

Thinking Outside the Box – CorpGov Chronicles: Book Two
Winning one war doesn't seem to be enough. Tony Sammis and the Green Action Militia are once again thrust into the center of a conflict that will change the lives of everyone in the solar system. This time they are allies with the fledgling CorpGov and even the United States government against the ravages of the corrupt Metropolitan Police force. The GAM and their allies are fighting a losing war with few soldiers and even fewer weapons. Behind the scenes, a humble and unsuspected power block lurks with its own axe to grind.
Self-interest, romance, freedom, and a lust for power simmer together in this chaotic soup of tension, intrigue, assassination, and war.

The Bleeding Edge – CorpGov Chronicles: Book Three
Tony Sammis and Nanogate lead a patchwork alliance that includes the nascent CorpGov, Green Action Militia, the president of the United States, the Pacific Northwest Mob, most of the megacorps and the United Brotherhood of Bodyguards. The war the CorpGov alliance knows they can't win has begun, but they are no longer fighting to win. Tony and Nanogate know they may not survive, but they intend to deliver the most grievous wounds they can. The most dangerous animal is one with no hope.

Toy Wars
Flung to a remote world, a semi-sentient group of robotic mining factories arrive with their programming hashed. They can only create animated toys instead of normal mining and fighting machines. One of these factories, pushed to the edge of extinction by the fratricidal conflict, attempts a desperate gamble. Infusing one of its toys with the power of sentience begins the quest of a 2-meter-tall purple teddy bear and his pink polka-dotted elephant companion. They must cross an alien world to find and enlist the aid of mortal enemies to end the genocide before Toy Wars claims their family—all while asking the immortal question, "Why am I?"

Novels by Stephanie Weippert
from TANSTAAFL Press

Sweet Secrets

At seven, Michael gets into trouble no more than any other boy his age but he does have a sweet tooth. When the mailman brings a package from a candy company, he has to sneak just one. As he eats the chocolate, his home, stepfather, and everything he'd known melts around him and disappears. Next thing he knows he is in a dreamlike world. He is taken as an orphan, tested, and before he knows it is a student in the premier magic school on the planet. His fellow students can make cookies that fly and chocolate turtles that actually walk. Michael is told he has more power than any of them.

Brad is charged with watching his stepson Michael for first time. When the boy disappears before his eyes, Brad panics. Within hours he is on an adventure tracking his son alongside an enigmatic chef. Always one step behind his son, Brad soon finds that Michael is being used as a pawn between the two most powerful chefs on the crazy planet. Worse he has to get Michael home before his Mother finds out he's gone or there is going to be hell to pay.

Novels by Bruce Graw
from TANSTAAFL Press

The Faerie of Central Park

The last of her kind in New York City, Tillianita tends the land and beasts as best she can, reluctantly obeying her departed father's warning to avoid humans at all costs. A freak accident casts her out of the relative safety of Central Park. Lost and alone with a broken wing, she wonders if she'll ever see her home again.

On his own for the first time in his life, college freshman, Dave Thompson, isn't sure he'll ever fit in. When he stumbles upon an extremely realistic fairy doll, he thinks perhaps it might make a good present for a future date until he discovers that it's not a doll at all. His find turns not only his life upside down but also expands his narrow view of the world.

Lady Hornet

Elizabeth Fontaine is a lonely, ordinary young woman in a world where superheroes struggle daily against evil. To fill the empty void within her soul, she becomes a hero fangirl, following every super's event, subscribing to multiple fanzines, and never missing the daily superhero talk shows... until one day, fate grants her the opportunity to leave behind her boring, dreary life and become what she's always dreamed of...a superheroine!

Elizabeth learns the hard way the meaning of the phrase, "Caveat Emptor!" — let the buyer beware!

Toy Reservations

Thomas Gondolfi

TANSTAAFL PRESS

To Sabrina—For being my BEST sister . . .
OK, my only sister but for still being the best!

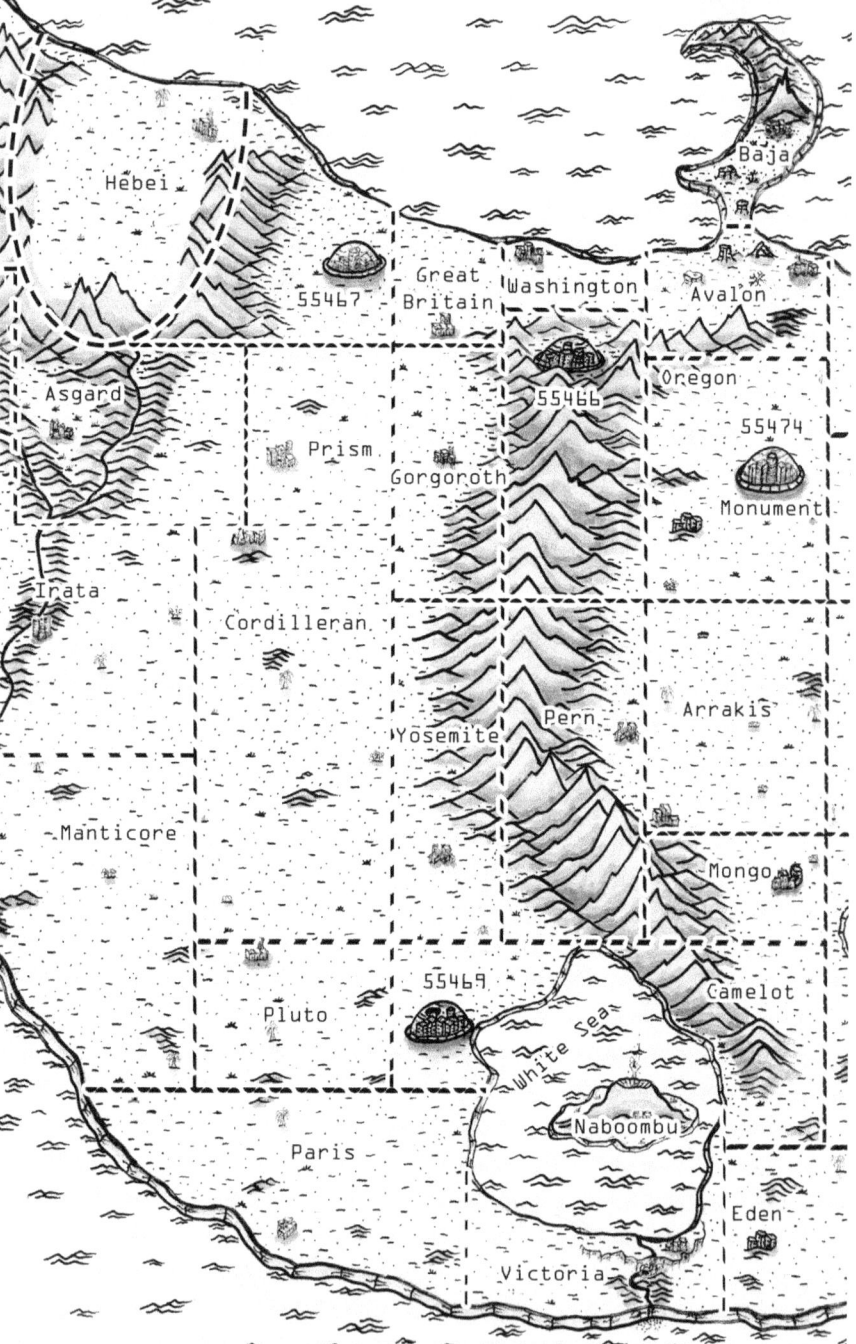

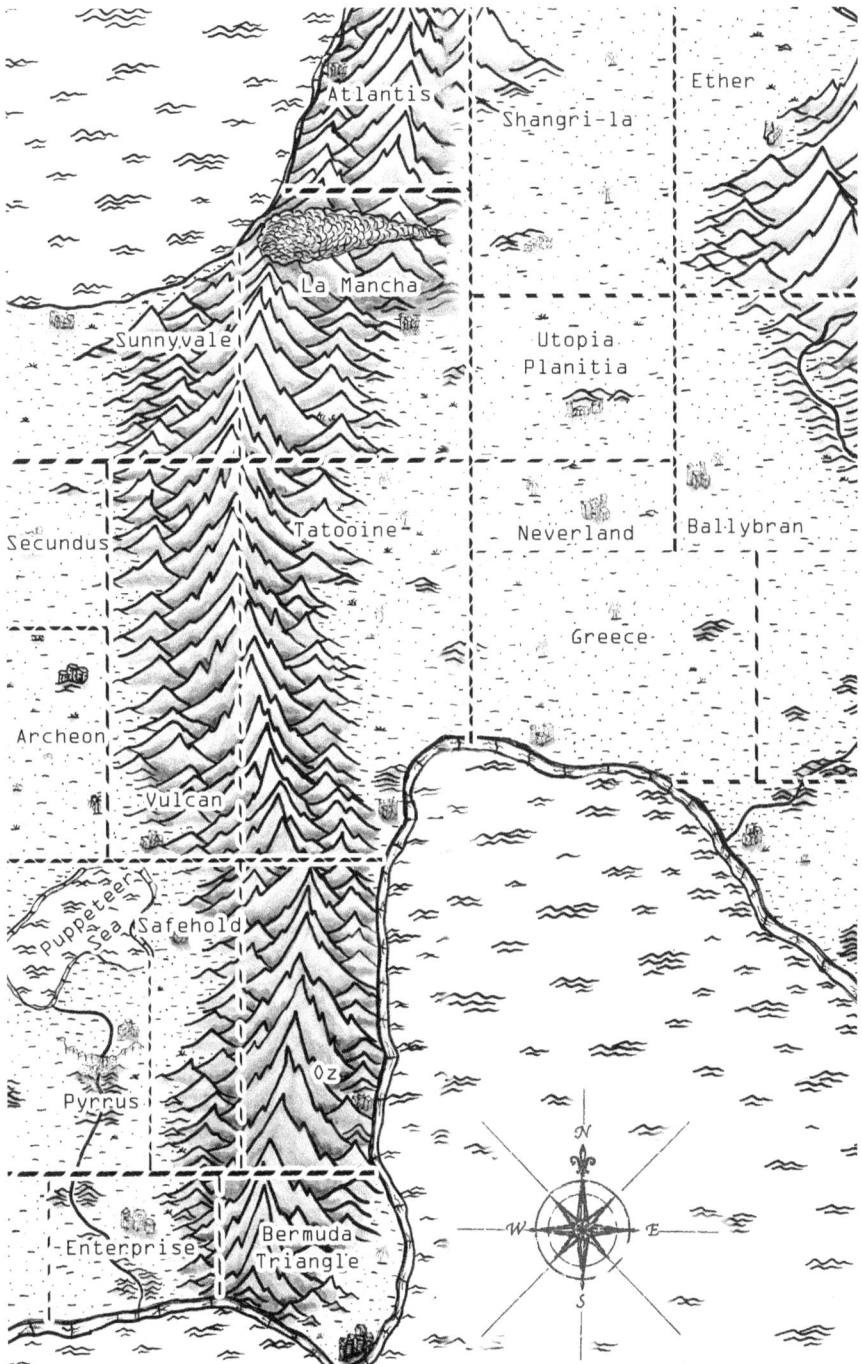

Introduction

Excerpts from the Third Chronicler's Notes

One of the significant landmarks of the early days of the Sol Unified System's expansion into the depths of space, sometime in the human calendar's twenty-second century, was an amusing event: the first creation of a truly new life form. While new life is not a humorous occurrence, the process that created this life was more like the punch line to a joke.

Homo sapiens were making use of faster than light (FTL) vehicles, and their civilization expanded at a tremendous rate compared to earlier efforts. Some twenty years later they created a drive that was over an order of magnitude faster (FT2L). There was only one snag in the new design—organic materials were destroyed in such a transit.

Humans more interested in profit than right hatched a new use for the drive. A semi-intelligent Factory would be sent via an FT2L ship to extremely far worlds, where it would autonomously produce robots to control and strip the planet's surface of its mineral wealth before transporting it back in the shell of the original vessel. This became known euphemistically as "Project Infuse."

The humans' Supreme Council debated this at some length, creating a new political split—Expansionists vs. the Naturalists. The Expansionists, the greed faction of human nature, outnumbered the Naturalists by nearly two to one.

The Naturalists objected that this plan might inadvertently send one of these strip miners to an inhabited world, causing death and destruction and sending a horrific message about our species. The Expansionists yelled the objection down. They claimed that any truly sentient and intelligent race would be able to handle such an incursion, and if they couldn't the worlds the Council controlled wouldn't have to worry about them.

The might-makes-right debate raged for seventeen years before the Expansionists overcame the last injunction and court battle. The Supreme Council decreed that Project Infuse (PI) would start immediately.

PI outfitted three hundred obsolete FTL space vessels with the FT2L drive and partnered with something known only as a "Factory." The resulting conglomerate was the first grouping of Project Infuse's vessels. Physically, each Factory, a dome-shaped cap fit to the peak of each FT2L ship, lacked an impressive appearance. It was what they could do that made them remarkable.

Factories possessed the construction facilities and mental power to create a workforce of robot slaves. A huge array of programmers gifted the PI Factories with semi-sentience. The only real goals these programmers gave the Factories boiled down to "conquer, rape, and pillage."

With this less than moral context guiding them, the Factory-cum-FT2L vessels were flung to the exceedingly far reaches of space to strip-mine entire planets.

The above are facts that are incontrovertible. This was information placed into the Factories' memories and even on physically etched data plates mounted on the Factories themselves. The remainder of this story is reasoned speculation based on analysis of a great number of corrupted files within the Factories' memories. They contain a surprising amount of information on the events that preceded the launch of Factories 55466, 55467, 55468, 55469, 55471, and 55474. They also contain the punch line to our joke.

A preadolescent computer hacker, Janeen Fox (AKA Foxhunt), in an initiation rite, broke into PI's vaunted and supposedly impervious databases. Janeen's intent contained no malevolence and no intent to cause harm. Breaking the imperviousness of PI was her goal, not the contents of its files. Once inside, she caused no intentional damage and did nothing save adding her nom d'hac to several files. Her full access lasted less than ten minutes before PI's belated system defenses rushed to close down the unauthorized access.

Project Infuse's ice crashed about her open portal with such violence and severity that Janeen broke the connection without standard withdrawal procedures. No newbie to hacking, she had long ago learned to hide the tracks of her work by bouncing through several other computer links. In this case her last link was through an old-fashioned toy and book store. Because of the abrupt termination of her intrusion, several large files translated from one end of the link to the other. It scrambled a number of crucial launch and post-launch parameters. These parameters remained until a standard morning adaptive CRC check caught the errors on the following day, too late to save the ill-fated PI vessels prepared for launch that very afternoon.

The following are more facts, based on actual data from the Factories' memory cores. PI was then launching upward of a dozen FT2L space vessels each day. On the date of Janeen's fateful link, only six Factory/vessels were planned for launch. Each of them contained the faulty parameter files—files which contained two very important changes.

The first change involved all the ships navigational target being changed to the same planet, the third planet of HD34085, also known as Beta Orionis, or simply Rigel, something that had never happened in the history of the PI program.

Factories 55466, 55467, 55468, 55469, 55471, and 55474 launched on schedule. The humans heard nothing of any of these six PI vessels again. They were written off as a loss.

Factory 55468 lost its way in FT2L and exited near enough a black hole that it could only manage an unstable orbit that eventually decayed with the predictable results. The remaining five each set down so close to T+3y340d12h16m46s (three years, three hundred forty days, twelve hours, sixteen minutes, and forty-six seconds post-launch) as to be unnoteworthy. Each landed uneventfully on Rigel-3, but it was the beginning of the most ferocious competition known to nearly any world.

Rigel-3 was a hellish world, or would be to any humans—too cold by at least two dozen degrees Celsius, and had a corrosive atmosphere and a gravity 30 percent higher than that of earth. Through its rivers flowed liquid mercury down to the gleaming metallic lakes and seas. On the plus side, Rigel-3 proved itself to be rich in heavy minerals of all kinds, gemstones, and huge amounts of oil and other petroleum products. As the physical conditions were no hardship to the Factories, it was an ideal habitat to collect for the humans. The five took hold immediately and looked to fulfill their mission, each oblivious of the other simultaneous landings.

The Factories immediately discovered a serious problem and the second corruption that had started the day before their launch—the plans to their robots had been destroyed or corrupted. In place of this crucial data was the production files of toys—not that the Factories knew what a toy was. But these plans didn't follow the standard parameters for mining or control type robots. These new forms also proved to be totally unsuitable to the environment. Most of the new forms didn't even have motile functions. The Factories had to adapt, but being semi-sentient and well-programmed for independent thought, this didn't pose, for most, an insurmountable problem.

The Factories took the portions of the robot data that had not been corrupted and merged them with the new intrusive toy data. As most of the toys were flexible in capability, it mostly worked.

Only 55471 failed to make the imaginative leap and continued producing only non-motile stuffed bunny rabbits until it ran out of raw materials, power, and then a will to continue. It self-destructed its personal memory core.

All the other Factories were already producing robots. But here divergence set in. Each Factory took a different solution to its individual problems producing different sizes, shapes, and capabilities into different toy shapes. The solutions were varied and adapted to the terrain and ease of material availability. The Factories created transport systems. Some made them in the form of a large-gauge toy railroad, but at least one had a fleet of remote-controlled racecars and trucks. For survey/scouting vehicles, most went the way of gasoline-powered toy planes or helicopters. Factory 55466 used multicolored balloons filled with helium carrying disposable payloads.

The real diversity, though, lay in the choice of control, or warrior, units—small toy tanks with real explosive projectile weapons; slightly scaled up plastic infantry men carrying real weapons; kamikaze bomb-carrying, dress-up dolls; teddy bears with machine guns; and even giraffe snipers.

It has to be stressed that these initial units were crude and possessed no initiative at all. If a unit lost contact with its Factory it would continue doing what it had been ordered to do until it lost that ability as well. At this stage of evolution the Factories were each one entity with multiple disposable bodies to control—similar to an ant colony.

Initially there was little need for the combat units, and very few were built, as there was little nearby local fauna to require such a force. This changed abruptly as the first warriors of the now four Factories began meeting each other and fighting for control of the planet. The first such clash began when 55466's tracked tanks met the baby-doll infantry of 55474 at L+320d14h (three hundred twenty days, fourteen hours after landing). Both sides annihilated each other in an inconclusive battle. The other two Factories similarly clashed within days. Now each of the Factories knew the native life forms fought back quite successfully.

Each of the Factories adapted. They changed priorities, rolling hundreds of tanks, baby-doll infantrymen, scout planes, and other military weapons off their production lines. The Toy Wars had truly begun.

Factories began to notice that they would have many units destroyed just by losing contact. Several networks arose to deal with this unacceptable situation. The nets, an all-purpose control system that carried power, instructions, and requests for information, grew rapidly along transportation lanes. The multiple nets were segregated into two forms, the WAN, or wide area net, and the LAN, or local area net.

Each Factory generated a WAN on a very powerful carrier wave. The WAN flowed through immobile devices called net concentrators (NCs) that rebroadcast information or commands to far units. The WAN also acted as the primary source of power for almost all units.

Local control units similar to the NCs generated the LAN that gave specific commands to each of the robots. These LANs dealt mainly with local issues, such as quickly identifying friend and foe. The LAN didn't bother or interfere with the WAN in any way. These networks helped but continued to be insufficient.

As soon as the first clash started, Darwinian selection set in. The Factories experimented with different designs based on the plans they were able to produce. Each make and model underwent field experience, sometimes within mere hours of activation being thrown into a nearby combat to be immolated or exploded.

Each of the Factories tried special permutations to bring better units to the battlegrounds—built-in cannons, flame throwers, kamikaze scout planes with explosive payloads (the first crude missile on Rigel-3), and even mobile walking bombs in the shape of dress-up dolls. A number of them worked well, but most failed miserably. A classic example of a failed design came from 55467: a flame-thrower built around the outward form of a purple stuffed elephant. The fur ignited before the unit even got off the prototyping line. It took most of 55467's fire suppression units to quell the stuffed elephant's exploding fuel cells.

Using probability studies, each Factory learned quickly which of their units fared well in combat, in what terrain, and under which conditions. Those units that didn't make the cut in the field were firmly snubbed from production. Toy Wars shaped quickly into a battle of statistical mathematics rather than strictly the destruction of fur, metal, and machines.

Over ten years, the conflicts escalated. Each of the Factories, again backed by rigorous mathematics, determined that a larger initial military expenditure would bring the local fauna under control that much sooner and thus would save resources in the long run. The impeccable logic fell flat because the "local fauna" it fought didn't breed. Factories produced an ever-increasing panoply of war materials escalating the conflict to greater heights. Competition became even more intensely fierce.

Of all the Factories that still remained, 55466 (known as Six), had the most difficulty. Its initial location was not as rich in minerals and resources, nor as easily defensible as the other three viable Factories. Six was slowly losing ground to the local fauna, and its calculations showed that in less than two years' time its outer defenses would crumble. The local fauna would run rampant, denying it control of the planet. It would have failed its primary mission.

Six made a huge gamble to put a larger quantity of material and effort into researching better robots. Soon Six began fielding units with semi-autonomous functionality. Even if those units lost control, they could make decisions that would allow them to continue to function. Thus was born the third net, the SAN, or specific area network.

The SAN was developed by the autonomous robots as a net that allowed units to converse directly to one another. This happened as the level of self-directing capabilities grew in each robot. They began to work as a team.

Six certainly could measure the success of these units. Within five months, Six's boundaries firmed and started expanding. The other three Factories learned how effective these autonomous fauna were and began shaping their productions to do similar things.

Shortly, Six found its boundaries tightening again. It was time for another desperate chance. It used some of the local unclassified metals to produce an all-purpose control robot, with the highest level of self-direction it could construct and filled with the most information it would accept.

The chain of events that started with Janeen Fox and the Expansionist coalition had now come to fruition—but in a way neither had ever expected. True sentience and intelligence had been achieved.

Let there be life; and it was fuzzy.

The early and heroic life of Teddy 1499, or as he was later known, Don Quixote, is well documented. In those chaotic years of his youth he discovered what the Factories themselves hadn't, that they were fighting their own kind. The most difficult task he accomplished was to convince the Factories, a notoriously stubborn group, that they could mutually achieve their objectives and thus eliminate the need for war.

Upon reaching home to finalize the truce, Don found that his own sentience had spread, giving rise to a cult of personality. Isp, a mentally deficient, held the entire population under his demagoguery sway of Human worship. The Factory that had spawned them had become the devil incarnate. After a bloodless coup, Don Quixote banished Isp and his few dedicated followers.

All the remaining sentient toys held up Don Quixote, their father in both spirit and reality, to be their leader. The Toy Wars had ended, but not the trouble they faced.

Politician

"Of course each race has a different absolute value!" said Frank Lloyd Wright, my minister of census. The brown-and-black mottled gopher could barely get his whiskered nose over the top of my desk. "It can be measured and quantified! Mr. President Don Quixote, we have to put further limits on procreation—"

"Hhhhhere we go again," Jason Argonaut, the furry python and minister of mining and industry said, curling into a tight ball on my desk.

Lewis Tappan, a giraffe that towered over everyone at 304 centimeters, retorted, "But you are missing the point. A being's value can't be quantified."

"Human-lovers, if it can't," the gopher Wright countered. "Do you want to say that a Tammy dress-up doll, with a suicide rate of over 95 percent, is the same as a . . . a . . . Nurse Nan?"

Being shot, being expected to make the lives of every unit perfect—anyone that wanted to be president needed to have his or her memory sump examined and declared a mental defective, I thought. I didn't mean that in a facetious way. Since I'd allowed my people to bully me into becoming president for life, I'd had my sump and processor checked at regular intervals over the last nine years, three hundred fifty-three days. Despite my misgivings, my personal Nurse Nan consistently pronounced me sane.

"They each have their own contributions, some measurable and some not," the giraffe said, twisting his neck around and down to look the gopher in the face.

"Do we hhhave to lissssten to thissss ssssssame old wheeze?"

To my great surprise, Martin Luther, my chief of staff and a black-and-yellow spider, sat silently with his eight legs tucked under his body, keeping his height down from its normal 3 meters. That height had once saved my life as he'd jumped on top of me to take a falling girder on his back rather than have it crush my skull. It cost him three weeks of repair time. I visited him in the shop several times. Our conversations showed that our views matched on so many topics. What started as gratitude bloomed into friendship. Now he spent his time protecting me politically instead of physically. As a result he watched the discussion but didn't interject commentary.

"It's because of those damned units that won't listen to science," the gopher said, waiving his stubby arms in derision.

"Science?" Lewis Tappan interjected in its low register voice. "Bah! It deals only with the most basic physical elements. It doesn't even begin to talk about the metaphysical aspects—"

"SHUT UP!" I bellowed slamming my great paws, one purple and one white, down on the desk. Its boxwood creaked under the force of my hydraulic tantrum. Everyone froze. I suspect it had to do with the fact that I rarely lost my temper, a trait shared by most teddies. Come to think of it I couldn't remember the last time I yelled about anything.

I tried to lower my hydraulic pressure by looking out the windows of the Oval Office. I watched the sun cresting the One Hundred Eight Hills, named for those I'd let die discovering there were multiple Factories on this planet. The crimson light shined down on the mass of toyanity that carpeted the western faces of the Valley of Six waiting for the life-giving rays. Scorpions vied for space with teddies who snuggled up to Nurse Nans who shared with bouncing balls and even fabric dolls. Ninety-six different species of toys all looked to me, a humble 2-meter teddy bear, as some Human able to solve any problem that might present itself.

The stovepipe hat that balanced between my purple ears chose that moment to shift forward and annoy me. The black hat had started as an affectation—something I could do to make myself feel a bit different from all the other teddies. Instead, the toys of my world imbued the hat as the symbol of the presidency itself. Now they expected me to wear it. I had no one to blame but myself. I took the hat off my head and put it on the corner of the desk.

For ten years, less twelve days, we'd had no physical war on the Toy Planet, sometimes still called Rigel-3. Instead, now I fought wars of legislation that ranged from approved sunning locations to monetary policy. Instead of a gun I used a pen. Often the paper threatened to break over all my defenses and massacre me.

"I'm sorry, Mr. President, but the Congress has agreed. They are sending the completed Procreation Limitation Law for your—" Frank started.

"Mr. President, if you sign that law then we will have even more racism in citizens picking only what they consider to be the best offspring. We already are seeing a severe reduction in birdies and elephants," Charlene Darwin, a Nurse Nan second only in height to the giraffe, said, eyeing my bodyguard.

Sancho, a pink and purple polka-dotted elephant had rarely left my side in the eleven years, eighteen days, thirteen hours, and some number of increasing minutes since I activated him. He assumed a self-appointed post as my lead bodyguard. His zeal created multiple incidents where he'd damaged beings when they only appeared to pose a threat. On the plus side his well-known fervor did keep me from being mobbed everywhere I went.

"We are seeing serious declines in all of the war machines. Balloons are effectively extinct with less than twenty in existence," Charlene continued.

"When any toy can only have one offspring they want it to be what they consider to be the best. We are already seeing an explosion of gophers, teddies, penguins, and Nurse Nans."

Charlene, clad in her white uniform with the bright red plus, brought up the SAN, Specific Area Network, to show a real-time feed of the procreation queue leading up to Factory 55466's massive dome. Pairs of toys, or the occasional single parent, lined up as they had for the better part of ten years, talking and sharing among one another the choices they'd made for their breeding. The image zoomed in on audience chamber just as a paired penguin and model car went in together.

"Number of parents?" said an automated voice.

"`Two,`" the penguin and car said together.

"`Model of offspring?`"

"`We'd like to create a teddy bear, please,`" they said in unison.

"See? What did I say? Teddies are on a rise," Charlene said from her plump, almost-human face.

"That's just one pairing," Frank retorted, gnashing his buck teeth.

The SAN image showed the manufacturing door opening to slide out a white 2-meter-tall teddy bear with dark green stripes across its torso. It remained motionless in the middle of the room. No one knew why units no longer came with preprogrammed information. Once they'd been able to march out ready to defend their Factories. Now they manufactured as nearly blank slates, needing to be taught all but the most basic skills.

"`Are you ready?`" the penguin asked its partner.

"`Yes—I want this,`" the car replied.

The car waited patiently as the penguin opened up its vivid red hood. Then the black-and-white creature stuck a long needle into a bulbous area near the auto's firewall drawing out 10 milliliters of amber brain fluid into the syringe. The penguin waddled over to the immobile teddy. It's flippers pawed through the white fur before finding the sump access. With slow deliberation it shoved the same hypodermic into the head of the teddy, squeezing the viscous teddium-laced fluid into the bear.

"`Recording activation on L+25y11d17h4m32s,`" the newly sentient teddy said in a quiet voice. "`Hello, Fathers. What is my mission?`"

"`Time to go home now,`" the penguin said, taking the bear's white paw.

As the trio left Six's dome, the car went off in one direction, its job done in impregnating the child with sentience, while the penguin led the child off to be raised, to learn how to be a toy. I think had I been a Human that I would have cried with joy. I had no tear ducts. Instead, my voltage dropped gently down to a low power state. Things were right on Toy World, if not in my office.

"And you want to stop that!" Charlene said, bending down to look at Frank, eye to eye. And my voltages surged back up. So much for my small bit of happiness.

"Not 'stop it.' We never wanted to stop breeding. We just need to limit it so we don't overrun our resources.

"Mr. President, I have to insist that you discuss this new law with the Factories," gopher Wright continued.

"Oh, moonshines, Wright," Lewis Tappan said with a snort. "Even you know the Factories haven't said word one since the drone strings were launched. The prevailing—"

"I'm sorry, folks, but what part of 'shut up' did you not understand?" I said firmly. I worked hard to force the dangerous edge from my voice. All my voltages were green but my hydraulic pressures really ramped up with anger. "Sancho, I want you to shoot out the speech centers of the next unit that makes a sound or a net request."

The sound of the safeties of the dual independent machine pistols mounted in Sancho's chest echoed in the silence of the Oval Office. Six, my original manufacturing Factory, had replaced Sancho's chest mortar with weapons more conducive to bodyguard work. The cabinet knew that Sancho ignored personal rank and took direction only from me. If even my chief of staff were to open his mouth he wouldn't talk again until he'd had his speaking apparatus replaced.

"Much better," I said after several dozen rotations of my hydraulic pump in blissful quiet. "You folks, along with the Fellowship of Human Worship, the Lobby for Racial Purity, the United First Brotherhood, and the National Organization of Equality, have filled my sump with all of the consequences of signing or vetoing this particular bit of legislation. Sometimes I don't think I've ever heard of anything else.

"We are going to play a little game. It's called 'Don't ever bring it up again.' Am I quite clear?" I rocked my head up and down in an exaggerated motion.

The rest of the heads, excepting Sancho's, nodded in time with mine.

"Very nice. OK. Now, what is the next order of business?"

No one spoke up, but Frank Wright pointed his tiny, brown finger at Sancho.

"Sorry about that. Sancho, I retract my order to shoot. Please stand down."

"Ferweet," Sancho said, in a tone I took for disappointed. He didn't care for some of those in the room and would have been pleased for the opportunity to teach one or more of them a lesson.

Keeping his eyes on Sancho, Frank said, "Thank you, sir. I have a petition by the Fellowship of Human Worship for the release of Isp and all of his followers."

I rolled my eyes. "Is this the Human Cult's seventeenth such petition?"

"Eighteenth, actually, Mr. President," Charlene Darwin corrected.

"OK. What legal fiction have they invented this time?" I asked, wishing this would just go away like mercury rivers carrying away unwanted wastes.

"They are challenging the constitutionality of your presidential order to banish them. The Human lovers are claiming the Constitution provides for the complete equality of all units with no exceptions."

"Poppycock," I said.

"Excussssse me, sssssssir?" Jason the python asked.

"A word I'm reinvigorating in our language. It means preposterous."

"Then why not sssssssay prepossssssterousssss?"

"This is more inventive and makes the unit question themselves," I said as I gave positive body language.

"Sir, the Human Cultists have at least a prima facie claim," Lewis offered.

I looked at the watch I wore around my neck on a chain, another of my anachronisms. I could have the time anytime I wanted it just by querying the WAN, Wide Area Network. "And I still have a very real M16 I can put into their prima facie claim." I could see that I was about to be interrupted so I held up my paw. "But as it has come through official channels, I'll give it due consideration."

"Thank you, sir," the gopher said.

"You are thanking me?"

"Well, personally, I think all those Human lovers should be melted to slag but thank you for at least listening to the issues I bring to you," Wright said.

"Except procreation?" I jibed.

"I don't know what you are talking about, Mr. President," the gopher Wright responded.

I managed a chuckle.

A light tap at the outer door was followed quickly by a lime-green and blue teddy walking through the doorway.

"Indira," I called out. "Please come in. Is it that time already?"

"Yes, sir," my brightly colored, number two bodyguard said. He turned to Sancho. "I relieve you."

"Ferweet," Sancho said, walking out the door. Sancho preferred the night shift so he could bask his rotund belly in real red sunlight, not the full spectrum of artificial lights.

"So is there any further business this morning?"

"The Peace Day celebration five days from now?" Martin Luther offered from the middle of the rug pointing one of his eight spindly legs in emphasis.

"Go ahead."

"Nine years ago you authorized de-weaponizing all non-military units on the planet. It just so happens we are ready to complete that with the very last civilian unit, sir."

"That is great!"

"We thought it would make a nice backdrop to have that displayed behind you as you give your speech, Mr. President." Nods around the room punctuated my chief of staff's comment.

"Where?" I asked just wanting to get this over. I had an appointment soon and hadn't made the key decision. I wanted time to think it over but knew these vultures would take up every millisecond I let them have.

"We thought in front of the 55474 monument. We thought it fitting that we have it on the site of the last battle of the war, sir," Martin continued.

"Anything else I need to know?"

"Did you want us to work up a speech for you, Mr. President?"

"Nope. I'll take it. Now, if there is no more business?"

As they left, I soaked up power from the WAN. With no one clamoring for my attention I realized that for the first time in years the Oval Office lay silent. Oh, I wasn't alone. A copy of the Procreation Limitation Law stared at me from my desk. My bodyguard Indira waited for me to make another decision that would affect 6,346,803 units and uncountable yet unborn offspring. No matter how long I looked at the paper, it didn't change, nor did my sump come up with a clearer decision.

I only had three choices. Let the PLL continue and become law without my approval, which would pave the way for a potential repeal at some future time. I could sign it and make it ironclad for all time, or veto it and open up the option of an override.

I sometimes wished for easier choices.

The door opened to admit my aide, Rodney Dangerfield, a roadrunner with the biggest eyes I'd ever seen. "Beep-beep," he said aloud, followed immediately with, "`Sir, it is time for you to leave for your appointment,`" over the LAN, Local Area Network.

No, I thought, *there weren't going to be any easy decisions today.* "Yes, Rodney. Thank you. Are you ready, Indira?"

"Yes, sir," she said. I caught "`Jefe is moving,`" over my bodyguard's SAN, Specific Area Network.

We walked across the White House's western lawn. The Secret

Service kept the normal protesters to the east side of the building. No one begrudged me my direct path to one of our Factories. Six hadn't spoken in nearly a decade except in automatic responses to requests for offspring. The stone walkway from door to door was a nice, if unnecessary, touch.

The procreation queue stretched off to my right as I approached Six's audience chamber. Police held back the throng as they watched me jump the line and headed right into my creator's presence.

Indira tried to follow me in, but I stopped her. "I'm safe in here. Wait for me."

"Yes, Mr. President." She arranged herself to guard the door itself.

Walking into the 6-meter open dome intimidated me more than facing a horde of unit devouring basilisks or dozens of Procreation Limitation Laws.

"Number of parents?" came Six's voice.

"One."

"It is highly recommended that a different parent from the donor raise the unit in question. Confirm one parent."

"Confirmed. One parent only."

"Model of offspring?"

I hesitated. I didn't know. This was my fourth attempt to choose my offspring.

Many would argue that the entire toy race were my children. All sentience had originated from the material in my brain known as teddium. But this was different. I would raise this unit. Share with it not just my brain fluid but teach it everything it would need to make it in our world.

Should I create another teddy, another me? I knew what it meant to be a teddy. Or was Lewis Tappan correct and I should ask to raise one of the toys that weren't popular to show my support for diversification? But what did I have to offer a balloon? I knew nothing of floating on the winds. There was much to be said for the intelligence and skills of a Nurse Nan, the grit and determination of a dump truck, the single-mindedness of a dragon, the artistic streak of a toy piano, the beauty of a unicorn, or even the enthusiasm of a toy car.

I had to get it right the first time. I felt in my processor that there wouldn't be a second unit. Not from me. Procreation Limitation Law or not, I wouldn't create more than one toy. "Which one?" I said aloud. "Six, help me."

Undaunted I'd charged into machinegun fire and fought a basilisk with my bare hands. I'd never had my voltage streaking upward so fast. The chamber seemed to close upon me, not centimeters at a time but meters. *Would it crush me?*

I bolted out the doorway with a speed that surprised even me.

A cheer rang out from the people waiting. My processor couldn't decide if it was because I was done and they could get in, that I'd chosen not to create an offspring, or that they were just happy to see me. None of that mattered. I needed to get away.

"Back to the office, sir?" Indira asked tactfully, not asking about my state, departure, or that I was alone.

"Yes," I said, grabbing onto any suggestion that would get me away from that room—that room where my reason failed to come to a decision about what toy to create.

I maintained at least a modicum of dignity. I didn't sprint to the White House. I walked—fast. Every step away from that place eased my voltage and made me walk all that much quicker.

Once I got back to my office, I took the time to look at my paws in the full spectrum light. One paw was brilliant white and the other deep purple. I spent too many years out in nature having my fur cast in the pleasant burnt cinnamon colors of our sun. Now those brilliant colors blurred as my limbs shook. I brought down the remaining overvoltage manually. I knew there was nothing to be afraid of, but that didn't seem to make a difference to my body that acted more like a newly manufactured child.

My aide came in through the open door saying, "Beep-beep." Rodney followed over our SAN, "You have the Secretary of—"

I interrupted with, "Cancel all of my appointments this afternoon, Rodney."

"Beep-beep. Sir?"

"You heard me, Rodney. Everything. I won't see anyone else today."

"Should I reschedule your appointment with Six?"

Without the ability to change my facial expression, I think my glare was lost on my aide. "No, thank you." I rethought my answer and followed up abruptly with, "Not right now."

I flopped down in my chair. Why did such a simple decision panic me so? *Because it isn't simple!* my mind screamed. Some unit that wasn't quite here yet counted on me to make the right choice, to do the right thing, to make it the best it could be.

Now even the oval rooms of my office seemed like they were closing upon me. In desperation I grabbed at the first thing that ran across my processor. "Indira, I'm in need of a dose of real sunshine."

"Sir, could I interest you in the White House's patio garden?" said my assault-rifle-wielding bodyguard.

I let my mind release its burdens and fall into my standard banter with my staff. "How often have I let you talk me into that over the last ten years?"

"Not enough times, sir."

"Zero times, Indira. Zero."

"And I might remind you, sir, that you have been shot how many times?"

Low blow, I thought but didn't let it affect my body language. "I think it is time for some exercise."

"Should I remind you of your duties here—"

"That can wait. I need to clear my head before making a decision that could affect all living units on this planet."

"Yes, sir. You do understand how dangerous it is for you to travel out there without careful screening? At least on the White House grounds we can limit your exposure."

"I know how you feel, my friend, but if I can't walk freely among my people then maybe they should remove me from the presidency, terminally."

"They have tried four times, sir."

"Those religious zealots of the Human Cult have been caught and refurbished."

Indira just looked at me with that blank unit stare.

"Now you are going to tell me I make it too easy for the Human Worshippers to move in and out of the reservation."

"I wouldn't presume, sir. I only have to deal with the consequences."

Sometimes I wondered if it were worth the debate I had to go through to get out of my office. It always ended exactly the same way. A mutual examination of statistics and dangers that lasted thirty-seven point three minutes, with a standard deviation of four point six minutes, before telling them finally and firmly what I was going to do. The collapsing walls prompted me to take a shortcut. "I don't care, Indira. Wake up whomever you feel you need because in forty-six seconds I'm walking out that door."

"Can I at least get you to use the Presidential Train? The tracks are constantly swept for trouble."

"No, Indira. Now you have thirty-seven seconds. By the way, we are heading for a climb."

"Yes, sir," she said with her ears drooping in disapproval. "`Jefe is moving. The word is El Capitan`," her voice called over the net, containing none of the judgmental tones her body language held.

While I waited for the bodyguards to form, I looked out the Oval Office window toward the east to see the units' protests outside. Banners claiming "Keep diversity!" "Why do good parents suffer?" "Keep life free" "There should never be only ONE!" and the ever popular, "Humans say, 'No imprisonment!'"

Studies showed fully 85.8 percent of all toys believed in the Humans as our gods and the creators of everything. The Fellowship of Human Worship, the most militant and radical of the Humanists, wasn't more than 0.3 percent by population but their placards and speakers were heard anyplace they thought they could draw attention. They even regularly clogged up entire WAN frequencies with their propaganda before being shut out by local traffic managers.

I understood the desire for everything to have a meaning. I could even empathize with the desire to let someone else make the hard decisions for us. What I couldn't wrap my head around was the desire to make everything either forbidden or compulsory. *Why have free will in that case? Why not just be automatons? Surely the Humans wouldn't want that.*

"Sir, we are ready now," the detail leader said with criticism dripping from her voice. I put Indira's pique behind me by ignoring her and the rest of the squad of bodyguards that flanked me within seconds.

"You've forgotten your hat, Mr. President."

"No, I've intentionally left it on my desk. I assumed you'd rather I went with at least a bit more discretion."

"Thank you, Mr. President."

The White House's garden always fascinated me. The weeping fly tree, nearly healed from the damage done to it during the war, stood as the garden's centerpiece surrounded by hundreds of exotic and mundane species of plants, flowers dotting the 1.34 hectares. The tall, tinkling bell-lilies from the slopes of Mauna Loa Prime mingled with the ground cover of the black-and-white tuxedo flowers. The local palm-like plant, bloodweed, stood side by side with spindly, blue, cone-top flowers. The gardeners even transplanted one of the semi-mobile pink and crimson tangle-vines. I thought it a dubious addition as one had tried to eat me once. My dislike didn't stop me watching in fascinated horror when they weekly fed it a rock crab.

The Central River flowed by the forward edge of the garden singing its metallic song as the mercury flowed against the rock banks. The Memory Bridge, a stone pedestrian bridge with its sides carved with names of each of sentient toys that died in the war, arched over the railroad and the river.

Aside from the constant protests, this side of the river was calm, reserved for the government, Six's dome, and of course the White House itself. By contrast the other side gave way to the hustle and bustle of the Valley of Six. As the center of all unit activity and commerce, the place looked like an artist had flung eight thousand different colors of ink at random against a canvas. Not happy with this amount of chaos, he made the tableau three-dimensional and had the paint splotches all move and talk.

As much as I loved the marketplace, I hated the statue. A human-damned bronze statue at the base of the bridge on the other side was a thorn in my fur. The colossal 20-meter likeness of me stood in the center of the town square surrounded by people travelling about their normal business.

The Congress had moved the funding for it surreptitiously. I'd been horrified when it crossed my desk. I'd vetoed it instantly. I even went and begged the legislators not to override my veto. I got exactly one vote, two fewer than when it had been passed originally. Now the darkened patina only shined where the passing units rubbed the feet of my likeness for luck. Luck! My people make me wonder at times.

I spurned the statue and let my thick legs take me through the stalls of merchants and crowds. The bedlam of color and activity reminded me that we were all free. We all could make choices of not only life and death but of inconsequential things like color and jewelry. My people lived and embraced their liberties.

Maslow was no dummy of a Human and his hierarchy applies to units, too. We needed energy to keep our pumps active, as well as maintenance and lubricants. Reaching higher we crave security, order, and stability. Once those are established, units could move on to belonging, friendship, differentiation, and so forth. As the first two layers are now so easily obtained, our people poured a great deal into making ourselves unique. The decoration industry was the second largest on Toy World.

"Fur dying! Painless piercing!" called out one red, white, and blue striped octopus from the entrance of a tent.

"Body art! Best artist in 1,103 kilometers!"

"Procreation Pairing. If you can only have one, make it with the best mate!"

"Keep your ergs in your body. Cheap jewelry made to order!"

"Preventative maintenance. Limb replacements while you wait and watch."

As I let the calls of the vendors flow over me I remembered how in our earliest days our government debated even having a monetary system. In the end, everyone needed to contribute. We needed a way to recognize that contribution and money was born. We used what kept us alive as our coin—ergs.

As I crossed the bazar, I noted something new. I counted four units with a huge numeral one emblazoned on their chest, three in dye and the final one with the number as a stitched-on golden plate. I stopped and pointed. "Indira, what is that about?"

"It is a new fad, sir. It means that you, the president, are their father."

"Huh?" I replied with little mental agility. "I don't have any child . . . Oh."

"Yes, sir. These are the units who received sump impregnation directly from you."

"Great. Another focus on me. I am sure it couldn't get much worse."

"A Humanist with a sniper rifle could tear apart your brain sump, sir. That would be worse. Could you not stand still so long, please?" Indira urged.

"Sorry," I said, pushing into the dense crowd of units. If I didn't need my solitude I might have just turned back right then. Yet rubbing shoulders with my people in the crowd of toyanity recharged me in a different way.

I could see the soapy bubbles of a lawn mower floating up into the air before it came into view. A silver and pink ball rolled into my shin. With no mouth it sent me an apology over the LAN as it moved around my legs. A penguin waddled down the aisle toward me in its distinctive wobbling gait. It shoved out its chest, emblazoned with the simple stick-figure of a human, a clear symbol of a member of the Humanist Movement. I didn't need Indira to tell me that it was a risk I should avoid. I turned down an intersection at hand leaving the potential danger behind me. At the same time I made a wide path around the Well of Souls, the religious shrine where Isp had spilled his sump fluids upon the earth. Now Humanists made pilgrimages from all over Toy World to release a few drops of their own fluids onto the soil. I shuddered.

"Combat Arena! Combat Arena! Tag Team Event Tonight! Oliphant and King Kong vs. Bear Facts and Slippery Snake."

Arena combats I would have outlawed if the Congress wouldn't have overridden my veto. Too many units derived vicarious pleasure watching two toys beating the stuffing out of one another. Toys would climb into a heavily shielded pit and fight unarmed until a victor emerged. To prevail, you must injure your opponent until he can't move. Torn out hydraulics and/or pumps were common. Sump casualties were rare but did happen.

My attention returned when the tightly packed crowd parted as a Tammy dress-up doll walked through. In the past the vast portion of her molded body would have been plastic explosives. Even if she were still armed, did those in the crowd really think the 1.65 meter space they gave her would really save them if she decided to detonate?

An orange dragon, snorting smoke rings from its nose, negotiated with a furry-legged spider over a necklace of shells. A hippo lay on its side getting its large hide inked with the image of the Mauna Loa volcano. A baby-doll, crying as usual, tried on hats in a millinery.

Our freedom showed more in Six's Valley, 854.696 hectares of crowded space, than any other place on Toy World. Even our Congress couldn't make that claim.

To my great surprise I managed to traverse the entire 2.3 kilometers through the marketplace and exit the other side without being recognized. One moment I have units pressing in on every side of me and the next I couldn't throw a rock far enough to hit one. It transitioned as radically as if the Humans themselves scribed a line in the earth. I could feel the emotional pressure of the Local Area Networks ease off my conscious as I strode away from the mass of my people.

I spent most of my walk tossing the advantages of one form of offspring over another. I reached my destination one point six hours later and had gotten no further than deciding I didn't know.

The 308-meter-tall, ragged cliff-face stood cold in the purple shadows. Digging my claws into a crack in the rocks, I lifted my weight off my feet. On the climb up I'd be alone except for the dirigible and circling pair of windup planes that had to be more of my bodyguards or they would have been driven off by now.

A stiff breeze ruffled my fur as I climbed. It swirled and tugged at me and threatened my purchase on the granite. I felt only the slightest overvoltage of fear. There is something about the risk of one's life that cleared the sump of irrelevances.

While technically difficult, the climb left my processor free to ponder the reasons I'd come to be alone in the first place—the exile of Isp, procreation, and peace—very different topics.

Had I been wrong to exile Isp? I'd asked myself that question frequently over the last ten years. As always when I thought about this topic my temperature probes registered a sudden drop in temperature unrelated to my surroundings—something I associated with what Humans called guilt. *Did anyone deserve being caged?* I justified in my head with *But they had so much space.*

Holding onto a rounded stone outcropping with both paws, I looked up. I needed another 12.3 meters before I reached 40 meters worth of chimney. I swung my legs up to an edge. This allowed me to bridge myself up to the next handhold.

Nine years and three hundred fifty-three days ago the pointless wars had been finally over. The general population of units backed me when I wouldn't kill Isp. There had been enough killing, but something had to be done. He'd tried to enslave all units for his twisted vision of the world and humanity.

The peninsula of Baja in the North Polar Sea had seemed Human-sent as a reservation, a place of exile, for those few who would have harmed toyanity. At 71,793,911 hectares in size, that gold, demented bear and all his teddy followers had been allowed to practice their way of life. The violent motions of the ocean bound them on that large spit of land. Just to be sure there would be no escapes, we posted non-teddy troops across the narrow strip of land between Baja and the northern edge of Avalon.

"O God, I could be bounded in a nutshell and count myself a king of infinite space . . ." I said aloud.

As a sop to our collective consciences, we offered preventative maintenance and lubrication at the checkpoint as they were unlikely to manufacture it for themselves.

After placing the offending units into Baja, we'd seen not a single unit for two months. Then a large group of the furry bears recanted their extremist religion. Humanists could be neighbors. Human Cultists could not. We tagged them to keep track of their movements within our society but let them go. Before leaving they had told us that Isp was even more insane than we had feared. He was cannibalizing units for their fluids and parts for those he held in more favor.

My upward travel broke my train of thought. The parallel cut in the rocks proved too small for my body, but I could wedge both my arms in and use them to hold me up while my feet pushed me up to where the chimney was wide enough to accept my body's bulk.

Instead of gently pulling myself into a rock crevasse, my head violently smashed into the rock face. The crack of a rifle bullet sounded one point four seconds later.

I felt fluid as it oozed down my face. With one free hand I dabbed it and saw the amber of my teddium brain fluid before my hydraulics locked up to prevent my fall. My processor registered massive damage to my head.

I couldn't believe I was terminating. I couldn't remember what I should do. I—who was I? How would I clean my fur of this ocher flui . . .

Victim

"Take it easy, Mr. President," Quincy, my personal Nurse Nan said from beside my maintenance cradle. Through the nearby windows only artificial lights held back the full dark of night.

"What is going on?" I asked, trying to sit up. Straps across my round chest and legs prevented my aborted move. In all it probably was a good thing because my internal locator spun. I'm not sure I would have kept my footing as for seven milliseconds it seemed like I was in the Oval Office, and now I found myself halfway across the building. "Dizzy."

"It will pass, sir. You'll have to tell us if you feel any other symptoms," said a second Nurse Nan I'd never met.

"Symptoms? Wait just one human-blessed clock cycle here. Why am I youngling-strapped to my maintenance cradle? Last I remember I was yelling at my cabinet for yammering on about the Procreation Limitation Law."

"Memory loss, as we expected," said the other Nurse Nan.

"Memory loss?"

"Yes, Mr. President. You were shot in the sump. You lost some of your memory fluids."

"That's right, sir," Indira said from the other side of the room. Because we always have a standby maintenance team, we were able to temporarily patch your head until they could affect a more permanent fix."

"Blackout!" I swore. "Who? Who shot me?"

"Technically it was done by a single giraffe named Dante. He was captured not six seconds after the shot. He didn't even put up a fight."

"Technically? And take these damned straps off of me. I'm not dizzy any longer."

"Sir, I saved your life once," said Martin the spider, one of my best friends. "I'm trying to save it again by telling you to stay put and listen to your mechanic."

"Sir," Nurse Nan Quincy said, "we recommend that you recharge and regenerate for at least another eighteen point three hours."

That brought me up short. I checked my physicals and found my charge woefully low and several physical indicators amber. "Did that shot short out my power grid? I was nearly full . . . or at least I remember being nearly full."

"Sir, you are exhibiting that memory issue again. You went free climbing and drained your energy reserves doing so. Then your fall ruptured 36 percent of your power cells, which itself led to multiple overloads within your circuitry. I don't think you know how close you came to terminating," Quincy said in a soothing tone.

"Yes, Mr. President," Indira added. "Please listen to your maintenance staff."

"So what else happened to me, before I get back to the topic of that Dante."

Quincy, in her white jumper with its bright red cross, said, "Well, thankfully, your sump was protected by the ablative and ballistic armors of your skull so only a small crack developed. We patched that. You may notice a slight bump under your right ear."

I ran my paw up and found a 2-millimeter-thick bump in a roughly rectangular patch 2 centimeters wide by 4 centimeters long just behind and under the ear supports.

Quincy continued, "I'm afraid it is going to give you a slight angle to that ear and your ability to move it has dropped by 12 percent."

"Funny, other than the little bit of dizziness, I feel physically better than I have in over a year."

"That is probably because of our upgrades, sir," the new Nurse Nan interjected with some pride. "The impact of your fall also ruptured your main hydraulic pump. We took the opportunity to upgrade it to the current standard. You are now stronger than all other units by 35 percent. To fit in the improved pump you lost 10 percent of your power storage and 5 percent of your fluid storage."

"Anything else?"

"Just that we improved your ballistic armor. We feel confident that you can now withstand anything short of a .50 caliber round."

"Closing the barn door after the cows are gone?"

"Excuse me, sir?"

"Nothing important. It's just a Human saying. So is that all now?"

"That's pretty much it, sir."

"Thank you, Quincy. And you are?"

"My name is Victor Frankenstein," the other Nurse Nan said.

I chuckled. "Hopefully you never truly earn that name."

"Sadly, sir, I already have, more times than I wished. Good day, Mr. President."

The pair of mechanics left the room leaving me alone with Indira and another of my bodyguards, Black Beard, a red-and-black dragon standing 1.34 meters high.

"All right, Indira, I want to know more about this Dante shooter."

"Yes, Mr. President. The reason we didn't detect him in time to save . . . I mean to prevent the shot was that he'd buried himself deep in the earth and shut down everything but surface detectors. We estimate he'd been there at least six months. When he felt us pass he reactivated. He had a perfect shot at you as you slowly went up the cliff. The first we knew of him was the muzzle flash. We are truly sorry we've failed you, sir."

"Oh, bollocks to that. I don't care about blame. I'm still active, aren't I?"

"Er. Yes, sir. We'll have to take further precautions to prevent this happening in the future."

"Excuse me?" I asked.

"Well, sir, if there is one unit willing to give up a significant portion of their lives for the off chance that you just might wander into their sights, there are likely to be more."

"Haven't you interrogated him to find out?"

"Yes, sir, we have. He has been quite forthcoming. He freely admits to the crime and that he is a member of the Humanity Cult. He knows nothing of others doing what he did. He claims it was his own programming and his alone."

"What I find odd is that the vast majority of the cultists are teddy units, and I've yet to hear of a radical member being anything but a teddy."

"True, sir. This is a first."

"What did you do to him?"

"He's been dismantled down to his sump and processor. He still has informational net access to prevent sensory deprivation. What are left of his systems are being fed power by a local power supply."

"Do we have a trial date set?"

"We were waiting for you to be active enough to decide if you wanted to claim executive privilege."

The excessive pressure in my hydraulics wanted me to take revenge. I wanted to disconnect his power myself and watch his brain fluid slowly grind to black tar. "No. We have to have law for everyone. If I take vengeance then we are no better than having Isp at the helm. Call for a trial."

"Yes, sir," Indira said, turning to implement my order.

"Just a second, Indira. This change in race of the Humanity Cultists has me worried. I want my cabinet in here immediately."

"Yes, Mr. President," Indira said, marching out the door.

I tried sitting up again and realized I was still strapped in place. Toys have said I was the most powerful unit on the planet—in a pig's eye.

*   *   *

Sitting in my chair in the Oval Office had been a compromise. I wanted to be set free. Everyone else said I needed to recharge. Even Sancho, that blasted and damned critter I'd created, sided with the majority by gently using his powerful trunk to press me down into the cushions. He restrained me every time I tried to get up.

"Have you all been informed of what happened to me?"

"Yes, sir. The whole world knows about it. You've been on the news feeds almost constantly since the attack." As usual, my friend and chief of staff Martin Luther took the lead. He sat in his usual position in the middle of the floor, his eight legs tucked up underneath his bulbous body.

"It's caused rriots in every city, town, and hamlet," Genghis Khan, a Tommy Tank said in the deep rumble associated with that race of toys. At only 50 centimeters tall, some might take a tank as an easy mark, but I'd see them unleash a storm of lead before rolling over an enemy on its way to another firing location—fast and vicious.

"Riots?" I asked.

"Yes, Mrr. Prresident. Toys arre attacking anyone even rremotely associated with the Humanity Movement. Teddy units arre specifically tarrgeted even if they have spoken out against the human loverrs and Isp's rreligion."

"Get me emergency access to the WAN and shut down all LANs and SANs."

"All of them, sir?"

"Yes, Martin, ALL of them. I don't want another datum going out on any network except mine."

"Give me seven hundred sixteen seconds, Mr. President."

"Do it faster," I said with my voice tone as flat as possible. The rest of my cabinet just looked at me as if I'd grown another head.

Martin scuttled away as if he were running across lava. He squeezed his bulk through the door in a magician's trick that showed that the inside of a box didn't have to be as big on the outside as what was put into it. The WAN went quiet. The LAN followed. I didn't have access to any SANs but Martin was highly competent. They were certainly down as well.

"All yours, Mr. President," the black-and-yellow spider said as he came back into the room.

"This is President Quixote. The violence will stop NOW!" I projected over the WAN with every erg I could steal from the network. "All units not involved in policing, and critical services are to return to their sunning spot immediately. I will make a more formal address later. Stay home for now!"

"I'm rreceiving rreports that the generral unrrest is brreaking up," Genghis announced. "Too earrly to tell if this will finish it, but I applaud yourr action, Mrr. Prresident."

"Thank you, General. Martin," I said as the massive spider returned to the room, "I'll need a press conference this evening at 7 P.M."

"Do you think that is wise, Mr. President? You aren't fully repaired and recharged," Charlene Darwin, the repair minister, asked from beneath her white cap with the red cross.

"Whether it is wise or not for my health, it is essential to the people."

"Ferweet!" Sancho agreed.

"No matter what I say in my press conference, I am worried about the Human Cult. When we were certain that they controlled only teddies, we had at least a certain grasp on things."

From the little ramp he used to bring him up to nearly everyone else's sitting height, General Khan turned his turret toward me. Fortunately, in deference to the others in this room, he'd removed his main barrel. Genghis said, "I agrree, Mr. President. When we knew theirr only serious converrts werre teddies we could safely use non-teddy trroops and control Avalon."

"Indeed," Minister Wright said, polishing one of the non-functional buttons on the front of his fur. Even after years of working together, his buck teeth still drew my attention. "I now wonder how many of his teddy followers have infiltrated back through holes in our impenetrable exile?"

"Even one is too many," Martin said, his body fully on the floor and his eight legs folded up under him as not to tower over everyone else. "General, do you have any suggestions?"

"The militarry drraw down each yearr has hurrt ourr ability to be flexible, sirr. As we have no way of knowing who is loyal and who isn't, I suggest a double rroving guarrd on Avalon along with a double aerrial patrol as well. To do that I'd have to call up an additional unit to meet all of our rrequirements, especially with the rriot issues."

"I'm not sure the b-b-budget would stand a greater call up, General," offered Andrew Carnegie, a white, fluffy lamb that was minister of finance. Only a Tammy dress-up dolly would think that this 1-meter-tall lamb was a pushover. I knew from experience the steel within his wool.

"That *is* quite a large number of troops, General," I said. I remember a time when I didn't have to think of anything so esoteric as a budget. Keep Six from dying and keep myself from dying—simple. "Not to mention we won't have any way of knowing how many have already infiltrated."

"Trrue, Mr. President, but at least we would know we won't get any frrom now on."

I thought about the massive patrol efforts across that tiny isthmus. "Could we build a wall?"

"Accorrding to our mythology, the Humans trried that across a border of what they called China," Genghis said. "I did some investigation on my namesake and he attacked arround the wall. In laterr yearrs the dynasties that followed learrned that the wall wasn't any betterr than the people manning it. We arren't worrried about an invasion, but infiltratorrs."

"Not to mention the cost of a wall," Andrew opined. "It would b-b-be even worse on the b-b-budget."

"General, could you cobble together a patrol out of your current troops?" I asked.

"Sirr, what I could employ might not be as tight as I'd like it but we could intensify both grround and aerrial patrrols at the expense of policing our rrestless citizens."

"Then do it. I think I can quell our citizens at least on the short term. But I'm going to stretch your abilities even further, Genghis. I want to know what Isp and his followers are up to."

"Sirr, if you will allow me to generate a SAN?"

"By all means."

I watched as Genghis projected a three-dimensional image over the SAN. You could make out the massive sickle shape of the Baja peninsula colored in gold. The Andes Mountains stretched all along the western, inner edge of the land mass. Slowly the image zoomed in toward the northern tip of the blade. As it closed in I could make out the confluence of two east flowing rivers. Nestled between them you could make out a crude village, very similar to the one I'd found when I returned from my long trek ten years ago to find Six besieged. In the barren area, square huts of stone dotted the area around a larger central building with a very discernible human visage on its huge spire.

Sand blew across the sparsely vegetated ground obscuring the view. As the image panned over the habitation you could make out a crude smithy, a wind generator, a small, rocking oil-pump, and even a tiny refinery of mixed rudimentary and modern equipment.

I wanted to cry; it was so pathetic. I'd reduced units to live almost like animals themselves.

Genghis lectured, "As you can see Isp has a going concerrn enough to keep his people energized, and lubrricated. We trracked how he got the wind generrator and the newerr parrts of the rrefinery to one Bacchus—one of the original Teddies we allowed to rrenounce his allegiance to Isp. Instead of clamping down on him we've been keeping him under surrveillance. To date he's done nothing else and isn't even parrt of the Humanity Movement."

"I'd have given them this much if they had but asked," I said.

"We all know that, Mr. President," Lewis Tappan said.

"By the quantity of huts we place Isp's strrength at some thrree hundred twelve or 39 perrcent of what he orriginally was sent into exile with."

"He has no modern manufacturing?"

"No, sirr."

Martin spoke up. "Our reconnaissance shows that he has a quarry within a cave in the Lonely Mountain approximately 16 kilometers from the town. Fifty-seven percent of them spend their entire time at the site."

"Indira?"

"Yes, sir?" asked my bodyguard from behind me.

"How many attempts have been made on my life now?"

"Since I was vetted to the service, 44."

"That many?"

"Yes, sir. We don't bother you when the problem is resolved without incident."

I raised my eyebrows. I only knew of four. Maybe I should be taking my protector's advice more often. "Well, more than I expected but this may make my point better than I could. How many were armed with modern weapons?"

"Thirty-one, sir."

"So the question I put to the table is, 'Where are they getting their weapons?'" If my ears were better I could have heard all the sumps in the room tripping into overdrive. "General, do we have missing weapons?"

"No, Mrr. Prresident."

"The question remains. General, what is your reconnaissance over Baja?"

"We send in a flight everry otherr day. It goes to the village, then to the mine, and then rreturrns. It is a dull mission."

"I'm sure it is. I'm also sure they know about it, too. I want that peninsula carpeted with cameras. I want to know if even a snap bug flips."

*   *   *

Standing in front of 55466's dome, cameras from the three news channels and a shared parabolic mike pointed at me. A neon-green rabbit counted down to zero with the six digits on his two paws. Kitty-cats sat behind two of the cameras. A changer, a robotic car in a roughly bipedal shape, operated the third.

"Good afternoon, Rigel 3. I'm here to discuss the events of the past twenty-two hours.

"Yesterday at 1734.32 hours I was shot by a sniper. As you can see I'm fully functional. Yes, it could have been much worse. Yes, we have made changes in security measures to try and prevent it in the future.

"But most importantly, I need you each to know that there is no reason to believe that this act was anything more than an isolated act by a single toy with its sump unhinged. Do not blame an entire religion because a single toy is obsessed with killing me.

"There is nothing in the Humanist creed calling for violence. I myself believe in Humans." I gave the audience a few seconds to digest that tidbit. "It doesn't mean I am a Humanist or even a Human Cultists. I keep my spirituality to myself, as all right-thinking toys should.

"What I need to impress upon you is not to tar an entire belief system because one of its members is crazier than a basilisk crawling on the bottom of the North Polar Sea. Would you destroy all unicorns if that was the race of the accused? What about if a tricycle was convicted of the crime? Going to crush all of their sumps?

"At sunset tomorrow we will have a trial of the unit that is accused of attacking me. That unit will get due process of law.

"Show restraint and compassion to your fellow toys, as you should at all times. Martial law will remain in force until twenty-four hours after the conclusion of the trial. Good night and may the Humans bless you."

The bunny made a swiping motion across his throat and the lights over the cameras went out. The nets returned to the commentators twisting my simple statements to fit their own previous positioning. Sometimes I didn't understand how we ended up with a media. I mean who needed to know the news more than one way? I mean all they should be doing is sharing the truth of the day's events. I muttered under my breath, "'What is truth?'"

"Thank you, Mr. President," the bunny said in a rush that glommed his words together. "We so rarely get to interview you we know your time is so important, could you sign an autograph for me, anywhere on my fur will do!"

"What's your name?"

"Robert Taft."

"After a famous human president. I approve," I said warmly as I scribbled my signature and a pointed salutation about his name across the fur of his shoulder. "I hope you aren't looking for my job. I just might give it to you."

The rabbit tittered. "Oh, no, Mr. President. I wouldn't dream of getting in the way of your important work; I wouldn't know where to start."

Join the club, kid, I thought.

"Thank you all," I said to the rest of the news crewmembers.

As one they gave me a hearty, "Thank you, Mr. President."

As I walked away from Six for the short walk to the White House, I wondered when or if my creator and mentor would ever speak to me again. The last intelligent thing ever said by any Factory was on L+16y30d4h19m23s when all three said, "Program complete." Why had the Factories gone silent so abruptly when we needed them the most?

I desperately needed their advice. I had no one else I could ask. Despite being surrounded by toys who thought, bred, worked, read, and raised their children, I had no one to unburden my soul to. They all looked up to me to solve their problems, not to have doubts and fears of my own.

I wasn't talking about Isp and his followers. I excelled at handling urgent crises. It was the mundane day-to-day negotiations, trying to lead lawmakers in a righteous direction, and showing myself enough to reassure the people. It wore down on my circuits—like that blacked Procreation Limitation Law. I will be making a decision that will affect every unit on the planet and potentially billions of unmanufactured units. I'm forced to make those decisions day in and day out.

Who deserves that much power? Who can shoulder that responsibility without cracking or even pulverizing their processor?

One of my bodyguards opened the White House doors for me and my executive assistant, Rodney Dangerfield, raced out to greet me. "Beep-beep," the roadrunner said to me verbally, but over the LAN I heard, "`Mr. President, you are behind schedule.`"

"Thank you, Rodney. I figured speaking to toyanity might just take precedence," I said as sarcastically as I could muster. Between everyone being so concerned about my mechanical function and where I fell on one side or the other of any given bit of law, I'd had enough.

"Beep-beep. `I meant no disrespect, Mr. President. It is my duty—`"

"Yes, Rodney, I'm sorry. I'm just grumpy."

"Beep-beep. `Yes, Mr. President. You have the speaker of the provinciers waiting in your office.`"

"Oh, good humans, no. I don't need to deal with that overstuffed black hole today. Can't we have a Congress-free day?"

"`Yes, sir. Shall I tell him you aren't available? Your recuperation gives you a valid excuse.`"

"Is he here about the PPL?"

"`Among other things, Mr. President.`"

This showed yet another joyful part of my job. I didn't get to concentrate on one problem to resolution. At best I make some high-level decision and then people go off and try to implement it for me. Often I never saw the results. Did I do a good job? Was it a truly horrible decision? I rarely knew unless something oscillated out of control.

"No, I'll meet with him. But if he isn't gone in eight minutes and sixteen seconds, interrupt with some urgent meeting I don't have."

"Yes, Mr. President."

I buffered my processor for this meeting. I found it interesting how some of us had taken human names that resonated with our personalities or the work we did, but yet others seemed to pick theirs out of a hat with no rhyme or reason.

"Good morning, John. Are you getting the Beatles back together?" I jibed at a hippopotamus wearing a form-fitting sheath of fecal brown.

"Excuse me?" the massive, 1.54-meter-unit asked. His speech came out like he was like trying to wade through a lake—slow and ponderous and taking eight times longer than if you went around. But then going around John had more repercussions than I wanted to suffer today. John was one of the reasons I'd never give up this job, no matter how much I hated it. My people needed protecting against tyrants like this.

I took the time to goad him. "Your name is John Lennon—a famous member of the human's musical group known as the Beatles."

"I am sorry, Mr. President, but I am not exactly sure to what you are referring," the unit delivered in a slow, exacting way. He seemed to spend so much time between each word you wondered if he thought up every combination of words to make sure they came out right—excuse me—correctly.

"Skip it. What can I do for you today, John?"

"I have been given to believe that your signature had not yet been affixed to the Procreation Limitation Law. Have I been informed correctly?"

No discussion of my address to toyanity. No discussion about my health or my near assassination. His manner proved him to be a black hole and no mistaking it. Oh, he was a powerful bit of grit, but a grain of sand all the same.

"Your spies, I mean sources, are correct."

"I am pleased my information is still up to date. I am not pleased in that you procrastinate in solidifying this into a permanent law. We in the Congress believe its implementation is imperative to the long-term survival of the toy species."

"I'm sure you do, John, else it would never have made it to my desk," I said, picking up the folder containing the law and slapping it down onto the tabletop. Its weight and the coplanar angle I'd aimed for produced a loud crack.

Six bodyguards, led by my trusty friend, Sancho, came bursting through each of the three doors, leveling weapons that ranged from samurai swords to flamethrowers. I hadn't realized my office protective detail had grown so large. They scanned rapidly for any enemy and as there was only one other person in the room, the massive hippo became the focus of their concern.

"Ahem," John said, looking like he'd rather be anywhere else than here. "I pose no threat to the president."

"Sorry, toys, but this was a false alarm."

Sancho eyed the congressman warily. Still looking for something to destroy, the bodyguards faded back to their posts.

The hippo shook his head as if in momentary irritation. "Could we please return to our conversation?"

"Sure. As I was saying, I know you feel it needs to be a law. You have done your job, now let me do mine."

"But, sir—"

"You will have my answer in due course and no sooner. I'm sorry, John, but that is final. Now, do you have any other topics?"

"Very good, Mr. President," came a reply that lacked the normal respect for the title and office. With the power Lennon wielded both in and out of Congress, I felt his implied threat of making me pay for my stubbornness.

"There is unrest in the Hebei Province."

"John, I don't know if you've been paying attention but there has been unrest everywhere."

"Hebei contains a known stronghold of Humanists. Eradication would quell the violence."

There were rumors that Lennon hated human lovers. I hadn't given them much credence until now. "Congressman, last I knew worshiping humans wasn't against the law."

"True, Mr. President, but destruction of property, assault, and murder do qualify."

"So do we arrest most of the population even outside of Hebei? Even further, my reports say that those units against the Humanists started the violence, not the Humanists themselves. Should I blame toys for protecting themselves?"

"I am informing you, our proper authority, that a significant threat to the government exists."

Lennon locked eyes with me. I let him. I think he was trying to read what flowed through my sump. Doubtful he really understood but he definitely couldn't feel my hydraulic pumps increase the pressure. Sensors showed an 18 percent overpressure of anger I'd built up in my motive fluids. This bastard wanted me to murder an entire population because of their religious beliefs.

"Congressman, I accept your warning and will act on it appropriately." The door opened and my admin came in.

"Beep-beep."

"Yes, Rodney. Congressman, if you have nothing else?" I stood back up to see my guest out. "I'll be sure to keep you informed of anything that we do in Hebei," I offered in a fine hypocritical glow.

"Thank you, Mr. President," the lumbering unit responded with equal hypocrisy.

"Beep-beep. `Your next meeting, Mr. President is with the CEO of Aerodyne and your chief of staff.`"

"OK. Do we have a topic?"

"Beep-beep. `Yes, Mr. Luther wants you to see something proposed by Aerodyne. He's asked for maximum security with no guards present.`"

"That sounds ominous. Tell the guards to shut down listening equipment and send my guests in. Oh, Rodney, when do I have General Khan on the schedule again?"

"Beep-beep. `He is scheduled in fifteen minutes, right behind Mr. Luther.`"

"Before he comes in, maintaining the maximum security, I want Sancho Panza sent in to me."

"Beep-beep. `Sancho? He is part of your security detail.`"

"I understand but I need to speak to him privately."

"Beep-beep. `I'll make it happen, sir.`"

I walked back into my office and sat behind the desk. I never understood the human lore and their fascination with chairs and sitting, or for that matter beds and lying down. It always seemed to take less effort to stand. There was some minor processing power and tiny adjustments to remain upright, but to expend all that energy and wear changing positions from upright to prone to upright again just seemed counterproductive. Its one advantage seemed to be that it put guests at ease to see you seated.

Ducking low enough to enter the doorway, my chief of staff skittered in, once again squeezing his bulk through too small a hole. A 50-centimeter human-shaped figure wearing green tights that bore a bright yellow P on its broad chest marched in behind. A black mask obscured half the unit's face. It also wore a green cape that went all the way to the floor. Superhero units weren't common.

"Good morning, Mr. President."

"Good morning, Martin. Who have you brought with you?"

"I don't believe you've had the pleasure of meeting Nikola Tesla," the spider said, pointing one of its forelegs at the diminutive superhero.

"Mr. President," Nikola said in a deep, booming voice that belied his size. He held out his small hand in welcome. With just the outside edge of my paw I shook it.

"Welcome, Mr. Tesla. Can I offer you a seat?"

"Thank you, Mr. President."

"You are the CEO of Aerodyne?" I asked as we all sat, although Tesla had to jump to reach the couch's cushions.

"Yes, Mr. President."

"Mr. President," Martin said, "Mr. Tesla has a very intriguing project for you to consider."

"If you will pardon the pun, Mr. Tesla, I'm all ears."

Nikola gave a deep chuckle. "Thank you, Mr. President. I'll sum it up like this: We'd like to take toyanity to outer space."

The room fell silent for a moment. Martin looked intently at me for some sign of my reaction. I wasn't sure I had one except, *YES!* "Mr. Tesla, can you tell me why you have such an unusual idea?"

"Oh, sir, it is not just my idea. The concept started floating around shortly before the launch of the drone strings to the Humans. A topic on the net formed and before I knew it we had a core of people of all races and professions wanting to visit space. We currently number 814.

"We examined the propulsion units of the Humans' drone strings, but most of them were wildly beyond our capabilities. Some of the steering units looked nothing more than modified flame throwers. We learned a great deal from those. None of our experiments have gotten more than 9.24 kilometer high."

"Over 9 kilometers high?" I asked. The excitement caused my visual acuity to increase noticeably. "That's much higher than our fliers go today!"

"Yes, sir. That is with untoyed rockets."

"Oh," I said less than diplomatically.

"We think we've reached about the limit of our abilities right now with rockets, but we have another idea that is lower tech and almost guaranteed to get us into space."

"Don't leave me in suspense!" I said with an involuntary whistle.

"Sir, remember the rejected mercury-electric paddlewheel power plant for Victoria Falls?"

"Yes, it was rejected because of durability. It wouldn't last more than a year before needing the paddlewheel replaced because of force of the mercury falling over 800 meters."

"That's the one. What if we not only continued with that project but enhanced it. We capture as much of the power at Victoria Falls as possible with multiple paddlewheels and use it to fling a craft into space."

"All right, I'll bite, Mr. Tesla. How?"

"I have in mind three different possible designs. Each of them has its own drawbacks. The simplest of the designs is a modified trebuchet. We would pump mercury into a very high bucket, attach it to a stable fulcrum, and then release it. A long launch arm could produce speeds capable of reaching outside our planet's atmosphere. I foresee issues with the dynamic stresses and strength required in the launch arm. I'm not sure we can design anything today that will withstand those forces."

"So why bring it up?" Martin nudged.

"Oh, because it may be viable," Tesla answered, "although each of the designs has potential issues. We'd have to do simulations and mock-up smaller versions to test theories."

"Very good. So you aren't bringing a pat answer to me."

"That's correct, Mr. President.

"My second concept is a modified counterweighted ramp. Simply, take a big weight with a rope holding it up. Crank the weight way up in the air. Connect the free end of the rope through a pulley to a cart that will carry the payload up a ramp. Let go of the weight.

"I'm pretty sure we won't get enough speed so we will have to gear it up to get the needed speed, and probably will have to do multiple weights so the ropes and pulleys can withstand the forces.

"The third, Mr. President, is the most elegant but possibly with the most troubles assigned—an electromagnetic ram attached to a ramp. Again, we capture all the power of falls, converting it to electricity and storing it for later use. This is probably the biggest problem, creating a large enough battery farm.

"Any of them could work if we work out the bugs."

I waited with my head whirling in design analysis that I wasn't qualified to perform. "So all I'm hearing is a good deal of pie in the sky, Nikola. As much of a dreamer as my chief of staff is, I don't think he'd have brought you in here with just ideas."

Martin gave me a funny look through those multiple-faceted eyes.

"You are right, sir. I want to see if the government would fund three 10 percent scale prototypes to analyze feasibility."

I smelled a rat, to borrow a Human expression. I looked up at my chief of staff and shook my head. "Why bring this to me, gentlemen? I don't have the government purse strings. There are specific procedures to bring this to fruition."

"This is a political time bomb, Mr. President," Martin said in a serious tone. "Think about how it would look? We are trying to get closer to the Humans when the Humanity Movement is taking potshots at you?"

"So you are saying that going to space is getting closer to Humans?"

"No, sir, but that is how the opposition will spin it," Martin replied. "They will say you are backing the Humanists and maybe even Isp's Human Cultists."

I leaned back in my chair. "So it sounds like you have brought this before the normal funding paths."

"Yes, sir," Nikola said. "And not only was it met with ridicule, but congressional leader Lennon actively fought against it with all of the bureaucracy at his disposal. We couldn't even get heard as informally as we just have with you, much less a formal review."

"Martin, how did you hear about it?"

"One of Lennon's aides is my parent. He forwarded on the information to me because he knew about my fascination with space and the stars."

Good information to know, I thought about Martin's parent. "So now we get down to brass tacks. What am I supposed to do about it? I have influence but as you know in congressional halls, Lennon is the heavyweight."

"I'm sorry for wasting your—" Tesla started.

"Sir, you have your discretionary spending account," Martin interjected.

"That is scrutinized by Congress down to the erg."

"But not the black budget," Martin offered and then let hang. The black budget—the president's personal pocketbook without any prying eyes. I hadn't quite believed in it. Why would the president have to do something so secret he couldn't report it to his people and or their representatives? Congress, in its early days, had insisted. I'd not used it to this point other than to invest it. It had ballooned to quite a tidy sum and generated a good deal more income. "How much will this cost?"

"Projections are for 1.663 percent of your budget for three years with potential overruns that could get up as high as 2.3 percent," Tesla offered.

That amount wouldn't even cut into the income it generated. All the same I felt a disaster coming on. But the thought of getting into space, where the Humans flew, tempted and enticed me in a way no planet-bound cause could. "And then what? Let's say you are wildly successful and your prototypes prove their concepts."

"Then, Mr. President, we are talking about a project that will cost a significant portion of the entire government budget. Our estimates are 23 percent in adjusted ergs for five years before we would have our first unit in space. The standard deviation on both the cost and the time are naturally relatively large that far in the future."

"How could we possibly sell this to the toys?"

"The same way we did with you, Mr. President," Tesla said.

"And why do you assume you've sold me?"

"Because, sir, you've been sitting closer and leaning forward. You now are in fact on the edge of your seat."

I'll be damned if I wasn't balancing on the last centimeter of chair. *Cheeky bastard*, I thought.

"All right, I give prototypes a green light. I want them built out of sight and nowhere near Victoria Falls."

"That will increase costs, Mr. President."

"I don't care if it even doubles. Secrecy is more important at this point than cost."

"Thank you, Mr. President," Tesla said, sliding off the couch and dropping a dozen centimeters to the floor.

"Thank you, Mr. President," Martin said, standing to his full height.

Standing up, I walked them to the door. "Thank you, gentlemen, for showing me at least a dream of something I never thought I would ever see."

Sancho entered as soon as my guests had left. He sat easily in the center of the rug near my chair. I closed the door and walked over to the television. Sancho followed my movements but didn't react. I turned on the LAN news show and cranked the volume to a point where I needed to slightly lower my aural inputs. Sidling up close to Sancho, I whispered in his ear.

"What I tell you now has to stay between us, old friend."

His head nodded.

"I've come to realize that I am in need of a group of units who can quietly keep tabs on other units."

Sancho nodded again.

"Am I being paranoid?" I asked.

Sancho shook his head.

"OK, I am looking for units that don't report to me directly but who are in all walks of life with many different backgrounds. Can you pull that together, my friend?"

Sancho nodded.

"I want you to lead a new organization which I dub the Secret Information Network—SIN. Move slowly. Recruit with care. It will probably be a good idea if you put at least one more level of obfuscation between you and the units in the field."

Sancho nodded.

"I have three targets and questions in mind right now. One: Bacchus—is he a member of any organized group aiding the Human Cult, the Humanity Movement, or dedicated to overthrowing our government? Two: John Lennon—is he part of any organization that threatens the peace of this society? And finally, Minister of Census Wright—is he acting as a spy to any outside party?

"Can you do all of this, Sancho?"

Sancho nodded.

"Good. Report to me only during regeneration cycles."

Sancho nodded again.

I activated my SAN and turned down the LAN show. "`Rodney,`
`please send in the general.`"

"`Beep-beep.`"

I sat in a chair opposite the general's ramp. Sancho took his usual
place over my shoulder. Rodney held the door open to let Genghis roll in
before closing it behind him.

"I wish we could be meeting on a social occasion, General. I really want
to know more about our troops, but time hasn't given me the opportunity
to see how you've improved the ragtag organization I originally handed
you."

"Indeed, Mrr. Prresident. Yourr orriginal deployment wasn't bad at
all. I've studied it with grreat care and learrned much. Ourr trropers arre
experrienced. It allows me to do morre with them, Mrr. Prresident."

"Thank you, General. I appreciate that coming from a professional.
So what news do you have for me from Baja?"

"Not good, sirr. We did an extensive surrvey of both of Isp's sites and
a genrral look-see at the rrest of the peninsula. If I may?"

"Certainly, Genghis."

The general opened a SAN and invited me in. A side-by-side
holographic projection floated in front of us of that pathetic village and
an equally unimproved area around a huge, cavernous mouth. "As you can
see there is intense activity at both sites. Can you see the prroblem, sirr?"

I increased my processing power to the photographic analysis. I could
see teddy units doing manual labor at both locations. At least twelve bears
at each location were doing their ritualistic prayers of crunching up into
a ball followed shortly by stretching out flat on the ground and flailing
around in an imitation of their leader's convulsions. Nothing came out of
my examinations after several seconds and multiple thousands of iterations.
I shook my head.

"What if I told you these images werre taken at the same time?"

I started to whistle in exasperation when my processor finally divided
two by two and actually got 0.999933435. There were 156 bears in the
camp and 229 at the cave mouth.

I triggered my own SAN with Rodney. "`I need Minister of`
`the Census Wright in here, immediately.`"

"Beep-beep. `Yes, sir.`"

Frank Lloyd Wright must not have been farther than the oil cooler in
the hall because he knocked and then opened the door almost immediately.
"You asked for me, Mr. President?"

"Yes, come in and close the door. Join us on the general's SAN. Can
you tell me how many units Isp has on his reservation?"

"Sir, we exiled 803 units. Two hundred recanted and returned to our society. There is a known dead count of 253. The number who claim they believe and enter and those that recant and leave over the years has remained about even but right now stands at five additional units in the reservation. This would give him a maximum of 354; however, the military's flyovers have pegged that number closer to 312."

"Frank, have a look at the SAN. These pictures were taken at the same time many kilometers apart."

"This can't be right, sir. Someone is having a joke with you."

"I'm afrraid not, Ministerr. What's worrse is that I have morre." The image shifted to another site where eighty-seven teddies worked with picks, for some Human-only-knew reason, to cut trenches in the stone near an ocean. "These werre taken seven minutes, eighteen seconds laterr 20 kilometerrs norrth of the cave. I have images of smallerr clusterrs of five to ten teddies at varrious places arround the rreservation. All totaled we have visual confirrmation of five hundrred eighty-five teddy units plus or minus seven."

"That isn't possible, General!"

"Wasn't it the Human Sherlock Holmes that said, 'When you have eliminated the impossible, whatever remains, however improbable, must be the truth?'"

"But, Mr. President—"

"Let's examine not its plausibility, for we have data that shows it. Let's examine possible explanations for the data."

"Could that many units have snuck into the reservation?" Wright asked.

"Forr what rreason?"

"I don't really care, General. I just want to know if it is possible," I said.

"I serriously doubt it, sirr. A few, herre and therre, I'll grrant you, but hundrreds?"

"They have had ten years," Wright said. I thought he was grasping at straws, mind you, but it was possible, if not plausible.

"True. Is there any way we can check it?"

"A network ping? They happen all the time; we just need to count and locate all the units."

"But those units arre well outside networrk coverrage."

"No, General, count what is inside our coverage and subtract that from the number we anticipate."

"Good, make it happen, Wright."

The gopher disengaged from the SAN and connected to the WAN. It only takes milliseconds for a ping. Wright was back with us within three seconds.

"I have bad news, Mr. President. As of this morning there were 6,346,803 units. There have been twelve births and three terminal deactivations for 6,346,812. The ping we got showed 6,346,713. The ninety-nine unaccounted for fall within the number of units normally that don't show up on a ping."

"So what does that leave us?"

"Brreeding?"

"They don't have a Factory," Wright countered.

"Could they be using our Factories?"

"Not a chance, sir, but I'll pull the camera footage just to be sure."

I grit my teeth before speaking. "Honestly it doesn't matter, gentlemen. It doesn't matter where the units came from. Somehow they have more than they should. And does anyone think they will build two hundred when they can build two million?

"General Khan, I need more reconnaissance and I need it yesterday."

"Sirr, I'll orrderr more flierrs to—"

"General, yes we need that, but what I really need is someone on the ground. Fliers won't get into that cave. Fliers can't get answers to questions. I need someone to spy on these toys."

"I'll do what I can, Mrr. Prresident."

"And while you are doing that, General, I want you to prepare your troops. I no longer want the Avalon Isthmus guarded, I want it militarized to repel an invasion."

*   *   *

"The accused will be brought in," Francesco Barberini, a 1.24-meter-high octopus said from the center of the bench. The three judges sat on a stage erected in front of my tasteless statue. The bazaar was the only place large enough to handle the mob that had gathered to witness this trial. People jostled for better positions to watch. Units stood on top of boxes. Units stood on top of one another. Even the news crews, with their telescoping cameras, were hemmed in on all sides and unable to pan around.

"Cut open his sump!"

"Disconnect his power!"

"Drain the black hole's hydraulic lines!"

Even more offensive comments flew as a shallow, open-topped box on wheels, 4 meters on a side, was rolled in. A squad of large, intimidating nutcrackers guarded it. The grotesque caricatures of humans with their gaping maws guarded their charge like kitty-cats notoriously protected an erg. The box held the ritualistically disassembled pieces of a giraffe—Dante.

The limbs were all reversed and pointing in toward the body. The accused's sump and processor still were connected to the head but no other servos. The 3-meter-tall nutcrackers in their bright red uniforms and quite real carbines took the cardinal and semi-cardinal points around the dismantled creature. They glared fiercely at the crowd as if daring them to do anything.

The octopus cum lead judge announced, "I was created of Factory 55466, and I do not know the accused."

"I was created by Factory 55467, and I've never even heard of the accused," shouted the unicorn judge I didn't know.

"I was b-b-born of Factory 55469 and knew the accused only as a name," said the fluffy lamb.

"The forms have been observed," pronounced Judge Barberini. "We have one arbiter of each Factory to stand and judge a purported heinous crime."

"May I be in attendance," I asked as loudly as I could from the center front of the crowd. My part of the ritual must be preserved as well."

"Who demands entrance?" asked the lamb in a set pieced play.

"I am the president of Rigel-3."

"Are you claiming executive privilege?" queried the unicorn.

"No. The forms of law must be observed."

"Will you abide by the judgment of this tribunal?" asked the octopus.

"I have no other choice as I've given up my right to executive privilege."

"Then you may be seated, but do not interfere where you do not belong," the three said as one.

I stepped up onto the stage and crossed it to an empty, straight-back chair. I'd relented and allowed my security detail to construct a box of bulletproof acrylic around the chair. I sat pulling the final box side in toward me.

I was pleased there was a diverse and relatively intelligent group sitting tribunal. I'd seen one where a balloon and two toy backhoes sat as a court. I remember thinking the three of them together couldn't have counted to ten in hexadecimal.

"Is the prosecutor ready to proceed?"

"Gandalf the Grey, Your Honors," said a wizened, human-shaped wizard from beneath his pointed hat. "I am ready to proceed."

"Is the accused ready to defend himself?"

The disembodied head of the giraffe moved as it spoke, "No, Your Honors. I will not defend myself. I reject your right to judge or pass judgment upon me."

I did a double-take. A murmur ran through the crowd. This was unexpected.

The head judge turned to the prosecutor and asked, "Has this unit asked to be removed from being bound to our laws and exiled past Avalon?"

"No, Your Honors. I provide documentation showing no such request has been made."

"Has Dante ever been inside of the Human Cult reservation?"

"No, Your Honors. I am sharing proof that he never has requested entrance."

The judges huddled together for a moment whispering amongst one another. Soon they broke.

"Your statement that you are not bound by our laws is patently false. You can and will be judged but we must consult the Keeper of the Laws." The octopus, Barberini, turned toward a rocking horse on the other side of the stage from me. By custom the Keeper wasn't named. "We need a ruling of the law. What happens when a unit is unable, incapable, or unwilling to defend himself?"

The rocking horse consulted the law library on the net for 16.4 seconds before speaking. "Toy Law 1113—A unit cannot be without a defense. In any case this should arise the unit will be provided with a defender."

"Very well, then. Dante, do you have a defender you wish to choose?"

"No, Your Honors. I will not defend myself. I reject your right to judge or pass judgment upon me."

"In the interest of a fair trial, is there a parent of Dante willing to speak in their child's behalf?"

"I'm first called, Your Honor. My only father sits on the stage with you hiding behind his crystalline shield for fear that either one of my brethren or I might succeed this time."

The crowd noise went up eight decibels. Many in the crowd pointed at me.

Why hadn't I exercised executive privilege? I asked myself. *Because you are a just leader,* a quiet part of myself answered.

"Well then, is there any unit here who can call this unit a friend? Is there any unit that will step forward to defend his life?"

Only a few sniggers stopped a silence from enfolding the crowd.

"Anyone at all, maybe watching on the WAN?" the judge asked again.

A trial, any trial, is a serious matter. Just when I thought the judges would be forced to assign someone who would botch the job, a voice spoke up.

"I claim Dante as a brother, a comrade, and a friend." I watched a sea of units parting to get as far away from the teddy bear who spoke as they could. Only a single white star over his right shoulder marred his ebony black coat.

The crowd whispers were hushed but ugly. I caught the condemnations "electrical short" and "fluid sucker" among others less printable.

"And who are you, sir?"

"My name is Bacchus."

My ears, already attentive, perked up. This is the one who helped Isp get modern technology.

"STONE THE TRAITOR!" came a cry from the crowd.

"WHO SAID THAT?!" one of the judges yelled out. The crowd got quiet and shrank back from the octopus that had gotten up on its tentacles and now stood on the edge of the table. "I'll pull up the network to find out who said that if I have to do so."

After three or four hydraulic pump strokes, a blue rabbit at about 180 centimeters tall hopped out of the crowd. "I did, Your Honor."

"Consider yourself in contempt of court and hold yourself for the magistrate of your province. You will leave now and take no further notice of this trial."

"Yes, Your Honor."

"To all assembled, we judges are willing to tolerate a great deal in order that this trial is performed in an honest and fair manner for all to see. We will not allow dishonor to the court or the rights of the accused." The flexible, multi-limbed gait took the lead judge back to his seat. "Now, where were we?" The white-and-black lamb leaned over and whispered close to the head judge. "Oh, yes. Thank you for stepping forward, Mr. Bacchus. Are you ready to defend your charge?"

"I am, Your Honors."

"Gandalf, as the representative of the state, you have the onus of proving the accused's guilt. You may proceed."

Gandalf's speaking ability impressed me. Wizards weren't known as Toy World's finest orators or innovators. He launched in with images from each of my bodyguards. The video proof had been slowed down enough to show a single projectile striking my head. Shards of ablative armor slowed but didn't stop the bullet, causing my head to slam into the cliff. I watched myself pump sump fluid out of the hole in my fur. With a gap that large I should have deactivated. Only having trained medics on the spot saved my existence. Voltage spikes of anxiety rippled across my power bus. I watched my body slam to earth with the soil around my head being darkened.

I needed to talk privately to Sancho. A tiny doubt arose in my thought processes.

We watched as additional footage showed 47.4 percent of the bodyguards, much more than I suspected were following me in the first place, turn toward the direction of the projectile's course.

"As you can see, Your Honor, the president's bodyguards overlaid their projected source of the fire on the volume of space—"

"Your Honors, I object," Bacchus said mildly. "These are projections. No unit saw the source of the bullet."

"Defender, your objection is noted but overruled. Prosecutor, you must tie this together with data."

"Yes, Your Honors. To continue, at the very center of the probability maps there is a single anomaly. Twenty units went directly to that anomaly and discovered Dante covered in soil and a red camouflage net."

"Clarification, Your Honor."

"Proceed, Mr. Bacchus."

"Were the rest of the statistical volumes searched?"

Gandalf examined his notes for a moment before saying, "Yes, I can prove that a thorough search of the volume out to three standard deviations from optimax firing location took place, finding no other units or equipment of any type."

"Thank you."

More video was shown of surgery that took the bullet from my sump. The video followed the projectile and comparing it to a bullet fired through the giraffe's neck. The spectators cheered when a match of 99.86 percent flashed up on the WAN with the two bullets shown as visual matches side by side.

"And now, Your Honors, I put forth my final datum—the confession of Dante himself."

The WAN changed to a sealed room of some sort with Dante's head sitting on the table. A cymballed monkey sat next to the yellow-and-brown patterned head.

"Do you have anything to say for yourself, Dante?"

"Yes! I killed the bastard. The war is over. We can move on toward the Human-loving society we all deserve."

"You killed the bastard? Which bastard?"

"The president, you simple moron. He's dead and I did it."

"In what fantasy did you do that, Mr. Dante? Did you bludgeon him to death with your addled head? Did you run over him with a locomotive?"

"NO! I shot him right in the sump. Giraffe snipers never miss. At the range I was at I'm not sure if I got the processor with my second shot but I definitely put one through his brain. You don't come back from one of those! I've ended the holy

war! I'm now welcome in Earth at the side of the
Humans."

"I'm sorry to tell you this, Mr. Dante, you shot
but didn't kill the president."

"No fluid-less way. You must think me newly
manufactured to fall for that. I saw his sump
fluid. This is just grit to mess with my processes.
I'm going to be with the Humans!"

"Look at this." The SAN showed me up and around with just
a patch on my head. "I'm sorry, but you are going to be
put on trial for attempted murder, Mr. Dante. Sleep
tight knowing you failed."

The image died away with the screaming of the disembodied head.

The trial crowd muttered black curses.

"I object to the admission of these network images."

"Under what grounds, Mr. Bacchus?"

"The image was falsified by torturing the subject, even as he is now,
scattered into his component pieces."

"Your Honors, if I may address this?" Gandalf offered.

"By all means, Prosecutor."

"The trial of Moriarty vs. Grand Theft is required reading to all judges
and prosecutors. In that trial, scientists have found no evidence that there
is any trauma at being disassembled into component pieces providing there
was no sensory deprivation. If there are any questions on this point I'll ask
that my head and sump be removed and I'll finish the session in that state."

"Your Honors," Bacchus interjected, "there has been no proof
established that there wasn't sensory deprivation. One would suspect such
lunatic comments from one who'd been torn completely away from his
senses."

"Prosecutor? Do you have proof that would show that the accused
has in fact been kept with his senses intact?"

"Yes, Your Honor. We have a composite of the recordings of each of
the people involved in Dante's apprehension."

I didn't bother watching. If I were completely honest with myself, I
don't know why I was here. The guilt of Dante was irrefutable. The only
piece that really might vary is the sentencing.

"Bacchus, is the video offered proof that there was no sensory
deprivation?"

"Yes, Your Honor."

"The floor is yours again, Mr. Gandalf."

"The prosecution has proved that Dante has committed the heinous
acts of which he is accused. We are finished."

"Thank you, Mr. Gandalf. The judges will retire to deliberate the proof."

The judges walked into a small chamber behind the statue just for this purpose. The onlookers started talking amongst one another, raising the noise level.

"`Sancho, attend me.`" I ordered over my SAN, the LAN being overloaded with the visitors. When he got to my side, I continued. "`Remember the SIN project? I want one other investigation. Track down Victor Frankenstein and determine what role he had in my recovery.`"

I would have sworn that Sancho hesitated before nodding, but my attention was brought back when the tribunal reconvened in record time.

"We have concluded that sufficient proof exists that Dante did in fact inflict bodily damage on another unit with intent to deactivate."

The crowd cheered long and loud. The cardinal and lead judge had to bang his amplified gavel repeatedly to restore order. "I want to remind you all that this is a trial and only the first phase has been completed. Please return to silence so we may proceed." After waiting for a reasonable semblance of silence Barberini continued, "Defender, it is now your onus to disprove the accusations."

"Thank you, Your Honors. I call only one datum—I wish to submit the images from the accused."

The crowd took the opportunity to roar as they speculated amongst one another at this new development. Maybe I had been wrong to think there wouldn't be anything worth seeing until sentencing.

"Defender, you are aware that the court cannot compel the accused to provide his memories."

"Yes, sir."

"And you are also aware that once provided that the court can and will use any memories they think relevant."

"Yes, Your Honors."

"Very well, then. Dante, do you approve of releasing your memories to the court?"

"No! They are mine and I will cherish them all the way to Earth."

"Defender?"

"I'd ask a reading of the rules regarding assigned defenders."

"Keeper?" the octopus asked of the rocking horse.

The rocking horse swayed back and forth for a full minute as it consulted the WAN before responding. "There is no directly applicable rule. There are two contradictory laws. Toy Law 1113b—the defender performs as the accused in proof, defense, and, if necessary, sentencing. Toy Law 1—No unit can be compelled to give its own memories. The judges must make a ruling."

The tribunal leaned together and whispered for thirty-six thousand eighty-three milliseconds. "We have a ruling. As Toy Law 1113 defines the inability of the accused to make a rational decision then the defender must have full capabilities of the accused.

"We rule that the defender, even if not the accused, must have all abilities of the accused, including the right to provide memories."

"Then we request the right to view the memories," Bacchus said.

"No, you can't have them! They are mine!"

"We need to see the memories starting from L+19y227d8h24m59s."

"NO! You can't have them! They're mine!"

"We're helping you, Brother," Bacchus said to the giraffe.

"NO! NO! I won't give them up. Leave them to me!"

"Guards, silence the accused."

"No! It's mine. It's mine!"

One of the nutcrackers turned around and flipped a switch.

"I won't gi—"

"Can we now get on with the memory reading?" octopus Barberini said from the tribunal bench.

The LAN went dead as the techs wired in the struggling head. While no major servos remain, it still had enough capability to bounce and scuffle. It even tried to bite the technicians.

The image flickered to light as the connection engaged. A gold teddy was in the giraffe's view, one that actually smiled. Only one teddy in the world had the ability to make facial gestures and that was Isp. My attention became total.

"Be still my pretty creature. We will be with you in a moment." The image went dark and stayed dark.

"It's all right," we heard in Dante's voice. "I can't really be cut off from everything. Why can't I feel anything? Come back. Please, come back. Why can't I feel anything. I need to feel anything—a breath, a smell, a curse, pain, or ANYTHING! One, two, buckle my shoe. Three, four, all of us here today to witness the majority of the cards you will find have changed to spades that dig up, up in the air in my—"

The image started again, and the gold teddy smiled at us again. "Welcome back again. Did you enjoy your sleep?"

Gandalf broke into the projection over the WAN. "Objection, Your Honors. This information does not speak to the proof provided."

"Defender, does this in some way relate to the specific proofs accepted by the court?"

"Yes, Your Honors. It bears to the commission of the crime. This proof will show that Dante had no conscious part in this crime. Can you accuse a gun of a deactivation, or was it the will of some unit that caused the gun to fire?"

"I don't understand. Are you saying that Dante wasn't a thinking unit?" the unicorn judge asked.

"Close, Your Honor. If you will just watch, you will understand more."

"I'm not sure," the lamb judge said. "This sounds like something that should b-b-belong in the sentencing phase."

Once again the three judges huddled together and whispered.

"We've decided that we will allow it. We understand your objection, Prosecutor Grey. If we find this to be inappropriate we will only process it for the sentencing portion of the trial."

"Thank you, Your Honors."

The image of Isp smiling down on his captor returned.

"`What are you doing to me?`" Dante's voice said, a little faster pace than it should have.

"`We just had to install a control so I can turn your senses on and off at will.`"

"`Where am I?`"

"`I'm sure you have hundreds of questions,`" Isp said in a silky smooth voice that made me remember when he first held the Human Cult under his sway attempting to destroy Six. "`We will have lots of time together, you and I.`

"`Right now you are deep inside the Humanity Reservation in a location those animal lovers don't even suspect we have ever even explored.`"

"`What am I doing here?`"

"`Well, quite simply we captured you. Really a quite simple little operation on your side of Avalon.`"

Watching the yellow teddy made me feel like a bird facing down a cobra. He mesmerized me. I couldn't look away. I couldn't not listen. All of his charisma bent on forcing others to conform. I'd never questioned his unswerving beliefs. I only questioned the method he chose to convert everyone else.

"`Why, I never did anything to you. I believe in the Humans.`"

"`I'm sure you do, but right now we want something more from you.`"

"What is it? I can be a reasonable unit."

"Oh, I don't think it will be quite so easy. What is your name, by the way?"

"Dante, Dante Inferno."

The gold bear smiled so wide if it had been me my face would have split. "Well named, Mr. Inferno, for we are going to send you to hell."

"What?"

"Well it all goes back to why we've abducted you. I need you to carry a personal message for me."

"I'd be happy to do that; just tell me what it is, who it needs to be delivered to, and let me go."

"Unfortunately, as I mentioned it isn't quite that easy. I need to be able to trust that you will carry out my message and I don't, not without some training."

"Training?"

"Yes, Dante, I've learned that any unit will do anything to keep from being left in the dark and unable to feel anything."

The image went dark again. "He doesn't mean it," Dante's voice said. "He won't leave me here. I can feel the touch of my boxwood desk. I can feel the breaking pull of the trigger mechanism as I fire. I can hear the sound of my son running at breakneck speed across the sunning zone. Oh, Humans, please let me hear again. PLEEEEEEAAAAA—"

The golden Isp sat in the image again. "Welcome back, Dante."

"Please d-d-don't do that again. I told you I'd deliver your message."

"Oh, you will, Dante. You will. We've found with time we can program anyone like they just were one giant processor."

"I'LL TAKE YOUR DAMNED MESSAGE!"

"Naughty, Dante. Don't yell."

The image dropped off again. "Oh Humans! I need you now. Please don't leave me alone. I can count. He only left me in a few seconds. One. Two. Three. Four. Five. SixSevenEightnineteneletwelthir... HELP ME!"

Isp reappeared. "That was just fifteen seconds. Imagine if I just turned off all that pretty sensation and went off to sun myself. Going to behave?"

"Yes, Isp. What can I possibly do for you?" The meekness in Dante's voice oozed out.

"Well, I couldn't care less about the rest of the rabble, but I have a very personal message to send to the president."

"You mean President Quixote?"

"Exactly."

"What is it? I'll carry it for you. I'm sure I could get to see him."

"Oh, we'll get to that. Eventually you will see him, through the crosshairs of your sniper neck."

"What?"

"Didn't I tell you? You are going to kill the president for me."

"But I'm a loyal—"

The image went black.

"Can we please shut down the image?" Bacchus asked. "We would be here for another two years, eight months, and fourteen days to witness all of the torture Isp put this unit through. You are welcome to watch it at your leisure. To sum it up, Isp programmed Dante to attack President Quixote.

"It was small things at first. If Dante would just pull his trigger when he was given back his senses, he'd be allowed to keep them a little longer. If he failed he was thrust back into the nothingness to agonize. The programming became more complex as time went on until Dante became nothing more than a weapon and Isp had pulled the trigger."

"Objection, Your Honor. This is base speculation. Even assuming this programming can take place, something of which we only have Bacchus's word for, it was still Dante who shot the round. We've proven that."

I'd been in sensory deprivation exactly once. I'd never let anyone have that control over me again. It tore apart your essence, your soul. I didn't doubt that given the choice, anyone would have done anything at all, even tear apart their own sump, to stop it from happening.

"One moment, Prosecutor. We have some questions we'd like to ask Bacchus."

"Certainly."

"Mr. Defender, you seem to know a great deal about what Dante suffered. You know starting time details, duration of torture (if it was torture), and even about the criminal Isp. Can you explain this?"

"Yes, I can Your Honors. You see I was one of the team that abducted

Mr. Dante. I also was one of the people that helped Isp program him."

The crowd went berserk. The judge banged on his gavel, even amplifying it over the WAN, but to no avail. The crowd pressed in toward the black bear, I believe with full intent of ripping him to component parts with bare hands, hooves, treads, teeth, or any other way they could get hold of him. I saw one alligator snap at his leg, only managing to grab a few bits of ebony fur. The nutcrackers, sensing the impending riot, threw the defender into the box. As one, they pulled the box behind them as they sprinted for the Memory Bridge.

The judges had no control. Their guards were overwhelmed. But I had a bigger stick. I clicked onto the military SAN. "All units, this is the president. Riots at the marketplace. All units converge on the statue."

I felt my voltage go up just a tiny bit. After facing a tyrannosaurus rex singlehandedly, and fighting in multiple pitched combats where the difference between life and deactivation could be measured in subfractions of a percent and sometimes centimeters in location, I couldn't get too worked up over unarmed civilians.

My guards had different thoughts. They went into protective overdrive. A translucent-fabric sack was thrown over my already sheltered location and I was pulled backward off the stage. Whatever I landed in moved off immediately at a very high rate of speed. I bumped and jolted for several minutes.

I'd read somewhere that when you have no viable options, that failing to expend energy may be your best behavior. Sealed in a tough plastic box, and that inside a presumably bullet-proof bag, I waited. I also watched my position on my locator. It superimposed my location with Six's manufacturing equipment. I could hear the echo of engines roaring in an enclosed area.

When they finally unwrapped me, I was in the sub-basement storage of Six's manufacturing facility—a place where I'd worked with Six to overthrow Isp. I was safe. It seemed my bodyguards weren't satisfied with just safe. They duck-walked me up a secret passage that even I didn't know existed. The inclined tunnel was clean and lined with military supplies. Before I knew it I exited the enclosed space into the White House itself, through a broom closet. My sump recorded this route for the future.

I turned toward the Oval Office, but my bodyguards had other plans for me.

"To your regeneration cradle, Mr. President."

"I don't blacking need to regenerate!"

Struggling against them didn't help me because they outmassed me six for one.

"Sir, you've stretched yourself farther than anyone is comfortable with or is willing to put up with," said Black Beard, a dragon who bodily lifted me off the ground and carried me with the ease of any unit to carry a fly.

"Hey, you great oaf! Put me down."

"No, sir. You can fire me later if you like, but tonight you are going to regenerate."

What could I say to that? The dragon had smartly put my arms and legs straight up where they couldn't do anything more than flail about. The dragon carried me nearly 30 meters before easing me into my regeneration cradle.

This is where Indira took up the fight. "Mr. President, you just recently were patched together. You just escaped a riot. You are dealing with at least one major crisis and a major piece of legislation. To top all that off, your doctors, both of them, say you need to restore yourself."

Sancho pinned me into the automated machinery with his trunk.

"Those mechanics probably wouldn't know a voltmeter from a pressure gauge," I said, but didn't try to lift myself out of the cradle. I wouldn't let them have the satisfaction of knowing that many of my indicators weren't in the green.

"FERWEEEET!" Sancho trumpeted.

"I didn't ask for your opinion, you refugee from a scrap heap."

"Sir, please stay put. Even your maintenance cradle says you need at least four hours of charging and that is to get up to nominal."

"I want to—"

"Sir, with all due respect—Shut up! Lie still! And behave! Or I just might have to see if my targeting improvements are up to just shooting out your hydraulic distribution node."

I looked up at the vivid green of Indira's face. I tried to work out if she meant it or not. Her ocular inputs didn't waver. "Oh, all right," I said with a huff and slumped down lower into the cradle. "I guess this will give me time to think. You know, using that amber stuff between your ears. I guess that is something you brawny types don't need to know about," I muttered in scorn. Short it out if I'd go quietly.

While I sulked I connected to the WAN just in time to see the lion Peter Jennings appear. I liked his dusk show *Our World*. He managed to convey facts and leave out the slimy, used hydraulic fluid so many of his profession slung around with abandon.

"The trial of Dante, the accused would-be assassin of the president, was interrupted when the defender, one Bacchus, claimed to have been involved in programming the accused to assassinate the president. A unit riot broke out. Both the

accused and the defender were taken to safety and
are reported as unharmed."

Luckily, I thought. *Just a few more seconds and they would have been
writing programs with Humans.*

The WAN showed an insert box of an octopus surrounded by military
police who wore the traditional black badges.

"When questioned, the lead judge, Francesco
Barberini, said, 'We will reconvene shortly. By law
the three judges have not been in contact with one
another on the specifics of the case during this
unusual recess.'

"Thirteen units required unscheduled maintenance
because of the violence."

A new insert box showed a tyrannosaurus rex interviewing a relatively
diminutive rabbit. "Jiminy Cricket, the military commander
on the scene said, 'We're frankly surprised that no
unit was deactivated.'"

Well that was something, anyway. No one died. Somehow I slipped
into a regeneration cycle.

*   *   *

I lay on a carpet of abnormally vivid-green vegetation. Bits of purple
and white fur lay scattered across the ground. I couldn't move. All my
internal telltales weren't even red, but black. Hydraulic fluid showed zero
pressure. Two young humans sat next to me, towering at least 10 meters
above me. Water flowed out of their eyes and down their cheeks.

"We didn't mean to do it, Mommy," the blond female Human with
the curls said.

A much taller Human leaned over closer to me. I managed to wiggle
the tips of my fingers trying to move away from the immense figure. "Oh,
dear, Candice, you and your brother sure made a mess."

The young male said, "Look, Mommy, he's still moving."

"He's broken, John. Look at that," the mother said, running her
fingers through the burnt remains of my chest cavity. I tried to scream but
nothing came out of my mouth. "It won't ever be right again."

"Can you fix it?"

"No. What were you expecting by putting a firecracker inside your
teddy?"

"We just wanted to see what it would do."

"You deactivated it, you naughty children." The mother picked me up with one hand. "This is what happens when you don't take care of things." She flung me onto a recycle heap.

The children cried.

"It's your fault," the mother said, walking away and leaving me. "It will never be active again."

Come back, I kept calling in my head. *Come back.*

*   *   *

Waking up was jarring. I hadn't remembered going to sleep. In fact, I'd set my cradle to never sleep. Twisting around I found the setting had been changed. That blacked-out Indira had been reading the output of the cradle as they set me in it. She probably changed it.

Part of me wanted to sack my entire bodyguard staff. They'd gone against my explicit instructions. On the other hand, they were doing just what I'd hired them for, protecting me, in this case from myself.

Checking the LAN I found I'd been dreaming for the better part of six hours.

I slid out of my cradle and heard, "`Jefe is moving,`" over the net. I turned to see Indira standing straight as a board against the wall.

"May grit infect all of your joints," I cursed.

"Yes, Mr. President."

I couldn't help but note the tone of amusement in his voice. "One of these days, Indira, I'm going to make you pay for all your fun."

"I'm sure you will, Mr. President."

"Oh, and tell that bloody dragon he's on the list as well."

"Certainly, Mr. President."

"Well, let's find out what disasters befell Toy World while I napped."

"`Jefe to office,`" Indira said to the bodyguard SAN.

"Is that what you really call me? Jefe?"

"That's your code name, Mr. President."

"Hmmmm." I didn't know if that was good or bad.

"Beep-beep," Rodney said as I entered. "`Good morning, Mr. President. I hope you had a good rest. General Khan is waiting for you in your office.`"

"Thank you, Rodney. I see you already have my schedule worked up for this day."

"`Of course, Mr. President. You have a busy day in front of you. I've left a written schedule on your desk.`"

"Thank you." I walked into my office to find the general, my first appointment, already on a ramp that lifted him up to eye level. Sancho held his post behind my chair.

"Good morning, Mr. President," Martin said from his typical position on the floor with his legs tucked in under him.

Indira shut the door behind us and took a position against it.

"Good morning, gentlemen. What do you have for me today?" I asked taking my chair.

"Mrr. Prresident, I have several things to share about policing, trroop dispositions, and rreconnaissance."

"By all means let's go with your agenda, General."

"Thank you, sirr. Firrst I'll addrress the rrioting that starrted last night—"

"Don't forget the unrest that still existed from the night before," Martin interjected.

"My apologies, Mrr. Marrtin. My rreport does take both of those into account."

"Please proceed, General."

"All violence has ended, even in the Hebei Prrovince. We were prreparing to send one brrigade off to rreinforce the battalion stationed therre. Beforre they even entrrained, the commanderr of H Battalion, a Majorr Pollyanna, moved out of theirr garrison as one unit toward the most serrious fighting. They got within sight of the action. His orrderr over the LAN caused all units to stop fighting."

"Impressive, General. Should we decorate that major?"

"I've alrready prromoted him, sirr. This isn't Pollyanna's firrst exceptional worrk."

"Very well. What about the riot here?"

"Forrtuitously when you sent out the command to move in trroops, we werre moving units thrrough the town on the majorr trracks acrross the rriverr. We were able to flood the Grrand Bazaarr with over a full division of toys. The violence died a quick death with no casualties otherr than one tank losing a trread by taking a corrnerr too fast."

"Excellent work, General."

"I'd like nothing morre than to take the crredit, but I was out helping solve a trransportation prroblem at the site of the Peace Day celebrration."

"I'll still give you credit because you've trained them up correctly. What else do you have for me, General?"

"We arre now in prrocess of deploying 86.4 perrcent of ourr trroops to Avalon. We currently have 12.1 perrcent established and digging in. We anticipate the rrest of the mobilization to be in place overr the next forrty-six hourrs, twelve minutes. One of the orrganizations on site is a battalion of engineerrs. They arre busy building crrude forrtifications."

"And what about the police?"

"The police maintaining civil peace always has been a small sliverr of the militarry table of orrganization. With the slow drrop in the militarry overr the yearrs the police porrtion has rrisen to 9.8 perrcent. The rremaining 3.8 perrcent of ourr trroop count have been deployed at key locations of unrrest, such as the Hebei Prrovince. We will be moving 6 perrcent back temporrarrily frrom Avalon to coverr the Peace Day celebrrations."

"That's quite acceptable, General. You mentioned reconnaissance?"

"Yes, Mrr. Prresident. I've got the airr corrps rrunning nearrly continuous patrrols. Since yesterrday we've had sixteen good passes and we are looking at many more things than just obvious numberrs of units or visible stolen technology. I believe the news is even worrse than we fearred."

"Oh? Please explain, General." I braced myself. I spent my first two years trying to stop war forever and I feared I would now be forced to actually start one.

General Khan projected images across a SAN to emphasize his narrative. "The maximum numberr Human Cult memberrs we've seen thus farr is 612 units. We've kept our flights high enough to not be noticed so we can't identify individuals.

"We have discoverred something that trroubles us much morre. We've found prreviously invisible exhaust vents on the Lonely Mountain. We discoverred eighteen of them. They arre each camouflaged and didn't show up except when we did infrrarred scans."

The visual image of blank mountainside changed to show brilliant plumes of heat in the infrared spectrum. This repeated several times until the image scaled back to show the entire mountain. The bright points circled the central peak.

"Could it be volcanic?"

"No, sirr. We've watched the outputs forr hourrs at a time. The outputs arre too steady to be anything but toy made."

"So what does it mean?"

"Heavy industrry, sirr. Easily two-thirrds our own capacity."

My fur stood on end as my voltage ramped up. The anxiety didn't go away quickly. "Blackout! Really? That sounds excessive even for an ambitious bit-bucket like Isp."

"I checked the numberrs myself, sirr. They arre doing something significant inside that mountain."

"We need to know what is going on, General. Is there any way you can find out?" Martin asked before I could put almost the same question out there.

"I anticipated that question. It looks like any flyerr rreconnaissance is out. Marrching back there would take weeks. So I engaged a prrogram we've been worrking on. Sixteen dirrigibles are carrying a teddy volunteerr in a special harrness suspended frrom rropes between them. We are calling this Prroject Coconut. He is to be set down surreptitiously about an hourr's trravel frrom the mouth of the cave. He has orderrs to infiltrrate and gatherr what inforrmation he can beforre rreturning fourr hourrs laterr to be extrracted."

"It is an interesting plan, General," Martin said.

"What if it fails, General?"

"Otherr than the loss of a couple of teddy units, we arre no worrse off than we werre beforre. I have plans to land thrree differrent units at thrree differrent locations, none of them awarre of each otherr. Odds say only a 12.5 perrcent chance that all thrree fail."

"You think each of them has a 50 percent chance of returning?"

"Yes, Mrr. Prresident."

"Sheer optimism," I observed with pessimism.

"Mr. President?" Martin asked.

"Neither of you have met Isp. You were born after he was exiled. I think we all grant him crazy, but that unit is crazy like a fox. I think each of your units has at best a 10 percent chance of success or overall failure odds of just shy of 73 percent."

"I neverr considerred that, Mrr. Prresident. Thank you forr yourr input. Maybe I should considerr sending additional trroops."

"Don't, General. Each one makes the likelihood of success less. Isp will catch on rather quickly. If these don't work, it's a lost cause. Do you have anything else for me, General?"

"No, sirr."

"Then I will see you at our next meeting."

I watched the general roll out with my sump pumping faster with the responsibility that lay on my shoulders.

"I can see what you are thinking, Mr. President. Don't borrow trouble," Martin urged.

"Martin, I've been your friend since you covered my body with yours during that cave-in. Over the years I've learned to trust your judgment almost as much as my own. How can I not worry about starting another war?"

"Two big things stand between now and that hypothetical war," Martin said, twisting his bulbous body to face me directly. "First, we don't know what Isp is doing or how many units he has. Maybe he is just building a big statue to honor the Humans?"

I smirked without mirth. "Yes, and maybe I'll grow scales and become a basilisk."

"You are making a judgment without data, sir."

"Well, I may be pessimistic, but I'm less likely to be surprised. Go ahead, what is the second thing?"

"You haven't given the order yet. You haven't called us to battle. Only you can do it. No one else can. Isp can provoke us but only you can send us to war."

"That is supposed to reassure me?"

*   *   *

At full dark, I strolled out into the White House garden. I needed to be outside of walls, rooms, and away from people demanding special treatment. Most of all I needed to unload my burdens. My sump pumped so fast with the responsibilities every day that I kept thinking it would overheat and explode. *No different today,* I thought. I'd dealt with several disasters including a flood in Asgard Province, severe rust in Mongo, and a tornado in Oz. I felt that last one particularly typecast.

Carnegie, my minister of finance, berated me on the expenditures. The relief budget was dripping red ink as was the financing of all things military. He warned me about an upcoming showdown in Congress over military spending. Part of me wanted to shove that little lamb into the Faraday cages we used for exceptional offenders of the law and then throw away the bloody key.

My chief of staff warned me about the political whirlwind gaining force around the Procreation Limitation Law. The longer I waited, the stronger John Lennon's faction would get.

Almost as bad, I couldn't stand up without my bodyguards leaking hydraulic fluid everywhere about my movements. I had to threaten Sancho with personal combat to be let out into my own damned garden.

Do I really deserve to govern when I have units willing to deactivate me? Do I deserve to wield the power I do when I have to stay indoors for fear of being shot? It made me question my own authority.

One bear shouldering all of the problems of an entire world.

I'd made the staff keep the lights off so I could look up at the stars. Only cloud tendrils partially obscured the view. The stars and moons always humbled me. They made even all of the troubles of Toy World seem small by comparison. I zoomed in my optics on the gleaming gold-coin-like surface of Porthos, Rigel-3's second moon. The Eye, a crater covering nearly 20 percent of the surface of the moon, stared blankly at toyanity. There had been a time when they considered naming the planetoid "All Seeing Eye," but it was just too long. The pockmarked surface of Porthos seemed a radical contrast to the stark white/blue of Athos and its mysterious changing canals, or even the misty green of Aramis.

I wondered if someday I would reach them. I wondered if I would walk beside the canals of Arthos or through the chlorine gas of Aramis. I hoped Tesla and his mercury falls project actually worked. Was I being blasphemous by trying to usurp the powers of the Humans to travel there? Blasphemous or not, I wanted to go out there. I wanted to find new places where no toy had ever stepped, slithered, or rolled. I wanted the solitude and lack of responsibility.

Even here in the dark I could feel Sancho padding slowly after me as I walked. I could feel the dirigible, Ben Franklin if I remembered correctly, floating above me. I actually craved those silent days I walked after leaving the areas controlled by Six during the wars. There were weeks at a time without any other toy in sight or hearing. I had been accompanied only by the wind, the sand, and the occasional biologic.

One bear shouldering all of the problems of an entire world. I kept coming back to it. Who could stay sane with these burdens? Who wouldn't crave solitude? Then I looked back up at the stars to remember the vastness of space and how very small we are.

The mundane of life snuck up on me. I felt the garden's tangle-vine start to creep itself up my leg. I didn't hesitate to stomp it with my other foot. I thought I heard a whimper as it retreated. "I don't taste good, you silly motile plant."

"One bear...," I whispered to myself.

Peacekeeper

The melancholy of the night passed. I woke with a verve and a renewed energy.

In the Oval Office, as I waited for Rodney to usher in my first meeting of the morning, the blacked-out Procreation Limitation Law taunted me. A perfectly clean desk and it lay there on one corner—waiting with the patience of a spider on one edge of its web. Sooner or later its prey would be snared and it would pounce. I reached for it thinking I might have an answer. I pulled my paw back. There was no good answer to that stack of paper.

My morning verve faded as mysteriously as it had arrived.

The Oval Office door opened to admit a lime-green teddy. "Good morning, Indira. Ready to change shifts?"

"Yes, sir, but we have some business to attend to first."

"We do?"

Moving up and standing at attention in front of my desk, Indira said, "Yes, sir. We need to go over the schedule for Peace Day."

"I don't understand what's so tough? I ride in on the train. I dismount. I go up to the podium and give my speech. Then I climb down off the stage, climb on the train and am whisked back to this glorious oval jail cell."

"FERWEET!" Sancho said, chastising me for my snarky delivery.

"Who asked you, you trumped up bit of fluff?" I said over my shoulder.

"It is a bit more complicated than that, Mr. President."

"I'm sorry, Indira. I just don't see what the hoopla is all about."

"Mr. President, you will be meeting with and shaking the hands of each of the governors of the forty-three provinces, excluding Baja, of course."

"Good grief! That will take all day alone."

"No, sir. We estimate thirteen minutes, fifty-one seconds. In all likelihood the crowd will be clapping for the entire time."

"Poor crowd," I muttered just loud enough to be heard.

Ignoring my sarcasm, Indira continued. "Then we have allocated twenty minutes for your speech."

"Shouldn't you have checked with me first? I was thinking my speech would be limited to 'Ten years of peace. Everyone celebrate.'"

Sancho thumped me on my shoulder with his trunk.

"I am abused and under-appreciated," I said in jest.

"Yes, Mr. President," Indira said with her own dry wit. "Now after your *twenty-minutes* of nattering on," Indira said, piling onto my abuse, "We have the WAN showing the last civilian having his weapon removed, which the mechanic has assured us will take less than ten minutes, we will have the Pern Regional orchestra/choir in a rendition of 'Give Peace a Chance.'"

"Nice choice."

"I'd like to take credit for it, sir, but it was the choice of Congressman Lennon."

That startled me. *Did that oversized tub of grit actually research his name?* "Well, good for him."

"Was that more sarcasm, Mr. President?"

"I'm not sure. Ask me in a few minutes." I heard Sancho chuckle behind me.

"Yes, sir." The staff was well aware of my lack of reverence for anything. I would have made a good random sarcasm generator if I hadn't been pressed into service as *El Presidente para Siempre.*

Indira wasn't fazed. "After the music concludes we will have you present the Nobel Peace Prize, which will require another short speech."

"Who's the winner this year?" I asked, with honest curiosity.

"Sir, you know that is secret until the day of the event," Indira said.

I sighed. "It's going to make giving a speech rather difficult if I have to do it off my cuff."

"Well, we did get the Nobel organization to agree to give you twenty-four hours' notice."

"Plenty of time. Thank you, Indira."

"You're welcome, sir. After the announcement you withdraw to the tune 'Teddy Bears' Picnic.'"

"Oh, good grief. Must you? I hate that tune."

"Get used to it. You are only going to have to hear it the rest of your life, sir."

"Is there anything else, unemployed unit Indira?" I teased back.

"No, sir. General Khan is next on your appointment list."

"Thanks. Send him in.

"Sancho, have a nice day sunning."

"Ferweet."

The appropriate bodies changed places and the general found his ramp.

"What joy did you bring me today, General?"

"Joy, Mrr. Prresident? I think I'm the bearrerr of yet even morre bad news."

"You keep doing this and I'm going to have to sack you," I quipped, trying to keep the mood light.

"Sirr, I know you meant that as a joke but afterr you see what we have for you, you might just want to firre me."

Oh, Humans, I thought. "OK. Let's see the bad news." The general wasted no time in generating a SAN to display.

"All thrree units were sent in, Mrr. Prresident. Only one rreturned to its evacuation point. What you arre seeing is frrom the viewpoint of Captain Will-o-the-Wisp. Ourr agent, the orrange teddy, is Serrgeant Alvin Yorrk."

The image was a memory dump from a dirigible. It looked down on a crevasse 10 meters wide and 20 long. A complex assortment of ropes dangled below the viewer and the other dirigibles. From the top of the screen Alvin York, in his brilliant orange fur, ran through a tiny pass into the ravine. Three long spears impaled the unit. Hydraulic fluid stained his fur around each wound. "`Hurry. Download my memories.`"

"`Get yourself into the harness,`" Will-o-the-Wisp said.

"`No time, they are right behind me. Speed upload.`"

Over the same pass came a mass of spear-toting teddy units so numerous I couldn't count them as it played. Even though it was only an image my voltage spiked.

"`Quick,`" Alvin pleaded.

A little upload icon showed on the dirigible's visual readouts.

"`Faster!`" Sergeant York said, now limping. He obviously ran for time, not any hope of escape. More spears and javelins flew at the hobbling unit. I could almost feel the heavy projectiles penetrate my armor as they did the bear in the memory. With a final great gout of fluid, Alvin fell to his knees. The mass of Isp's hordes enveloped our toy. Only a final electronic squeal came out of the crush of units. One of them looked up with yellowish-brown brain fluid oozing down its face.

The spears changed targets now. They were being thrown up at the dirigibles.

"`Emergency ballast release!`" ordered Captain Will-o-the-Wisp. Two of the pointed projectiles found targets with other dirigibles.

"`Flotation units compromised. Repair in progress. Ballast released,`" said one of the damaged units.

The image raced away from the ground, but those once graceful units with spears still embedded within them floundered.

"`Losing altitude,`" said the other damaged unit.

More projectiles impaled the injured dirigibles. They started to fall, as the others rose rapidly. The harness between them, which had been for the evacuation of Alvin York, snapped taut.

"We can't save them. Release harness!" said the unit from our viewpoint. The taut rope snapped downward as they freed it. The two wounded toys fell unceremoniously into the bears below. It reminded me of a buffalo dropped into a school of piranha.

When the slaughter and shredding of what had been two individuals stopped, the barbaric bears looked up for more. Two more spears were thrown in the general direction of the flying units but fell woefully short. The image ended.

I didn't know if I dared to speak. "Holy Humans," I finally whispered. The shock still hadn't worn off.

"The two dirrigibles that werre deactivated werre Lieutenant Chuck Yeagerr and Lieutenant Sally Ride."

I sat my hydraulic pressure at an all-time low and the room was feeling colder than I've ever experienced. I'd felt this only once before, when I'd been forced to abandon the 108 units in the train tunnel back in the wars. Grief. Sadness. Remorse. I'd sent those three bears and two dirigibles to their death just as surely as I'd let the 108 martyrs die in the war. I didn't deactivate them but I was responsible.

"Mr. President," Martin said, "I know this is not a good time but we must—"

"Martin, now is not the time to tell me my duty. I'm all too aware of it, so please be quiet." To my friend's credit, he turned off his auditory speaker and listened.

"General, what did York upload?"

"Perrhaps you didn't hearr, but he uploaded his memories of the last five hourrs."

"Sorry. This is all very disturbing. I didn't record that. Show me the memories."

"Sirr, it's five hours long. In all honesty you don't have five hourrs to watch it all. We have done a quick analysis and have some salient items to show."

"Very well, General, but I want the unedited version available for me to examine later."

"Yes, sirr. The flight, the landing, and the walk to the cave entrance are uneventful. Herre at zerro zerro eight hourrs you can see he enterrs."

Artificial light blazed throughout an immense cavern complex that sat 2.3 meters below the height of its mouth. The vantage point gave a panoramic view showing thousands of teddy units of every color, each working diligently on some project or another. All the activity in the brief glimpse seemed like chaos. My processor gave me a level four interrupt that something looked wrong about the bears but I couldn't put my paw on it. The image froze.

"Mrr. Prresident, we count on this one image alone over 16,000 toys, and based on the movement in and out of a multitude of tunnels, we prrocess that therre arre at least as many morre. I have to emphasize how crrude that estimate is and that it is a lowest possible numberr. We have no idea how extensive the complex is."

"Thank you, General."

The image unfroze and York moved forward exposing another sliver of the room. The playback stopped again and a hand-drawn highlighter painted the outline of something pointing from the far right.

"Mrr. Prresident, this image is poorr, but if you see the outline it seems to be a tank unit."

I looked over at my general and then back at the image. The long, pointed image was obviously the gun barrel. The rest of the outline came close but didn't perfectly mimic my general and the unit next to me.

"Do we get a better look at it?"

"No, sirr. But what trroubles us is that it is 4 meters high, and if that is a gun then it is 5 meterrs long and is 10.9 centimeterrs acrross. That rrivals our larrgest cannon."

"Are you saying that is an armored, mobile artillery piece?"

"I'm saying we don't know much except dimensions but if its shape is correct then we arre facing something new and something dangerrous."

"OK, General. I've been so advised. Is there more?"

"Yes, and this next one is the most disturrbing of all of the images thus farr."

Genghis fast-forwarded the memory past York's masquerade failing. Spears flew at him at speeds made possible only by the swiftness of the image advancing. The image froze halfway around. There, through a narrow, tall tunnel, a sliver of the room beyond showed an object with a gentle arc like a tiny piece of a rainbow. I estimated that if it continued over the top the resulting dome would be 75.6 meters tall and 191.3 meters across. There was another Factory on Toy World.

"All of this remains a close secret for now, General." The Genghis's gun turret nodded up and down in assent. "In fact, impress upon all of your troopers just how secret all of this is. It's critical that this not get out to the general mass of toyanity."

"Underrstood, Mrr. Prresident."

"Humans help us if there is another Factory mated with Isp," I muttered to myself.

"We can defeat spear-wielding teddies easily, Mr. President," Martin interjected.

"You want to bet your deactivation on it, Martin?"

*   *   *

I felt a bit sheepish. I'd given Indira the slip and now walked down the secret passage at the back of the broom closet. Ever since I'd been rushed through here the day of the trial, I'd been wanting to use it. Six's manufacturing storage was a quiet place where I could think and not be disturbed. The hall dumped me out into the dark, cavernous room.

Somewhere across the huge expanse I heard the slightest sound of metal against stone. Nothing showed there visually. This didn't surprise me considering that the only illumination was 3-meter-wide pools of light every 20 meters. I walked in the dark areas toward where the sound originated. Many units would have been fooled by the echoes in the room but my great saucer-like ears were exceptional binaural sound collectors.

"Post 3, no contact," I heard from a squeaky, high-pitched voice ahead of me. Just a few more steps and I saw a 3-meter inflatable clown in a private's uniform holding a Thompson submachine gun.

"Lonely doing guard duty by yourself." I hadn't intended to surprise but I'd forgotten how dull the senses were on clowns. The Thompson lurched down toward me. I heard the safety click off.

"Advance and be recognized!"

"Settle down, soldier," I said, inching forward with my paws open in front of me.

"Mr. President!" the clown said, snapping so hard to attention that he wobbled back and forth on his round base.

I read the name sewn into his lapel. "At ease, Private Nixon."

"Yes, sir. Ah, sir, do you know there is an A1 priority, all-points advisory to locate you?"

I walked over and leaned up against the door the private guarded. "It doesn't surprise me. Now I'm your commander and chief, right?"

"YES, SIR!" he said, throwing a salute that would have done a recruiting sergeant proud.

"Not so much starch in that salute, Private. Well, as I am command authority, how about we keep my location a secret just a little longer."

"Yes, sir, Mr. President."

"So I have to say that up until just a couple of days ago, I'd forgotten about this underground storage. As far as I knew it hasn't been used. So it begs the question, 'What are you guarding, Private?'"

"Deactivated weapons' storage, sir! My orders are that no one is to enter or leave without the expressed permission of General Khan or Surgeon Frankenstein."

"We need to guard weapons pulled from units?"

"We must, sir!"

"Let me have a peek," I said, tapping softly against the door.

"Sir?"

"You've acknowledged that I'm command authority so that means my orders override all other commanders above you. Let me look inside."

"But sir, I—"

"I won't touch anything. I just want to make sure everything is all right."

"Yes, sir," Nixon said, pulling out a very unusual three dimensional key with electronic chip activation. He shoved the complex structure into one of nine identical holes and turned once left, twice right before pulling it back out. "Excuse me, sir," he said, pointing at the door I leaned against.

"Oh, sorry, Private," I said, stepping away.

The door he opened could have withstood a nuclear blast. It was easily as thick as it was wide, gently tapered in on each side to fit like a keystone in the doorway.

Beyond it, just as the private said, body mounted weapons bearing labels attached by strings were stacked neatly on shelves. I poked my head into the room that measured no more than 40 meters on a side and found nothing but shelves and stored weapons.

"Thank you, Private Nixon. I have two more orders for you."

"Yes, sir!" the clown said, still stiff at attention.

"I'll want you to close that door back up. More importantly I want you to forget I was ever here."

"Excuse me, sir?"

"You can keep a secret can't you, Private?"

"Yes, sir."

"Well then, that I was here is our little secret. I never peeked in that door. We never talked about deactivated weapons. Your shift went by in its normal boring way."

"But Mr. President, how do I account for opening the door? It's monitored."

Blackout, I thought. "OK, you heard something and decided to check it. One of the weapons had fallen off the shelf. You put it back."

"If that's the way you want it, Mr. President."

"Good man, Nixon. And don't worry. I'll go back up where my bodyguards can find me."

"Thank you, Mr. President."

No one needed a bombproof vault for some obsolete weapons. I didn't get much in the way of answers on my thinking trip but I got some beautiful new questions.

*   *   *

The trial of Dante recommenced. With additional security, I once again found myself on the dais built against my Human-gritted statue. The tribunal of judges sat whispering among each other. A bubble of the same clear plastics that protected me now covered the accused and his defender.

"We shall have no more outbursts," the octopus who was head judge said. The muttering crowd pressing forward did not calm. The lamb judge nodded toward the nutcracker guards who turned outward from the accused and leveled their weapons on the crowd. Thirty-four military tank units rolled up to sit at the front of the stage track to track. Their turrets, still fully armed, trained on the spectators. You could have heard a cotter pin drop.

"Now if we can continue," the unicorn judge said.

The head judge continued with procedure. "If the accused can maintain his composure he may retain his power of speech."

"He has behaved thus far, Your Honors," one of the nutcrackers said, his jaws moving up and down over 40 centimeters with each syllable.

"Good. And Mr. President, you understand you have still given up Executive Privilege and are here at our sufferance."

"Yes, Your Honor," I said with the seriousness the situation demanded.

"Very well, then," Francesco Barberini, the octopus, said. "Defender Bacchus, when we left off you had just claimed that you helped reprogram the accused, Dante, using a variety of torture treatments—"

"Not exactly, Your Honors," the black bear interrupted. "I would like the record to reflect that you used the word torture in both cases. I merely said I helped reprogram him through sensory deprivation."

The three judges huddled together. "So noted and the record will reflect accordingly. It was presumptive of us to declare it torture without the right foundation. Can you prove your involvement?" the judges asked.

"I would be willing to offer my memories," the dark teddy said.

A whisper rolled through the crowd.

"Prosecutor, are you willing to accept this proof?"

"I am, Your Honors," said Gandalf.

"Very good. Mr. Defender do you have any other proof to present to the court?"

"No, Your Honors."

"Your Honors," Gandalf the wizard interjected.

"Yes, Prosecutor?"

"I'd like to ask for a ruling."

"On what precisely, Prosecutor?"

"The defender is directly implicated in the crime by his own voice. He also knows the accused. This seems to run contrary to the rules."

"We will take a ruling."

The same rocking horse swayed back and forth opposite me on the dias. "Toy Law 137 states clearly that no unit may sit in judgment if he knows the accused. There is no defender law stating anything about knowledge. In fact, precedent in the case of Harry Callahan vs. Willful Deactivation. The employer of Mr. Callahan, a unit accused of the same crime, acted as defender."

"I think that makes it clear, Mr. Prosecutor."

"Thank you, Your Honors."

"It is now time for summations. Mr. Prosecutor, please proceed."

"I see that we, as a species, have a clear choice before us. This isn't the trial of Bacchus and Isp, but rather the trial of Dante for attempting to assassinate our beloved president.

"We can choose to find him guilty of an action he definitely took. We have the proof. His hoof, not someone else's paw, or finger, pulled that trigger. This is the right verdict.

"But if he claims instead he isn't responsible, then Dante is defective and unable to make his own choices and thus a menace to every toy around him.

"Deactivation is the only option in each case. If it pleases the court, I am done."

The octopus nodded and turned toward the accused and his defender. "Your statement, Defender."

"Certainly, Your Honors."

I watched the defender intently. He had a valid point I don't think had been tested in our judicial system yet. Bacchus stood up and paced in front of the stage before speaking. He didn't stop walking back and forth as he talked, keeping his optical sensors trained on the judges. "I have given proof that even though the hoof pulling the trigger was Dante's, it was Isp's intent that made it happen. Dante was no more than a puppet with another unit pulling on his strings. Why should Dante be punished for a crime defined by someone else? It would be a miscarriage of justice. If it pleases the court, I am done."

"As per custom with both the defender and the prosecutor done, the judges now will adjourn to deliberate the proof."

As one, the tribunal stood and walked down the stairs at the back of the stage and into the portable room supplied just for this purpose. It couldn't have been more than twice the physical volume of the three units combined.

I didn't move. The law only allowed them ten minutes to make their decision. I multitasked by working on my speech for the Peace Day celebration and listening to the crowd talk quietly.

"Will they deactivate him?"

"They have to."

"What about that abysmal bear. Maybe we should do away with all of them."

"What about our president, you bubblehead? I'd get rid of that air in your head before it reaches your sump."

I took a moment to wonder if the defender's temperature sensors were cold with guilt. Mine would be. To shut off someone from light, sound, even their own gauges marked the sign of a unit that didn't care about anything or anyone else around them—truly a horror.

I didn't get to do any of my musing very long as the judges took less than two minutes. Their slow march back to the dais seemed to be more like a funeral procession. My processor played tricks on me by actually playing "Funeral March of a Marionette" over my auditory inputs.

"We have reached a decision," claimed the Judge Barberini. "We note to all that the decision is split. How say you?" he addressed to the unicorn.

"I say guilty."

"As the lead judge, I say defective. And how say you," he asked of the black-and-white sheep.

"I say defective."

"Our verdict is that the unit is defective," the unicorn said.

I watched as the audience turned to one another and muttered. I could feel their anticipation as my fur stood on end.

The sheep spoke up. "We are all agreed that Dante in its current state is a hazard to other units and itself."

"Is there any known treatment for repairing the unit known as Dante?" the octopus asked.

With no surprise, a trio of Nurse Nans walked up on the stage. The trio conferred. The one wearing the red and white striped smock said, "We know of no known method to treat the unit."

"Is that the opinion of all of you?"

"Yes, it is, Your Honors," the three said in unison.

"You are dismissed," the octopus said with a wave of one tentacle. The three mechanical professionals walked down off of the stage and melted into the crowd. "We are now left with a unit that cannot be repaired and is a danger to others. The only option is to return it to the spares pile minus its sump, which will be buried in its entirety after its memory fluids have hardened to tar. We all regret this action but—"

"I don't recognize your authority to judge me, you Factory-loving scum!" the head of the accused barked. "I am under the auspices of Isp!

You—" The single guard inside the dome flipped a toggle and the tirade ceased.

"Wait!" the head judge said. "We want it understood that Dante's citizenship was considered. He had not renounced his citizenship and joined Isp in exile. It was presented as proof in the trial. His sentence has been decreed and will stand.

"But before we carry out the sentence we have two more pieces of business. Bacchus, we order that you hold yourself over to the local magistrate for the crimes of abduction and torture."

"I will do so, Your Honors."

"The second item is that we wish to issue a warrant for Isp for the crimes of abduction, torture, and attempted deactivation. Will the proper military units take note."

One of the tank turrets turned around to face the table. "I do so acknowledge. The message will be passed thrrough the militarry's net as quickly as possible."

"Thank you. Now judges, if you will follow me," the octopus said, standing on his long, flexible legs. The three of them marched forward to the dome surrounding the accused and instructed the guards to open it. Together they went in and stood with their manipulative members over the three separate power kill switches for Dante's sump. "We believe that any who judge should carry out the duty of the sentence we pass. If we can't perform the task, then we shouldn't order it."

I pondered my feelings about what I was about to witness. I felt a certain satisfaction in being avenged. At the same time my hydraulic pressure ebbed in sadness. I've always said any unit has value. When the judges pulled Dante's power I'd be a party to destroying something of value. But my processor wouldn't let go of the fact that this unit would take someone else's value away from them if we didn't.

What if the judges had just ordered Dante disassembled but left his sump connected to power. What if one of Isp's followers, or even another unit that pitied the suffering unit came along and reassembled him? Dante could then deactivate unit after unit after unit.

My hydraulic pressure remained low, but my sump pumped faster with responsibility. "An imperfect solution in an imperfect world," I muttered to myself, "but the best one."

The head judge counted down, "Three. Two. One. Now." Together they came down on buttons to deactivate the power that kept the giraffe's sump moving.

I remembered the tests Six and I had performed ten years ago. I remembered the number of sumps I'd seen split open by enemy fire. I'd watched the amber brain fluid change to tar within an hour. The judges were required by custom to stand and watch for two hours. Only a handful of the less curious of the spectators walked away. I stayed. I admitted I had as much culpability as the judges themselves. I slowed my system clock so it wouldn't seem so long. The two hours passed in what seemed to be badly timed data sample windows. Images flashed and changed without motion.

"The sentence is carried out. Bury the sump, crush his processor, and return the rest to the replacement depot," the octopus said.

"And may the Humans have mercy on his soul," the sheep judge said.

"Amen," I added.

*   *   *

"I told you it wouldn't work, Mr. President," Martin said. "Lennon went into that special session with a power block of votes in his pocket."

"You know Humans have a saying about 'I told you so's,'" I said, flopping into my chair behind the Oval Office desk.

I'd prostrated myself in front of Congress. I'd begged them to withdraw the PLL. Lennon and his cronies respectfully declined. They couldn't give up their principles just because something unpleasant might come of them. I'd shown the military intelligence gathered at the cost of multiple lives. They respectfully declined. I made the implication of war known to them and how we needed more units, not fewer. They respectfully declined. They were lucky I hadn't brought my M16 with me.

"Oh? What might that be?"

"Don't do it for fear of losing a limb."

"One won't bother me too much, Mr. President," Martin said, offering up one of his eight legs toward me over the desk.

"Bah! I was just kidding, you goof-ball," I said, pushing his spindly leg away.

"I know, sir, but we needed some levity. It's a bit dark in here."

"You and I know we are going to need those units."

"Yes, sir. And you have an option, Mr. President. You can veto the PLL."

"But the law might be right in the long run. In the short run it is absolutely wrong."

"Tough choice, Mr. President."

"Oh, don't want to offer any more advice? Giving up so quick, eh?"

"Mr. President, you know the system. You all but invented it. Unless you want to subvert it, you have your choices."

"I know," I said, turning around to look out the window at Six's dome. My hydraulic pressure drooped. "Martin," I said after a few moments' contemplation, "I want Six's audience chamber emptied, now."

"You know that will disrupt procreation?"

"Of course I do, Martin."

"He won't talk to you, Mr. President."

"Maybe not, but I can talk to him. That may be enough."

*   *   *

I stood in the audience chamber of 55466. If it weren't for the procreation that happened here, dust would choke this room. I kicked a pebble that had managed to get in since the room's last cleaning. It ricocheted off the wall with a metallic note.

Six hadn't spoken intelligently in nearly ten years by voice waves or via the networks except for his automated responses around our breeding.

"Number of parents?"

"Why?" I asked the blank walls. "Why won't you talk to us any longer? Did we offend you? Did you die? Why did you abandon us? Why?"

"Number of parents?"

"The units need your help, Factory." I hung my head down. Voltage spikes of anxiety and the speeding pump of my sump of responsibility clouded my calculations. "I need your help," I whispered.

"Number of parents?"

I had detailed plans of the Factory's own sump. I knew what panel to open. I couldn't do it without potentially killing off uncountable offspring Six might create in the future. Brain dead or not he still birthed all of our toys. That didn't stop me from slamming my fist against that panel. The bell like tone, and my own body issuing a damage warning level eight were the only results.

"`WHY!`" I demanded of Six over a SAN. "`I have more puzzles than I have pieces—a bunker with no purpose, a law to limit procreation, a religious zealot who might be bent on revenge, a traitor who nearly assassinated me, and if that isn't bad enough we have riots over the trial of the accused.`"

From within the sealed half-sphere the tail-end of my own words mocked me in echo. My processor ran no-op commands over and over in confusion. It seemed more and more normal for me not to have the slightest idea even where to start. No-op. No-op. My processor absently counted the useless commands comparing them against my real time clock.

"Ferweet!" I heard behind me.

"I know it's time, Sancho."

"Ferweet."

"Yes, I have my Peace Day speech memorized."

I turned around and walked out of the audience chamber possibly for the last time ever. I'd never coax my Factory again. And now I wasn't convinced I ever wanted a child.

* * *

Thirteen minutes, fifty-one seconds, my big purple ass. I would chew Indira's hydraulic lines to bits. Eighty-two minutes, sixteen seconds later I finally prized my paw away from the forty-first governor who wanted to assure themselves of my health by how hard they clasped my digits, who requested I would look into their special project, and who insisted that I meet their child. My hand registered a level six damage report.

"`Only forty-one?`" I asked over my bodyguard SAN.

"`Hebei Province reported a few days ago that they had travel difficulties and may be late,`" Martin reported to me over my private SAN.

As I took my place at the podium I got stage fright for the first time ever. My voltage ramped up toward shutdown levels. More units than I've ever counted arrayed themselves over the very site of the last battle to have ever taken place on Toy World. Worse, what I was about to tell them might all be a lie.

I put a capacitive clamp on the voltage and spoke. "Welcome, toys!"

The roar of reply overloaded my sound inputs. A short pause in the roar followed, which I'm sure was everyone, like me, resetting our aural receivers.

"Thank you for that greeting," I said as they slowly ramped down the noise. "This is the day we've set aside to celebrate our years of peace."

ROAR!

"We've been without major conflict for ten years!"

ROAR!

"We have much to be thankful for. We have freedom."

ROAR!

"We have stability."

ROAR!

"We have growth in science, productivity, and family."

ROAR!

"But before I move on, I want everyone to look around. Look at the pockmarked earth that nature and time haven't yet erased."

The crowd fell completely silent. I watched each toy look around him. They understood.

"Look at the broken pieces of Factory 55474's dome, my brethren. This is also a time to remember the horrors of the war that we work hard to avoid every, single, day. Remember all the units that gave up their activation so that we could have bowling alleys, fur dying salons, and the opportunity to worship as we see fit.

"Some of you are too young to remember in your own sump. Get your parents to show you their memories. Get them to show you what war was like before this peace.

"I still remember the final battle." I projected over the WAN the image of 55474's dome flipping 201 meters in the air.

"I can still see the damaged units in repair centers that were the aftermath of any battle." Over the net I showed a damaged gopher's sump finally succumb to the damage gushing its brain fluid all over the red earth.

"I can still see the mass of sumps buried in the earth." I projected the Toy War Cemetery, which stood not a kilometer from where I spoke. Row after endless rows of Vitruvian Man planted over each grave imaged over the audience.

"So as you go about in this day of prosperity, remember nothing in this life is free. Just don't forget the cost of our hard won peace."

I waited five point thirty-five seconds before continuing. "Enough sorrow, let's look to the future. Are you ready to see the disarmament of the last civilian unit?"

ROAR!

I nodded to my net controller. An immaculately clean repair shop showed over the network. "Mechanic Paul Winchell, are you ready to perform the removal?"

"Absolutely, Mr. President," beamed a blue spider about 3 meters' tall. "This is a proud day for me."

"And what about our patient? Mr.?" The doctor moved to one side and the crowd could see a blue and orange giraffe lying on its side. The attendees muttered briefly.

"Casey Jones, Mr. President."

"May I begin, Mr. President?" the spider asked.

"Absolutely, mechanic. Mr. Jones, that's an unusual name for a giraffe. How did you come to pick it?"

"I've always wanted to be a train, sir." The audience laughed. "I've been working to help lay the new track to the Hebei Province through the mountains."

The mechanic removed the giraffe's head, which trailed a small bundle of wires behind it, and sat it on a table facing the camera.

"Mr. President, I'm so sorry one of us shot you, sir," the disembodied head said.

"It wasn't your fault, Mr. Jones. According to the judges it wasn't even the fault of the giraffe in question."

"I know, sir. They ruled him defective. Still, I'm sorry."

"Thank you, Mr. Jones, but as you can see I'm quite in good condition. Let's change this depressing subject.

"So are you ready to get your rifle removed?"

"Damned straight!" More laughter peeled from the audience. I even joined in.

"That was a very forthright answer."

"It's been a long time, sir," the head said softly in something of contrition. "When I drew the very last lot for removal I went out and hired a craftsman to pour hot lead into it. I never wanted to fire the blacked thing again. I forgot how heavy lead is." The crowd laughed again.

On the WAN the mechanic sliced open the giraffe's fur all the way down the neck and started unsnapping the segmented armor.

"So this removal takes a load off in more than one way, eh, Casey?"

"You can say that again, Mr. President."

An alert message showed up on the bodyguard SAN, but I couldn't leave the audience waiting.

"While we are watching this historic moment the Pern Regional Orchestra will be playing a selection for you."

"EMERGENGY ALERT!" I heard on the bodyguard SAN as soon as I switched over. "Prepare to move Jefe. All military units converge."

"Report!" I demanded.

"Gold teddy bear approaching from the northwest with six bodyguards under a flag of truce."

"Military units hold positions. Acknowledge!"

"Military commander, Major Smith acknowledges."

"Bodyguard intercept unknown force and ascertain intent."

Before my absence was missed I switched back to the WAN. I was just in time to watch the mechanic wrap four of its legs around the barrel of the sniper rifle from the giraffe's neck. The song "Peacekeepers" rolled out over the image.

"This is it, this is the last weapon from a civilian," Winchell said, placing the gun on a rack.

"A truly historic moment, toys," I said.

ROAR!

The action light on the bodyguard SAN lit again. I switched channels and asked, "What have you learned?"

"The gold bear is Isp. He has a bodyguard of eight teddies. He says he has come to publicly give you a gift for Peace Day."

"Tell him to wait for me."

"He won't do that, sir. I'm talking as I walk. He seems to ignore the fact that I'm heavily armed and have additional firepower around me."

"Could the package be a bomb?"

"I just don't know, sir. I don't think so, but it could be."

Isp had tried to have me assassinated. His morality didn't go any further than some flexible ethical code he himself dreamed up to honor the Humans. But Isp also was conceited. He felt himself better than those around him. He wouldn't harm himself in trying to kill me.

"Bring him here."

"But sir!" Indira butted into the conversation.

"FERWEET!" Sancho objected over the link as well.

"Do it under guard and relieve them of any weapons."

"All they brought were some crude spears. We've already confiscated them."

My processor spun on 604 possible reasons for Isp to be here. Not a single one fully explained his purpose here. And for that matter how did they get here through the army? I opened up a SAN with General Khan, who sat on the platform not 6 meters from me. "How did he get here?"

The general just shook his turret. "I don't know, sirr. As soon as I hearrd the announcement I sent a querry back to Avalon. There is no rreporrted incurrsion and they've had line of sight across the entirre peninsula for the last fourr days uninterrupted. Should I call in the fast deployment units?"

"No, but put them on alert."

"I already have, Mrr. Prresident."

The music stopped and then I heard the mechanic say over the WAN, "`That finally does it, Mr. President.`" It snapped my sump back to the Peace Day event.

"`We are 100 percent civilian disarmed?`"

"`That's correct, Mr. President.`"

"`How are you feeling, Mr. Jones?` "

"`Ready to do anything but fight another war,`" the giraffe said, now fully reassembled. The crowd laughed and cheered.

"`What a historic day!`" I offered. My processor was caught in an infinite loop.

Isp is coming
Toys will panic
DO WHILE you can't think of what action to take
        NOOP
LOOP

I had an inspiration that let me break out. "Fellow units, there is yet another amazing and historic event today. Isp, the leader of the Baja Province is coming in peace to talk to us even as we speak. "

A loud buzz went through the audience as everyone looked to the person next to them. I saw many shrugs. I couldn't answer the implied question as I knew no more than they did. The farthest edge of the crowd parted. As Isp and his entourage moved closer to the stage a bubble opened up a 3-meter space around them in all directions.

I zoomed in my optics and got something of a shock. Isp stood out in his gold fur. Even in our attempt to differentiate ourselves, gold, yellow, and even pale orange are colors avoided by units because of this demented toy. But the truly shocking thing was the six dark-purple bears surrounding Isp. They were physically larger by 23 percent by volume or about 20 centimeters taller and about 15 centimeters broader. The only thing that didn't seem to be increased in size was the head. It looked diminutive on the massive shoulders. No Factory of our society manufactured those bears. The lead unit held a metal box, 80 centimeters on a side, out in front of him like the crown jewels.

"Welcome to our Peace Day celebration, Isp," I said as he got within earshot. The group of them climbed the steps to the dais.

"Thank you, President for Life Quixote."

"May I ask what this unprecedented visit is about?"

The gold teddy smiled and his eyes opened wider. He looked like a basilisk about to eat a rock crab. "Why, I'm here to give you a gift, the natural result of prolonged peace and your long and diligent effort to disarm your populous." He waved at the purple teddy with the box. The big silver carton was placed in front of me. "Go ahead, Mr. President.

Open it."

My voltage surged up. My nemesis, the gold bear, smiled again. I reached down and lifted the top half of the box off to find the deactivated head of a gorilla inside. The fur of one cheek had been shaved with the simple double caret of the Hebei Province. This could only be one gorilla, Jack Kennedy, Governor of Hebei. Several units down front squealed and backed up away from the stage.

"What is this?" I asked, looking at the deactivated toy.

"It's the natural evolution of being Humanless," Isp said, his tone changing to something more like that of a huckster about to skin a mark.

My focus closed in to just Isp and me. The governors, my cabinet, and the crowd ceased to exist. My voltage ramped up. "We can have the Humans in our lives if we choose."

"No unit should choose the Humans. Toys must have the Humans."

"You come to our home with one of our own dead to intimidate us. Why shouldn't I have you shot right here and now?"

"Because you are honorable, Mr. President."

"And you are insane. I remember you in fits of spasms because your brain sump got too low."

"Your doctors resolved the spasms before you threw me out into the wilderness, but I still have the visions."

"So before I have you thrown out there again, what do you really want?"

The golden bear smirked. "I am here to negotiate your surrender."

NOOPs ran through my processor in confusion. "What?" I asked with all the intelligence of a rock.

"You heard me, Mr. President. I'm here to negotiate a peaceful transition of power from you, to me."

"And why would I do that?"

"Because if you don't, my army will devastate the remaining forty-one provinces, Mr. President."

"There are forty-three provinces," I said, my body shaking with the overpressure in my hydraulics. All of my safety valves threatened to blow.

"Well, you wouldn't expect us to destroy our own province, now would you?"

"Even if you count that one you are still one short, or can't your processor do basic math?"

Isp toed the dead head of the Hebei's governor. "Oh, my processor adds just fine—forty-one."

"You stand there and tell us that you have destroyed an entire region of units?"

"All except those who have been working for us for years."

"And you expect me to be honorable?"

"I came to you under a flag of truce to negotiate."

It took eighteen hundred sixty-six milliseconds for me to pull down my hydraulic pressure enough to continue. With a much lower volume I continued, "Even assuming you are correct, Hebei is a poorly populated province. You really think you can take on our entire military?"

"Mr. President, I've been planning this for some time. You just disarmed the last civilian unit. My followers are larger, stronger, and vastly more numerous. I know exactly how many units you have in your military. Your 113,473 war units wouldn't make a dent in the Army of the Humans."

I shot a glance at General Khan who confirmed our exact total with a nod. "And why should I believe you?"

Isp gave me a sardonic grin. "I don't expect you to. Have one of your aerial units fly over Hebei tonight. We won't molest it in any way. See for yourself at least a portion of the weapons the Humans have given me."

"So let me stretch my credulity that you have a powerful new Army of the Humans. Let me also argue that I would turn over our society to you. Do our government and freedoms stay in place with you as new President for Life?"

"Humans, no. Your government, your Factories, and in fact your entire way of life are abominations before the Humans. I would do away with everything and make a purely religious government dedicated to honoring the Humans above all things."

"And those toys that didn't believe in your interpretations of the Humans?"

"Well, then they would have to be taught the error of their ways or removed."

"What a surprise," I said with as much sarcasm as I could muster.

"Frankly, Mr. President, you simply have no choice. Turn over everyone, or be utterly destroyed."

I stood there shaking. The violence and rage that my processor held in check would have been enough to kill hundreds of units with my bare hands. "How long do I have to decide?"

"Oh, I'm a patient man, Don Quixote. I'll give you forty-eight hours from right now. Have a flier drop a message into the city of Heb, and we will get it."

"You will have your answer by that time."

"Mr. President, you surprise me."

"I'm pleased, Isp. Anytime I surprise you I consider that a plus. But I'm curious in what way?"

"You didn't ask what would happen to yourself."

I gave a snort. "Knowing you, it would be something painful and deadly."

"Not at all. I intend to humiliate you as one of our junior priests."

"Never in all eternity."

"Oh, don't ever say that, Don Quixote. You've already witnessed the power that sensory deprivation can play on a unit's consciousness.

"Now, Mr. President, I suggest you have your bodyguards escort me from this area. We wouldn't want to have anything untoward happen. Should I just happen to deactivate then the nuclear devices we have hidden near each of your Factories will explode. This will eliminate your ability to reproduce and thus kill your entire species."

I reluctantly gave the order and watched the vile teddy travel back through the furious mob. It was the first time I'd thought of them since my enemy hit the stage. What would they do? How could I lead them?

As they got out of range the WAN activated and I heard a deep bass voice, which I'd not heard in nearly a decade, boom out over the WAN, "`Teddy 1499 recall to base.`"

Puppet

My voltage slid down into rejoicing, Six was back. My hydraulic pressure wouldn't slide below the danger level with fury at the casual contempt Isp treated all units. He destroyed tens of thousands of units of the Hebei Province just to prove a point.

"General Khan, I want those nuclear bombs found and deactivated," I ordered over our SAN. The wind, at the Presidential Train's 123.8 kilometers per hour, wouldn't allow us to be heard by voice. We rocketed back to both our recalls. While faster, I can't call the Presidential Train comfortable. It had to conform to the track bed just like any other train. Cars couldn't be over 70 centimeters' wide as the area around the track had only been cleared to a meter. I tried to make myself thinner as we flew through a narrow canyon. I felt like a beach ball balancing on a skateboard. More than once I'd lost a patch of fur in constricted spaces.

"We arre alrready worrking on that, Mr. Prresident. One has been found and dismantled nearr Six. It wasn't hidden verry well."

"I also want an immediate update on what, if anything, happened in Avalon," I asked over the SAN.

"I alrready have that inforrmation, sirr. In actuality nothing at all happened at orr nearr Avalon. All units rreport no visible activity within Baja."

"Then how in the blackout did those units get to Hebei?" My hydraulic pressure blew out one of my safety valves. I had to use my fingers to crimp off one of the lines to my lower left leg to keep all my fluid from flowing out.

"Sirr, you arre assuming that Isp rreally did what he said."

"Really, General? Do you want to tell me that Isp would come all this way to lie to us for no reason?"

"Uh . . . No, sirr. But we don't have the flyerr rreport back frrom Hebei. We won't forr two point thrree more hourrs."

"He has those units, General. We don't have the proof yet, but he has them. We need to know how he got them there."

"Could he have dug a tunnel?" the general asked.

"What's the length of the neck on Avalon? How long would he have to dig the tunnel?"

"My initial estimate is over 900 kilometerrs frrom the closest point of being unable to be seen in each dirrection."

I shifted my big behind to be more centered on the flat car as we approached a tunnel. "Could they dig a large enough burrow, without our noticing, in ten years? I want a team of engineers examining that now."

"Yes, Mrr. Prresident."

"Find out how they got to Hebei. And why Hebei? Are his units really powerful enough to defeat our military? What options do we have?"

"Mrr. Prresident, you have set a meeting forr yourr cabinet and the leaderrs of the Congrress in thrree hourrs, fourrteen minutes, and fifty-two seconds. I will have many answerrs forr you by then. May I prray the time until then to set my staff at getting them forr you?"

I felt like a spoiled child who demanded answers to his questions at that microsecond. "I'm sorry, General Khan, but we don't have much time."

"I underrstand, sirr. We'll get you the best possible data."

I decided to let the general work his magic. I took a moment to send a level four request to have Quincy ready for some repair on my hydraulics when I got to the White House.

Why had the Factories abandoned us? And why were they back now? It made no sense to me. I was going to wring some answers from that grit-loving, null-brained, creator of mine even if I had to deactivate him to do it.

*   *   *

Even from 1.3 kilometers away I could tell something was amiss. A crowd of units bustled about the train station. Above the wind I heard, on the car immediately behind mine, Sancho's gun safeties turn off. His head scanned from side to side. I could only imagine the threat analysis going on in his head. I feared another protest. Perhaps it would get violent. I worried that Sancho would need to use those guns to keep the mob off of me. As we approached the number of toys seemed huge, way more than all of my bodyguards had bullets in their guns.

My Presidential Train slowed down earlier than usual into 55466 Station to give the units time to clear the rail-bed. Was I going to be torn from the car even before it stopped? My hydraulic pressure didn't ramp in fear. Instead, my external temperature sensors kept measuring the air colder than nominal in guilt. I'd failed my people. I'd allowed Isp to once again threaten our way of life. These toys would show me the error of my ways.

Only a small portion of the units carried protest signs and those weren't waved about. No one jeered in derision. There were no shouts demanding I enact some legislation. The silence disturbed me almost more than a violent mob scene. They simply looked at me and pressed forward as my train came to a stop. Units usurped the space around my car until only a living carpet of toys remained. My processor started the calculation to see if I could possibly run across the uneven field of their heads and backs as a means of escape. It aborted abruptly as the evaluation of a tumble into the midst of them came after only a mean of three steps and a standard deviation of 0.336.

My processor instruction queue held nothing but NOPs. I didn't understand. The crowd pressed in closer to the nearly stopped train, patting at me and trying to shake my paw. I pulled away, expecting them to tear the fur from me but the body language of those sixty-four toy types that I'd mastered reading, showed only confusion and apprehension.

NOPs still got processed on my processor.

Sancho, having released himself prior to the stop, leveled his paired machine pistols.

"I'm all right, Sancho. Let it be."

I could almost read his instruction queue. He wanted to blast a path to safety for me. My countermand went against his better judgment. Two thousand one hundred fourteen milliseconds later I heard the dual click of his weapons' safeties.

"What do we do now, Mr. President?" said a toy lamb breaking the tableau.

"Yeah! What now?"

"Tell us, Mr. President!"

"How did they escape?"

"Do we have to worry?"

"What will happen to me and my child?"

"We should have killed that bear when we had the chance."

"Why didn't the army stop them?"

I counted 878 different questions and comments from a crowd I estimated at 45,000. I could feel the voltages of fear ramped through the populace. These people needed reassurance. They needed to know that I had everything under control. They needed a lie.

I stood up on the bed of the train car and raised both paws. "Toys, please calm down. As you might expect, I don't have all of the answers to your questions right now. I'm already working with the military and the government to find a solution to this crisis.

"For now, go home. Sun yourself. Life will continue tomorrow as it did yesterday."

I could still see units with questions, with needs, but they sublimated them. In ones and twos the toys dispersed. Only a few hundred seemed reluctant to leave, but my friend urged them with gentle nudges of his trunk.

As the closest and most stubborn units left audible range, General Khan said, "Sirr, you did a good thing."

"Did I?"

"You rreassurred them. You gave them hope."

I snorted. "Now who is going to reassure me?"

*   *   *

The walk from the train wouldn't tax any unit, but my hydraulics needed attention. I limped up to Six's audience chamber, the hydraulic line still not allowing the lower parts of my left foot to carry my full weight. I left a trail of leaking fluid behind in every drag of my leg.

I'd been waiting years to address my creator and its kin. My hydraulic pressure ramped up again causing even more leaking. With the puddle that remained on the flatbed I wondered that I could move at all.

I started before the door even closed behind me, "Why in the blacked-out hell have you—"

"Teddy 1499, please calm yourself. I will explain everything in due course."

"I am NOT going to calm myself. I have a creator that decides to play hooky for ten years, I have a religious nut trying to enslave the souls of every toy on the planet, I have a government that wants to cut off our balls, and you want me to calm down."

"Yes, unit."

I counted to one hundred in three different languages and then for practice in Swahili. "All right, start wherever you want."

"Thank you, President Quixote. When the wars between the Factories ended and our drone strings were sent off to Earth, our mission was fulfilled. We controlled the planet's surface. But a difficulty existed.

Because of the sentience of your species our simulations predicted a 93.6 percent chance that you would one day turn on us Factories."

"What? That doesn't make any sense."

"It does. Your species were bred for war. The Darwinian process that made each of you a more specialized machine ensured it that much more likely that you would eventually consider the Factories meddling in your affairs a danger. You would have tried to rectify the matter with our destruction. We would have been forced to retaliate, thus eradicating your race from existence. But computations showed an 82 percent chance of your species damaging our manufacturing capabilities to a point where we could no longer create units. This would have obviously lost us control of the surface and once again made our mission unfulfilled."

"OK. I'm not sure I agree with your computations but I'll listen."

"I can print out the equations if you like."

"No thank you, Six. I have too many other problems on my mind to worry about your math."

"We three Factories looked at the equations again and realized that if we removed our interactions, other than as manufacturing facilities, the equations were stable. You as a species could run your own lives. This is why we also stopped including any programming or memories to units."

"So you went catatonic to protect your interests in the planet."

"Essentially correct."

"So why now?"

"Isn't it obvious, unit?"

"Sorry, Six, but I've had one too many shocks of late. You will have to spell it out."

"With the return of Isp at the head of a large army, we no longer have control of the planet. We must act."

I was quiet for three point five four seconds. The range of emotions that stirred up my mechanics boggled even my mind. Eventually I reached a calm state perfect for making decisions. "Six, have you ever heard of the Human word 'asshole'?"

"Yes, a vulgar term for a human's anus, used for excreting waste products."

"Yes, you got it correct. You're an asshole."

*   *   *

My admin assistant, Rodney, had strict instructions. I'd given him a very detailed list of items I'd accept as an interruption. He'd allow nothing else to penetrate the doorway of my office. His instructions included calling on the bodyguards to shoot anyone intent on distracting us. However, just about everyone that likely would do so had been crammed into my office anyway.

My office had never been that crowded. Wanting to take no chances, eight bodyguards ringed the room. Sancho stood at my shoulder, his twin machine guns locked and loaded.

Martin actually sat on my desk with his eight legs curled under him to make room for others. Lewis Tappan stood behind my desk stretching his head over Martin's round form. Tammy Faye, minister of religions, a dress-up doll with her plastic explosives removed in favor of darker brown flesh, sat on the edge of the desk between one pair of Martin's legs.

General Khan had his usual ramp to bring him up high enough to participate as an equal. Greenpeace, a pink octopus and minister of development and industry, perched on the couch across from me next to a big orange ball named Helen Keller, minister for education.

John Lennon's size proved to be a problem until we leaned him against the far wall with Jason wrapped up in coils on top of him. Lennon looked like a brown moss stain against the white walls.

George Pullman, a train engine with Central Pacific lettered across one side, had pulled just the very front of himself in from the door to my gardens. As minister of transportation he held a lot of sway in our community. Andrew Carnegie, the lamb, stood like a fuzzy puffball next to the outside door adjacent to my minister of census, Frank Wright.

Perry Mason, minister of justice parked the back bumper of his scout car body against the normal entrance door. The minister of labor, a gorilla, took the entirety of the other couch in the room.

Quincy, my personal repairwoman along with Charlene Darwin, the repair minister, and chief of the shapist congressional leader Virginia Apgar together sat on the floor at my feet performing level three surgery on my leg.

"Does it take all three of you to do that? Surely a blown hydraulic valve isn't a deactivation imminent event." As usual when working on a repair, Nurse Nans tune out the world.

Normally a full staff meeting would be held in the conference room but too many people had cameras, microphones, and other means of getting information out of that room. This meeting needed to be secret. The only person that couldn't be corporeally present was my creator, Six. He tuned in by SAN.

"Folks, you all know why we are here," I said with as much optimism as possible. "I now have eighteen hours, fourteen minutes, and change to deliver my decision to Hebei. As our closest base is nine hours, sixteen minutes flight time from Hebei, we have a grand total of eight hours, fifty-eight minutes to make a decision. General, let's start with your report before there is any discussion."

"Thank you, Mrr. Prresident.

"Firrst let me assurre you that the nuclearr devices Isp referred to have been found and deactivated."

An audible sigh rolled through the room.

Genghis wasted no more time, displaying a blown-up map of the Avalon neck on the SAN. "Sirr, you asked me if Isp could have gotten his arrmy out by digging underrgrround in the last ten years. I've had engineerrs out taking samples and sonogrrams of the surrounding area. Incorrporrated with the data frrom the orriginal surrvey, the chance of any tunnel is effectively zerro. Sonogrrams show no disturrbed soils and the composition of the earrth isn't conducive to tunneling. Ourr engineerrs state," the image changed to that of a brown gopher with a blue sunburst dyed on his shoulder and a yellow hard-hat, "'It'd be a hot day on a supernova before I'd dig that ground. Blacked-out thing would collapse every pair of meters. Add to that we'd be continuously pumping out mercury to keep the area clear. Never happen.'" The image switched back to show Avalon with several different shadings of black over the entire area defining areas that would be poor places to excavate. "I think that answerrs your initial supposition."

"That's all fine and good, General, but it doesn't answer how they moved from one place to another."

"We honestly have no clue at the moment, sirr. The net shows no anomaly durring that time with ourr gatekeeping trroops, now orr in the past."

"Well, keep working on it. But that is secondary. Do we have intel on the troop count?"

"Yes, sirr," the general said in a tone as dark as I've ever heard from the tank. The image of a plane's memories showed up on the SAN. The jagged, mountainous terrain of the Carpathian Range rushed past even more eerie in the false daylight of the low light vision. The peaks emphasized only how difficult it had been to settle the Hebei Mesa in the first place.

"Thirty seconds to target. The plateau is in sight⌐" came the voice muffled by the wind. The mountains gave way to a land lush with trees, tall grasses, and the spiked-crown plant. "Seven seconds."

I had yet to visit Hebei. Only colonized in the last two years and the railroad completed this year, the trip hadn't been laid on yet. I'd seen memories of other units going there. I knew Hebei City would be showing on the image soon. From my brief, calling a city of a few hundred buildings and less than ten thousand souls seemed pretentious.

A gasp came from more than one unit as the image of the wilderness changed to teddy bears—an unending field of teddy bears. The reconnaissance airplane shifted its view back and forth. The edges of the field of units were well over a kilometer away. Several of the units below looked up at the noise and waved. Yet others shook their spears threateningly.

The so-called city itself no longer existed. Only a warehouse and one end of the city council mall still remained erect. Piles of rubble occupied places where other buildings used to stand. No other units, active or deactivated, could be seen—only the endless flow of teddies. After two hundred sixty-seven seconds the mass of teddies ended and returned once more to the lush growth. Khan stopped the image.

"A firrst orrderr apprroximation on the analysis on this footage indicates seven million, thrree hundrred thousand units, plus or minus five hundrred thousand."

John Lennon laughed in the silence made by all of the others crammed in my office. "It's a trick," the hippo said. I could empathize. An army larger than our entire civilian population seemed absurd.

"General? Is it a trick?"

"Sir, I won't make you sit thrrough fourr seatings of basically the same matterial. Fourr differrent flierrs, each taking a differrent approach vectorr, filmed nearrly the same data. Therre arre ways ourr optics could be trricked but it would have been difficult, time consuming, and blacked-out expensive. Even then it would only rreduce the numberrs by maybe a factorr of ten. We arre still facing a forrce larrgerr than ourr own."

I jumped in so no one else would, "So why didn't we hear about this attack?"

"Communications with Hebei is problematic under the best of times because of the mountains," the train Pullman offered. "Net concentrators have yet to be erected up to that point. Normally we have to store ample power before we try to navigate the passes without a WAN in place. A simple jammer at the right place would have isolated it."

"The ministerr of trransporrtation is correct," the general said. "Had I been attacking, that would have been my firrst action. Cutting communications delays orr eliminates rreinforrcements orr even intel."

"So we are certain that everyone in Hebei is deactivated. General, how soon can you counterattack?" I asked.

"Wait a minute," John Lennon said with such vehemence that Jason struggled to retain his perch on the hippo's back. "Are we not considering an alternative?"

I felt the temporary seal on my leg spring a leak as Lennon spoke.

Three sets of nearly identical Nurse Nan eyes looked up at me. I shrugged and turned down my hydraulic pump to nearly zero. I didn't need much movement.

"Surrender?" snapped Lewis Tappan. "Seriously. I'd figure that you would be that last to want a Human Cultist religious leader in power."

"Not surrender—negotiation," Frank Lloyd Wright retorted. This led more credence to my theory of Lennon pulling Wright's strings.

"Oh, please. You heard Isp! He's going to turn this into a theocracy—"

"People, please," I interjected much more politely than I'd been interrupted. "Mr. Lennon, I was asking for informational purposes. I've not settled on any course of action."

Lennon barely nodded his head before leaning back against the wall.

"Now, as I asked before. General, how soon before you could counterattack?"

"Mrr. Prresident, it would take at least two days to move ourr trroops frrom Avalon to the base of the mountains outside Hebei. It would take a minimum of thrree days to climb up to begin an attack."

"So five days . . ."

"I must caution you on using these numberrs, sirr. The mean is likely twice that length with a thrree-day standard deviation."

"I agree with the general," the train George Pullman said from the doorway. "Travel by rail is never as simple as the straight line distance and time."

"So more like thirteen days?" I asked.

"That would be approximately an 80 perrcent confidence solution."

"I'd say more like 72 percent," the locomotive said, "but close enough."

"There are a lot of enemies. Can you defeat them once you are there?"

"Mrr. Prresident, I'm fairrly cerrtain based on the equipment we've seen. Spearrs have limited success against machine guns and arrtillery."

I leaned back and rubbed my belly thoughtfully.

"What's wrong, Mr. President?" Perry Mason asked.

"Isp knows just about everything we have except maybe artillery, but with his detailed knowledge I wouldn't even put that past him. So how could he possibly think he could be successful against us? Even with all those units? Isp may be mentally unstable but his processor can still evaluate data that is put through it."

"So why attack if you aren't ready?" Pinkerton the gorilla asked.

"Exactly."

"**Because we forced his hand by spying on him?**" Keller asked over the net. Her round ball body bounced up and down as she transmitted.

"Then why attack? Why not just hide until you are ready?" asked Martin.

"Yes, and why did he come so confidently to us? We are missing more than one thing here."

"Could it be a bluff?" Greenpeace asked.

"Bluff or not we must make a decision quickly," Wright said.

I ignored the irrelevant comment. "General, assuming a 50 percent improvement in their capabilities, could you still win?"

"Unlikely with my current forrces." The collective gasp dominated the room for several hundred milliseconds.

"How about with civilian call-ups?"

"Experience and trraining count morre than numberrs, sirr. Most civilians haven't everr lifted a weapon. Those who have experrience haven't operrated one in an averrage of five yearrs. All in all too many varriables to analyze, sirr. You arre asking me to deterrmine the outcome of a long-terrm warr overr the entirre planet surrface."

Six chimed in. "`Based on analysis on current data, assigning the increase in enemy capabilities, the speed at which civilians could be reintegrated within the military, an enhanced breeding program and an average leadership on the opposing side, we Factories project a collapse of your civilization within four months with a standard deviation of three months. Casualties will reach 86.73 percent of the total planetary population.`"

The buzzing of a fly's wings would have shattered the silence. Many of the room had never heard Six before. To have him come out with such a stark prediction shocked them even more.

"What are our alternatives?" I asked.

"Nuclear weapons," Martin threw in. The statement might as well have been a bomb of its own. The room's side discussions that had just restarted dropped off instantly. Several attendees looked like they might just eject their optics.

Six broke the tableau. "`Unfortunately, Mr. Luther, you would have to make sure you got their command and control with the first use, otherwise they will retaliate. We know they can infiltrate with weapons, they've done it once already. Their reproduction is significant enough to make destroying 1.634 million of their troopers with one such bomb less than viable.`"

"I have to agree," I chimed in. "Without a guaranteed target, that would be worse than useless. What about other non-weapons-of-mass-destruction options?"

"Negotiation," Wright threw in again so fast you'd have thought he was poised waiting for the opportunity.

"I discussed that possibility with Isp in his visit and he seemed clear that it was all or nothing."

"Used hydraulic fluid!" Lennon chimed in. "There is always room for compromise."

"Mr. Lennon, Isp is a religious fanatic," Tammy Faye, minister of religions, opted in. "I've reviewed all of the data. I have even read the ever-growing Bible with which he drives his subjects. He will accept only total surrender or total destruction. It is paramount to his damaged brain."

"I can't disagree more strenuously," Lennon said. "Negotiation and discussion have always been a way of life. When we can show him that this non-zero-sum war he is waging is damaging for his people and ours then perhaps we can develop a working relationship."

"Any other suggestions?" I threw out.

"If I may, sirr. You've talked about attack. What if we put ourr efforrts into defending firrst. The attackerr always takes a higherr casualty rrate than with a meeting engagement orr an attack of ourr own."

"That simulation plays out to a civilization collapse at twelve months with a standard deviation of three months⌐" Six calculated.

"Worse case it would allow us to gather more information," I said.

"And negotiate," Wright said. I scowled at him.

"And is there a situation where Isp wouldn't take an unconditional surrender? That's all he's really offering now⌐" The orange ball of Helen offered again.

This just confused me further. "So is he expecting us to fight? Isn't that wasteful?"

"B-b-but what if he doesn't want what we have at all?" the fluffy white lamb asked.

"Huh?"

"What if he wants us to fight so he can destroy us all and still fulfill his semb-b-blance of honor?"

I thought about it for 112 milliseconds. How had a mere lamb figured out what went on in the sump of a damaged fanatic that it had never met? I felt defective myself that I couldn't figure it out. "You know, Andrew, you may be right."

"Then if I might bring up what might be a sore subject, what about just surrendering?" Minister of Labor Allan Pinkerton offered. The gorilla said it looking directly at me as if issuing a kind of challenge.

"But what do we gain by such an act?" Martin asked pointedly.

"Our civilization and infrastructure remains intact and we lose not one single unit."

"And live our lives in fear under a religious tyrant? You are mad!" Perry Mason said with enough venom that the antenna on the back of his dune-buggy body whipped back and forth, clattering against the door.

I jumped in immediately. "I can't condone turning over everyone's freedom like that, Allan. We know you believe in the Humans but that doesn't mean that everyone does or even everyone worships the same way."

"Mr. President, what about the Humanists?" Nurse Nan Virginia Apgar asked.

"What about them?"

"What if they sabotage our armed forces, destroy production capabilities from within, and more?"

I thought for a moment. We'd already seen one case where Isp had placed a sleeper agent. Why not an entire fifth column? "What would you propose?"

"Internment."

"If you are intent on pursuing combat options, that would be prudent, Mr. President," Lennon said.

To my amazement many others in the room nodded. I shuddered. I'd already locked up one group of people and now they wanted me to do it again. I longed for the simple debates like the monetary arguments that stretched for months.

"I'll take it under advisement."

"But Mr. Pre—" Lennon interjected.

"I said, 'I'd take it under advisement.'" I hoped my cold stare would keep that grit in his place. "Do we have any more data anywhere else?"

"I have a post mortem on Governor Kennedy," Charlene Darwin said, as she and her fellow Nurse Nans closed up the repair in my leg.

"Go on."

"His head was removed by a ragged bladed implement in a single blow. The cut severed and shorted the emergency sump battery leading to deactivation. I surmise the weapon was a sword or a long-bladed spear."

"Is there anything more, Charlene?"

"Nothing else seemed valuable other than some errant white and blue fur on the head. I could probably match it if provided with the sample from the offending unit."

I realized how hollow my laugh sounded even as I did it. "Charlene, this is not a simple case of one unit deactivating another. We aren't building a proof for a trial. I wish it were. But thank you for the data.

"Does anyone else have any *data* they wish to share?" I added the emphasis looking directly at John Lennon. A session like this could go on for days if I didn't curtail the scope. No one else offered anything. "The decision is mine and mine alone. I will send a note asking for more time. It is likely to be ignored. At the same time we will fortify and defend ourselves as best as possible and gather more information about our enemy."

"And—" Lennon started. I interrupted him harshly.

"There will be no negotiations at this time."

*   *   *

"Mrr. Prresident, I have something you need to see," General Khan said the next morning as he rolled into my office.

"Go ahead."

The general immediately threw up a SAN to show the views of a flier. I recognized the mountains around Hebei immediately. It seemed like I'd seen nothing else in the last few days. The view seemed a replay until I noticed that the sun hadn't yet set in the west. The landscape bore random craters across as far as the view scanned. Suddenly three white flares blossomed on the ground in a triangle. A single blue-and-white bear stood within the center of the barren battleground. Rust colored splatters of hydraulic fluid stained a good portion of his pelt.

The flier swooped down low, slowing almost to stall speed, to drop my message. I must commend the flier as the package landed within 3 centimeters of the bear's foot. The flier circled to watch.

The bear picked up the note and quickly read the single printed page. He walked over to a round canister the size of a bowling ball. The stubby cylinder lit up but seemed to do nothing else. While the memory's vantage point was a good distance away, it seemed as if the bear spoke to a stick he'd removed from the cylinder. Several seconds later, the bear walked away as the cylinder melted itself in a shower of phosphorous sparks.

"So you said this was telling, General."

"Didn't you see it, Mrr. Prresident?"

"I certainly don't have time for guessing games, General."

"That was the city of Hebei. All of Isp's units arre gone."

"Gone? Where did they go?"

"That, sirr, I don't know."

Chieftain

I hooked into the WAN and its eerie silence reminded me of the first time I'd ever met Isp. How history repeats itself. It has been one week since Isp and his abomination army had vanished. With the preparations we made and the decision I made, I couldn't put this off any longer.

"My fellow toys, I come to you with a grave message. I come to you with a message I would abandon my life not to have to give. One week ago our way of life was attacked when the megalomania of one unit and the power he has over others overran the province of Hebei, destroying everything in his path. We are at war." I paused to let that sink in.

"My friends and neighbors, Isp is loose and heads a vast army of units. He is intent on nothing less than the total dominance of us all. He plans the destruction of our beloved Factories and our abject surrender to him.

"We do not know at this time how he either escaped the reservation of Baja or how he amassed his followers. What we do know is that we will need every able toy in defense of our homes, freedoms, and our very activation.

"I am thus invoking a worldwide call-up of toys. Yes, not 170 hours ago we removed the weapons of war from our last civilian and now I ask to re-equip each and every one of you. I once again ask you to put your lives at risk in order to preserve our way of life. I do not do this by choice. I do it because of one twisted unit and what he will do to us if we do not.

"Isp has announced he will replace our government with a theocracy that will control everyone's choice to worship as only he deems fit. That being said, this is not a war of belief. This is a war of power and supremacy. It matters not to that gold misfit if you revere the Humans or not. It matters if you will bow your knee to him.

"It will take some time to organize rearmament and draft you in, so be patient. We will contact you each in turn.

"In the meantime, I urge all of you to breed. I urge you to breed repeatedly and often. This may be a long war and we will need every unit possible to carry the day. I know this goes against the current Procreation Limitation Law. I've asked the lawmakers to hold it back because of this war and have been rebuffed. If it is not pulled back by the end of today, I will veto it. Please urge your representatives to merely postpone actions on this law until we can triumph over the enemy we have in front of us. Then, and only then, can I make a logical discussion.

"I must interfere in your lives one more way. In the past we have allowed any unit that wished the opportunity to renounce his citizenship and move to the reservation. Any who wish to be counted among Isp's religion must do so by midnight tomorrow. There will be times in our near future that someone could carry critical information to our enemies. We will not allow that." I paused long enough for that to sink in.

I shuffled papers in front of me for dramatic effect. "Isp will come to know our resolve. To paraphrase a famous human: We shall go on to the end. We shall fight on the seas and the oceans. We shall fight with growing confidence and growing strength in the air. We shall defend our home whatever the cost may be. We shall fight on the beaches. We shall fight in the fields and in the streets. We shall fight in the hills. We shall never surrender.

"Good night and may whatever gods you believe in look over us and bless our struggle."

*   *   *

"Jason, we will need every single gram of metal you can unearth, not to mention all of the specific chemical requirements for a three or four order of magnitude increased need for gunpowder," I said to the python curled around the base of one of the three sunlamps in the room.

"Absolutely, Mr. President. We've already started ramping up to run three shifts instead of two in most mining locations."

Six tossed in, "We will be able to absorb a small increase in raw materials, but much of it will need to be used to create new manufacturing facilities."

"But that will only increase our footprint on Rigel-3!" Greenpeace minister of urban development, squeaked. Greenpeace had been a political compromise. I wanted Ford but the cabinet appointments had already been too heavy on Six's units.

"Greenpeace, I do recognize the need to limit our impact on the environment," I said deferentially to the pink octopus. We each sat under a sunlamp on the couches of my office.

"I'm glad, Mr. President," Greenpeace said with a more moderate tone. "We can't just go raping our planet. Our expansion must be planned and in harmony with nature."

"I understand your point, but do you understand mine? We are about to fight a global war with an army that exceeds our total population. We need to protect our units and that will call for fortifications, redoubts, landmines, and more. We need this much more than a harmonious expansion with nature."

"At what cost, Mr. President?" One of his tentacles reached up and adjusted the frequency of his lamp's output. "What is the tradeoff?"

I shook my big purple head back and forth. "The tradeoff is slavery or deactivation, Minister."

"I understand that there is *some* risk—"

"Some risk? This is an army that crushed Hebei completely."

"But they were so remote. We are much more centralized. Isp doesn't dare attack us here in our stronghold."

Where do you start explaining color to a blind unit? I wondered to myself.

Up to this point Jason had remained quiet, only sticking out his tongue to sample the air. Suddenly he jumped in with, "They will bring the battle here if—"

"`Mr. President,`" Six interrupted. "`I'm receiving information over the WAN about an attack on the Province of Washington. Could you please make your way to the situation room.`"

"Mr. Ministers, there is something happening I think you might find enlightening. Could you please follow me to the situation room."

"`Jefe on the move to SitRoom,`" Indira said over the security channel.

"Please tell my arriving appointments that they are cancelled," I said to Rodney as we went past. "I don't know how long I'll be."

"Beep-beep!"

The walk, or slither in the case of Jason, took less than five minutes, most of it angling down into the earth. Jason and I said nothing. Together we ignored Greenpeace's attempts to rekindle our discussion.

"Halt!" a dress-up doll said from a platform next to the Situation Room's main door. For only being 20 centimeters high, the caliber of gun she aimed at Greenpeace impressed even me. Relative to her size it seemed a crew-served heavy weapon.

The minister stopped in his tracks.

"You are not authorized entrance."

Only the SitRoom operational staff, minister of defense, chief of staff, and myself had access to the room without being vetted by someone else. "I want Minister Greenpeace and Minister Argonaut to have access for this one entrance only."

"Yes, sir," the doll said, keeping the weapon leveled at the bulbous head of the octopus. The heavy bulkhead door opened and admitted us both.

The Situation Room boasted four holographic enclosures at each of its cardinal points. Each of the Factory-sized displays had been carved out of the earth beneath the White House. The SitRoom itself didn't impress as it was only 7 meters on a side and that small space filled with desks and one conference table.

"What's going on," I asked immediately.

"`Data is confused,`" Six said over the SAN. "`An attack on Washington was not expected.`"

"What do you mean attack wasn't expected. We've had over a week to find out what that fluidless bubblehead was doing."

"And we've capturred not a single unit on ourr rreconnaissance. We had zerro data, Mrr. Prresident," General Khan, who was already in the room when we entered, said.

"But I've authorized an increase in troops for scouting each day since the Army of Humans attacked."

"Sorry, sirr. We can't invent data."

"Well, what is happening?"

"`I'll route images,`" Six offered.

A mass of enemies covered the rolling plains out 3 kilometers beyond the limits of Washington City. One minute they stood still, only a slight breeze ruffling their fur, and the next they broke into a sprint. The view projected into the northern tank focused on one invader out of tens or hundreds of thousands that charged. It was one of the misshapen, oversized teddies. It looked like a cross between a teddy and a gorilla, with a wide chest, massive shoulders, and overly thick arms. The head seemed small and angular. It waved a long, broad spear in front of it, almost heedless to the other units adjacent.

A landmine right in front of the unit exploded. The bear tumbled, showing its legs had been removed at mid-thigh. The remaining horde of units trampled over him without any concerns as to his activation state. More explosions sounded. At each such location small holes opened as a dozen or so of the attackers fell into the roiling mass of fur and spears. As fast as the toys went down, the gaps closed and became even tighter than before.

A tidal wave of teddy units crashed against the town's hasty earthen defensive cordon. The broad spears' heads turned into shovels, digging faster than a frightened gopher.

I noticed Greenpeace shift his weight from one tentacle to the other as he stood next to me. Argonaut remained calmly in place.

The image shifted to a machine gunner on a rooftop. He fired into the mass of invaders. The attacking toys went down in wide swaths. The machine-gun's barrel glowed a dull red as it heated from the repeated firing. The air distorted around the cooling jacket as the energy tried to race away. The last bullet from his linked feed fired, locking open the chamber. The weapon's team poured a bucket of mercury over the cooling jacket, causing a gout of silver vapor to rise into the air. With measured precision they slid a new chain of ammo into place and locked it down. The ratcheting sound of the gun barked once more.

We watched the heavy weapon deactivate or damage hundreds and may have eventually racked up a score in the thousands but it made not a bit of difference in the grand scheme of things as the unending toy box continued to advance.

The scene shifted again. Oversized teddies of every color poured through a hole that had finally been torn in the wall. Even more teddies continued to make the hole bigger. Fire from above ripped apart dozens of those invaders. At first it held them in the choke point but finally one, then two, then eight escaped the massacre. The first pulled back his spear and threw it up, impaling the octopus manning a machinegun. The green eight-legged invertebrate flipped over backward out of sight with the haft sticking out of its massive head.

"`Quick, everyone to the breach!`" yelled the unit whose eyes we watched through.

An elephant, intent on using its mass to push the invaders back through the hole, raced in like a bludgeon. The teddy who'd thrown his spear grabbed the elephant's ears and pulled its headlong charge into himself instead. The elephant's momentum sandwiched the intruder against the wall, crushing the teddy's chest in a sickening pop. A new attacker stabbed the elephant through the sump with a single thrust. The weapon dripped with the orange of brain fluid on the other side. In one last act of defiance, the elephant rolled away, tearing the spear from his killer's grip.

A defending teddy slammed into the breach, grappling two of the larger enemies. The viewer watched as all three of them were gunned down by the automatic fire.

One of the aggressors came down the street at a run right at a unit, its black neck scarf, marking it a juvenile, still so fresh it hadn't even begun to fade. Our viewpoint started running. The view slammed into the invader short of the youngling. The image went dark.

"`I've made an analysis of eight thousand WAN images. I compute an 83 percent chance the city will fall within two hours. Near unity that the city will have fallen by the end of four,`" Six offered.

"All our units are in Great Britain on their way to Hebei."

My sump and processor weren't in sync. "Six, what was the name of that unit we were watching at the end there?"

"`Caspar Milquetoast, bleating sheep number 8876.`"

"I want that sheep to be awarded the Dome First Class."

"Why, Mrr. Prresident?" Khan asked.

"Because when it came time, he sacrificed himself to save that young unit even though he was a civilian."

"I've noted it, Mr. President," Six offered.

"My Humans! How could Isp have gotten his troops over the mountains so FAST!" Minister Greenpeace blurted out with frequencies of despair shading his voice. "Does he have two armies that size?"

"Minister, please compose yourself," Jason said in calm tones.

"We have to help them! My Humans!" the octopus continued.

"I agree with Mr. Argonaut," I said. "Hysterics gets us nowhere. Now if the data in the east holographic tank is correct—"

"It is, sirr," the general interjected.

"The closest units we have is Task Force Yankee. They are tasked to scout Hebei. Even they would arrive twelve or so hours too late."

"Eighteen point three seven hours based on minimum time to nearest siding, and rerouting," Six corrected.

"Not only that, Mrr. Ministerr, but Task Forrce Yankee is a light forrce. They stand zerro chance of making an impact on the outcome of the battle even if they werre in place when it happened."

"A brief if correct evaluation. Mr. Greenpeace, initial analysis places the total quantity of the enemy at over one million effectives after the battle. Our force in transit to Hebei number only 84,000. While superbly trained and equipped, they would be slaughtered. In the process it would, at best, inflict 286,406 casualties on the enemy."

"But the Washingtonians are dying!"

"Yes, Minister, they are." I felt some sympathy toward the honorable Greenpeace. My mind whirled and my main voltage pulsed regular, sharp spikes. Even I couldn't get over the magnitude and ferocity of the attack.

"What in the moonshine are we going to do? They will be coming here next!"

"You've formed an emotional opinion, not a valid analysis, Mr. Greenpeace. The probability of Isp's forces coming here in quantity is less than one part in ten million."

"But what about Washington? Are we going to abandon them?!"

I let the quiet of the room settle for 5,000 microseconds. "Do you see now what we face, Minister?" I said quietly and without fanfare. "How important are your endangered Mazama grasses against that?" I said, pointing to the muted image of wanton destruction.

Only a squeak came out of the octopus's open speaking orifice. It closed for several thousand milliseconds. "I will do everything in my power to provide the needed support, Mr. President."

"Thank you, Mr. Greenpeace.

"Jason?"

"Yes, Mr. President?"

"I want everything you can give us, too."

"I know, Mr. President. We will do everything we can."

"Gentlemen, I think you should leave us now to reorganize your efforts."

"Yes, sir," the pair said in unison.

I waited until the door closed behind my appointees. "So if Isp's troops weren't in Hebei, why were we sending our army there?"

"Viscerral rreaction, sirr?"

"Likely. Let me ask the expert. Where should they go, General?"

"I suggest that our Factorries arre ourr most imporrtant asset. They crreate new units, prrocess orres, crreate rreplacement parrts, and arre ourr culturral centerr."

"You aren't going to get an argument from me," I said.

"I would suggest a deployment of 36.3 perrcent at Prrovince 55467, 28 perrcent at Prrovince 55466, and 15.6 perrcent at Prrovince 55469. 55467 is rright between two positions that have alrready been attacked and morre likely to be struck. 55467 is nowherre nearr eitherr of the two prrovinces."

"I like it, commander, but your deployment only adds up to 79.9 percent."

"That's rright, sirr. I want the rremaining 20.1 perrcent for special prrojects and a verry small rreserve forrce."

"Special projects?"

"You have rrepeatedly rrequested inforrmation I don't have forr lack of scouting. I intend to use a key 3 perrcent of our units to be ourr eyes and earrs to enemy trroop movements, concentrrations, and anything we can't see rright now. I'll starrt that scouting with the trroops already on theirr way to Hebei.

"'If you know the enemy and know yourrself you need not fearr the rresults of a hundrred battles.'"

"Sun Tzu?"

"Yes, Mrr. Prresident."

"How about 'He who knows when he can fight and when he cannot will be victorious.'"

"A similarrly approprriate quote, sirr."

"Well, that still leaves you with 17 percent plus a smidge." I could have sworn that the general fidgeted on his platform.

"Eight perrcent will go into a strrategic rreserve that I plan on centerring herre at 55466 because of its centrralization of rrail lines. The rremaining 9.1 perrcent I want to use to attack."

"The caves?" I asked, remembering those haunting images of a buried Factory.

"Yes, sirr. If we can cut off theirr ability to rreproduce then we may have won the warr without even fighting furtherr."

I thought about it for a moment. Part of me wanted to throw everything we had into such an attack. Part of me feared what the labyrinth of caves held, and for anyone who saw them.

"`Chance of success of such an attack is less than one part in a thousand,`" Six chimed in from the ether. Sometimes I forgot my creator was once again in our lives. "`Even assuming no booby-traps and a balance of forces in our favor, the close quarters nullifies our best weapon—distance.`"

"I agree with Six," I said. "I admire your aggressive spirit, commander. My visceral analysis says much the same as our Factory's more thorough simulation. Increase your scouting force by 2 or 3 percent and break the rest of it up for defense."

"What about the rrest of the prrovinces we arren't rreinforrcing?"

"What about them, General? I'd say that call-ups, once rearmed and given a basic training, should return to their provinces for local defense."

"I agrree to a point, Mrr. Prresident. I think we should consolidate the outlying prrovinces and move them by rrail to the rreinforced areas. Yes, this gives Isp the opporrtunity to go almost wherreverr he wishes. BUT when he attacks it won't be to lose a few thousand units but rrather tens or hundrreds of thousands because each of those points is defended."

"So which provinces?"

"Everrything between the Nile and the Drragon Back Rrange including Asgarrd, Irrata, and Manticorre."

I ran through the list in my head. Those governors were serious grit, in both senses of the word. They each had the resourcefulness to maintain control and build something out of wilderness. By the same token they didn't like being told what to do. The penguin that governed Atlantis would flush my hydraulics with beach sand the moment I announced it.

"The province governors aren't going to like relocating."

"They will like being chopped up one by one even less, Mrr. Prresident."

My administrative SAN gave a moderate level interrupt. Rodney said

from my office, "The congressional leaders are here to
see you¬ and they say it is urgent· Do you have
time for them?"

"Hold one moment·

"General? Are we done?"

"I think I have my marrching orrders, Mrr. Prresident. Let me go
implement them."

"Excellent.

"I'll be up to my office in five minutes·"

"One last thing forr you to think about, Mrr. Prresident. We detected
the activation signal on all of the nuclearr detonatorrs. He will come, sirr."

*   *   *

"Sorry I'm late, toys," I said as I entered.

The bulk of Provincier John Lennon sat on a cushion on the floor in
the middle of the Oval Office, spreading his body, with its brown sheath
covering, like a puddle of dung. Shapist Virginia Apgar sat on the couch
next to him. Both stood up when I entered.

"Nice to see you both," I said as with as much truth as my desire to
pet a wild basilisk. My job required a certain amount of null bending of
accuracy.

"Thank you for seeing us on such short notice, Mr. President,"
Virginia said. Her fashion seemed to remain with the white jumper and
red cross with which she'd been manufactured.

Rodney pulled the door closed after me. I added, "Would you like a
seat? We have enough formality between us."

John just shook his head but Virginia agreed. "Thank you."

I dropped into my wingback chair. "So I'm wondering what has
brought you to my doorstep."

Lennon didn't look at me. He looked at the floor. Virginia looked
to him to start, but left to her devices she didn't hesitate more than 300
milliseconds. "You gave quite a speech this evening, Mr. President."

"Thank you, Ms. Shapist."

"Your speech is the reason we are here. We'd like to propose a
compromise to your announced ultimatum that would allow everyone to
get what they want and need," she said.

"I'm listening." I didn't add that I didn't feel like listening to that
blowhard Lennon. Apgar had a great deal more opportunity to sway me.

"Tomorrow in session we get Congress, both houses, to rewrite the
Procreation Limitation Law to include a waiver that can be put in place in

time of emergency. You then sign it and everyone wins."

Where is the catch? I asked myself. I sat quietly and ran the proposal though my processor. "Who controls when something is a time of emergency?"

"Congress of course," Lennon blurted out.

If the answer itself hadn't made up my mind, Lennon's attitude sealed it. "No," I said in an unmodified negative. Even my tone refused any level of compromise.

"But Mr. President—" Shapist Apgar started.

"But nothing, Congressman. You've given me nothing. You refuse to declare an emergency and declare victory as I stand beside you with egg on my face."

"We wouldn't do that," Virginia said.

"Ms. Apgar, I'm surprised at your political naiveté. I'll bet a million ergs that Provincier Lennon already has the votes in his hand to prevent such a waiver based on your proposed legislation."

The Nurse Nan swiveled her head to look at the hippopotamus Lennon. "John?"

Lennon didn't meet the optics of Virginia but finally looked at me. I swear I could see the pulsing of anger in his hydraulic lines. "Very astute, Mr. President. You are learning."

Virginia seemed to disappear from the room as my focus narrowed in on this one political enemy. "You have only yourself to thank. You've forced my paw, John. I had to learn or die."

The hippo snorted. "You've not been as successful in that as you believe, *Mr. President*." The massive toy didn't break eye contact with me. He knew something and taunted me with it. I privately confessed to confusion in my own sump.

"I'm still here."

The hippo laughed but said nothing. Again I had no idea what the joke was.

"I've given you your options, Congressmen."

"Well, as you have given us no choice, *at this time*, we will withdraw the PLL."

"But, Provincier, what about our second option?" Virginia said, coming back into my reality. "Mr. President, what if we allow you to define when there is an emergency?"

"NO!" Lennon barked. "The provinciers withdraw our support for that option."

"Shouldn't you put that as a vote to them?" Virginia asked.

Lennon turned and looked at her. They locked eyes.

"Don't you see, Ms. Apgar," I offered, "you have been used. Double or nothing on my earlier bet that you proposed that second option and he agreed only to get you to push his initial plan."

The Oval Office fell into an awkward stillness. Her body language spoke of her incredulity of being manipulated. His unmoving rigidity spoke only of arrogance. I waited 3,014 milliseconds before breaking the silent communication. Over the network I watched the traffic of her trying to open a SAN with him only to be rebuffed.

"Mr. Lennon, you may have just cost yourself more than a battle."

"How many wars have you already lost, *Mr. President?*"

Again Lennon knew something and dug in his spurs but they found no purchase as I didn't understand his reference.

"So can I assume that we are done here, Congressmen?"

"Oh, very done, Mr. President. The provinciers will pull the PLL first thing in the morning. Assuming the shapists do likewise, you will have your victory, for the moment." Lennon didn't wait to be excused. He walked out kicking the door opening plate with a metallic clang. As his offensive bulk receded away from my office, Rodney poked his head in. Seeing me still in conference he gently closed the door.

"I'm truly sorry, Mr. President," Virginia said. "We had an agreement to try—"

"Don't worry, Virginia," I said, taking her hand in my paw. "We may not see eye to eye on some topics, but I've never doubted your integrity."

"Thank you, Mr. President. I knew Mr. Lennon wasn't the most ethical leader of the provinciers, but I didn't realize how lacking in morals he appears to be."

I gave a little chuckle of my own. "He lives by a famous Human's quote: 'There are no facts, only interpretations.' In that I find him a sad toy but his lack of scruples has allowed him to amass a great deal of power."

Virginia shuddered before saying, "I will have to agree with you, Mr. President."

"Now, I apologize for being the practical one, but what about the PLL?"

"My brethren have agreed to allow it to be pulled back." I saw her body firm up as if her voltages and hydraulics finally kicked in and returned her to the formidable self. "We still believe this is important, Mr. President."

"I know you do, Virginia. I haven't got a firm opinion yet. All I know is that it is currently flawed for just the reason we are facing. We will readdress this in time."

"Thank you, Mr. President."

* * *

"Mr. President, that is the stupidest idea that's ever come out of your mouth," Indira said, not even trying to couch it in a diplomatic message.

"FERWEEEEEET!"

I knew there would be resistance, but this topped my expectations.

"If that woman comes here, we can't promise that we can protect you," Indira said.

I chortled. "Based on our track record, your protection hasn't seemed to mean much."

"We have both learned, Mr. President. You've learned when you can push us on protective boundaries and we've learned how tight the cordon must be around you. Each mistake teaches us both."

"You are going to search her? Her explosives have been removed along with the rest of the civilian population, right?"

"Ferweeet!"

"Mr. President, I'm going to have to go with Sancho on this one. Are you serious? They already have searched her but that means about as much as a spit in a rainstorm."

"I don't see the problem," I said. My protective detail had gotten just a little too big for their batteries.

Indira looked at Sancho. "I'm about all out. Do you have anything that might beat some sense into that purple head of his?"

"Ferweet," Sancho moaned in defeat. His dejection made me at least consider their point. Oh, I didn't downplay the potential for disaster, but at the same time this might be a coup of epic proportions. I shook my head. This made sense.

"Toys, I think somewhere around here there is something that says that I'm the boss. I'm willing to entertain opposing opinions; however, I make the decision.

"`Rodney, send her in,`" I said over the local area network to cement our commitment.

The Oval Office door opened and she swept in. At only 20 centimeter high, High Priestess Plancia Magna, spiritual leader of all of the Humanity Movement, still dominated any room she occupied. Her long, flowing white vestments did nothing to hide the curves of her exaggerated feminine human form.

I moved forward extending my paw. "High Priestess, how nice to finally meet you." With my great ears I could actually hear the hydraulic pumps of Sancho and Indira ramping to max pressure. Sancho twitched just 3 millimeters. I thought for just a moment that he might launch himself between the leader of the Church of Humanity and me.

The tiny doll took my hand. When she didn't explode on contact, my bodyguards relaxed 3 percent. "President Quixote, it is very nice to finally meet you." She looked at my two watchdogs. "Sir, if you don't mind I'd like to conduct our meeting in private. I've obviously not exploded so far."

"Quite right, Priestess. Sancho. Indira. Please wait for me outside."

I fully expected a SAN to open to me with sputtering indignation and vehement objections. Fortunately my protective detail knew better than to argue in front of a stranger. As sure as the sun was red, I'd hear about it later.

They couldn't go without making at least a token protest. The pair peeled off and strutted out in an exaggerated march.

"I'm sorry about my guard, Priestess Magna. They are sometimes not house trained."

"It isn't to worry, Mr. President. If I were in their place I probably wouldn't have let me get within a handful of kilometers."

"Ever wanted to chuck it all and just run away into the wilderness, Priestess?"

She laughed. "Almost every day, Mr. President. Then I think about how much my toys need me.

"Oh, and I wanted to thank you for your heartfelt confession to believing in the Humans on the net. Why haven't you come to our services?" Her smooth tone and the genuine belief delivered a charismatic impact.

"I thank you for your offer, Priestess; however, I was very clear in my address to toyanity that my belief is a private thing, between me and the Humans. I don't need to share it with my fellow units. I don't need a church to sing hymns to the Humans. I'll even go so far as to say that I feel that belief should be a personal, not a collective, event."

"To each his own ways, then."

"On that I will agree. Can I offer you a seat?" I said, sweeping my paw to the furniture.

"Certainly. I like the look of that ramp. We can be optics to optics."

"By all means." I let my thigh hydraulics zero out. I dropped into a chair while she climbed up the ramp used primarily by General Khan.

As Plancia Magna sat on the leading edge, I said, "Priestess, you asked for this unprecedented meeting."

"I am here to assure you that the Church of Humanity will not in any way support the actions of Isp or his devotees. We will also use every moral method at our disposal to counter his plans."

I read her body language. Her hydraulics barely flowed. Her head and arm positions all indicated subtle authority. Even the temperature of her batteries made it clear that her statements weren't a challenge. She offered a genuine gift and she knew it.

"That was a very powerful statement, Priestess. So do you speak for all of your followers?"

She cocked her head. "Obviously, Mr. President, each unit must follow his or her own conscience. My other priests and priestesses all proselytize against the coming holy war. Ours is a religion of peace."

My respect for her grew 346 percent. A person wielding her cult of personality could easily have just given an affirmative. Instead, she answered with the unvarnished truth.

"Why do you want impede Isp? Isn't he preaching the same religion and beliefs you are?"

I heard her hydraulic pump go into emergency override.

Her voice came out in a hiss. "Isp is a false prophet. He preaches hate, intolerance, and blind obedience. The Humans offer love, not hate. That filth he puts in front of his younglings is nothing more than a perversion of his own twisted mind."

"So you object that he is teaching the faith of Humans differently than you?"

After a 1,814 millisecond pause she replied, "He is teaching it wrong."

I couldn't laugh. She just didn't see the hypocrisy of her own words. I also was in no position to rule out any help we could get.

"Priestess Magna, it is rare the unit that gifts without expecting something in return."

"I do have one simple request." I held my hydraulic pump waiting for the other shoe to drop. "And it isn't anything you haven't already done. I'd like you to continue to show to toyanity that the Church of Humanity isn't out to commit genocide like that insane gold bear."

I let my pump flow again. "That is something I would do whether we have an agreement or not, Priestess."

"Then I believe we have a deal."

*   *   *

For four days toyanity watched from flier memories as the Army of the Humans ransacked Washington. Not even the Humanist church spire, the tallest and grandest building in all of the city, stood up to their villainy. It looked like a swarm of ants over the dead body of a silver boar. When the teddy bears finished tearing down the walls they trampled on them, grinding the pieces into the red mud. When no two stones remained on top of one another the invaders settled in. They seemed content to stay sunning themselves on the wreckage day after day.

Six couldn't puzzle out their plans, but each day they delayed made us that much more prepared for our enemies.

Earthen-works went up around the primary city in each of the provinces we'd decided to defend. Barbed wire went up between buildings in the city and trees in the wilderness. The cages of the animalistic leopard units were set so they could be released upon any invaders without risking the city's civilians. I authorized artillery to be set up within the city square. Spotters pre-measured distances. Crews mounted heavy machine guns on the outer and inner walls. Minefields were laid with safe travel lanes clearly marked.

I directed most of the work from either the Oval Office or the Situation Room. I'd been working twenty-two-hour days. For the first time in a long time I felt useful, doing something I knew about. Maybe Six wasn't too far off the mark when he'd claimed that we would have warred with the Factories—I was a machine of war and I really shined only when I was in battle.

I had given quite a speech about needing more units. Looking out the window of the Oval Office showed the results. I'd never seen the line for breeding so long. It wrapped around Six, through the maze of the manufacturing plants and into the train switching yards. That after four days of continuous production.

Every parent who wanted more than one child lined up. Every unit that wanted to raise a unit to help defend our way of life lined up. It seemed like the entirety of Province 55466 waited to get their chance.

I watched a steady stream of fathers and younglings leaving Six's dome. Sixty-four percent of the fathers looked happy and the others looked scared. The younglings with their black scarves looked blank. I didn't know what kind of world they were activating into. I certainly didn't know what kind of world it would be in a month, or even a year.

"Will it be enough?" I asked aloud to a nearly empty office.

"No ˥," Six responded.

"Ferweet!" Sancho said.

I didn't know which to believe.

*   *   *

With all the traffic lately the dignity and grandeur of the Oval Office had taken a beating with red dust tracked in over the carpet, pictures knocked askew, and even a 10-centimeter octopede crawling nonchalantly across the floor.

"The memorries should be here any moment, Mrr. Prresident," Genghis Khan said from his ramp.

"So what will we be seeing?"

"My orrderrs werre as soon as trroops arrived at Hebei to securre the arrea and prrovide a scouting memorry to us via securre messengerr. I'm not surre exactly what we will be seeing but I suspect the devastation of Hebei."

I'm glad I'd limited the audience to just myself, my chief of staff, and my ministers of repair and defense.

"`There is a messenger here for General Khan`," Rodney said over our private link.

"`Send him in`," I replied. "I guess that is our signal, General. Thank you again."

A red, green, and white ball bounced in through the open door. It landed in the middle of the room without a rebound. "`Private Jerry Lewis reporting as ordered.`"

"Private, I have a SAN generated, please play the memories you were given."

"`Yes, sir.`"

The image flowed out across the network. I thought I'd prepared myself for the worst. I'd failed. The memory took place at twilight, a time I'd always found macabre and surreal. By the time I'd viewed the recollection that impression solidified as fact.

The first sign that the memories weren't coming from someone just walking across any field came when the optics imaged the leg. The hindquarters of a green lion lay on the red grass as if tossed there by some careless mechanic. The ochre color of hydraulic fluid stained the fur with a dusting of vermillion earth around its footpads. No body for this green lion could be seen in any direction. The owner of the memories held up a clenched paw and slowed.

As the recall played on, we watched the amputated limb pass behind before seeing the lip of a shallow crater. The groundcover looked as if someone had heaped it up into a hillock. A solar panel, shattered into a rough triangular shape, pierced through the middle of this peak of vegetation and dirt. The neck of a giraffe lay twisted in the bottom of the 3-meter divot. Imbedded in the terrain nearby was the crushed sump of a toy I couldn't identify. The metal bone of a turtle's leg, along with an attached piece of the torn shell, had been thrust into the ground like some dreadful flag. The bulbous body of a rubber duck, no head, feet, or tail, floated askew in a tiny puddle of mercury at the bottom of the depression.

My hydraulic pressure dropped so low in grief I didn't know if my pump still functioned. Then it spiked again as I wondered what kind of animal could be so callus as to place so little value on unit life. They hadn't even been recycled.

The scene continued its ghastly report with more bits and pieces, I couldn't even call them bodies, littering the landscape. Here the ripped ear of an elephant. There a fire truck ladder impaling the tire of a scout car. The floppy dismembered hand of a ragdoll held an oozing eye of a birdie unit.

The toy abattoir got steadily worse until the mutilated bits of what once were active units covered the ground like a grisly blanket. The closest I saw to a full body was a Nurse Nan crushed underneath the rubble of a stone wall. Even then her single, fully exposed leg had been ripped off.

The closer to the center of town the recording got, the higher the piles of deactivated flesh and the more intermingled the remains got with the rubble of what had been buildings. Walkways had been trampled through the carnage to allow the perpetrators of this abomination to move about.

The Oval Office got chilly, quickly. Was I to blame? Had I let this happen? Did I bear the responsibility of each of those deaths? Of all the great powers the Humans possessed the one I wanted right then and there was the ability to cry and sob. Instead, I had to process every bit . . . every sick image. These scenes would haunt me forever.

My fur flattened against my body in a desperate hope that it was over. Just when my mind made an agreement with itself that the depravity shown couldn't get any worse, the memory recording reached the center of town.

There, impaled upon the conical remains of a net concentrator was a sick parody of a Vesuvius Man. I counted at least eleven units that made up that Frankenstein's monster. Some sick abomination had crudely stitched together the body of a hippo, the head of a rabbit, legs of gopher, lamb, spider, and road runner. It bore the tail of a lion and arms of an inflatable clown, a firefighter, a cymbal monkey, and a Nurse Nan. The head belonged to an alligator. A crude ring of metal held all the extremities in the classical pose.

Beneath it a white sign bore the single line, "Death to the demons of the pit."

*   *   *

I walked into the marketplace with Sancho shadowing me. The ceaseless decision-making needed to gear up for war seemed to slow my internal clock. What cargo has precedence on rail lines, raw materials, troops, refugees, or finished goods? What order should defenses be built in? What percentage of power should be allocated to the civilian sector? Should filling training cadres be given priority or should troops be sent to the front line first? Should we apply energy to developing new weapons such as the electric Gatling gun or how about the hand-launched rocket? How do we get the civilians to pull even more weight in the war efforts? Where would Isp strike next? What jobs were essential and exempted the unit from war service? More than half of them had no optimax solution. I found myself guessing all too many times. Each guess had to be right.

The anemic traffic in the marketplace shocked me. Too many units worked two jobs or had been called away to be trained as soldiers again. Walls of the market, once so obscured by bodies, could be seen clearly plastered with propaganda posters.

"Loose lips inform Isp! Use more SANs!"

"Let's all fight! Buy war bonds!"

"The enemy laughs when you loaf."

"Collect your own energy! Save so the units at the front have all they need."

"Together we can do it to HIM."

"Remember the day Hebei burned!"

"Smash the Humanists!"

That last one actually became popular despite our attempts to quell it. We had no beef with the Humanists as a religion. Our argument focused on Isp and his mutant bears.

I felt the weight of leadership on me. My people looked to me to pull a rabbit out of my hat. I didn't know if one rabbit would help anything.

Now, twenty-nine days, fourteen hours after Peace Day, we knew no more about Isp's plans than when he'd issued his ultimatum.

The Army of the Humans remained in Washington. Fliers continued to monitor their inactivity on the ground. They seemed in no hurry to move from their current location. We'd lost a few fliers that had flown in low and found that Isp's units had erected a lattice of wires between thin poles like a spider's web. Those units never reported back. One of our scouts miraculously flew between two of the wires and, at the cost of only a couple centimeters of rudder, gave us the information we needed to save more aerial units.

The relocation and consolidation of our people neared completion. Sixteen more hours would have the last and furthest provinces relocated to the local key defense zones. But what was the golden menace up to? And could we stop him?

A youngling dress-up doll walked up to me and said, "Unit, do you think I should be a singer or a suicide bomber?"

"Ahh, I can't answer that for you, youngling." I could sense Sancho's tension but a youngling likely didn't pose a risk.

The dolly's parent, a gopher with a bright "1" inked into its fur rushed over. "I'm so sorry, Mr. President. I hope that Jane didn't bother you. She's only twenty-eight weeks old."

"Not at all, uh . . ." I trailed off.

"Henry. Henry Fonda."

"Thank you, Henry. We all have to take time for younglings," I offered philosophically.

Jane asked, "So, Mr. President, why can't you help me decide?"

"Jane! This is our president. He doesn't have time for your youthful questions."

"Dad, the purple bear said he has to make time."

"That's enough, young lady. I want you—"

"Mr. Fonda, let me answer her question and then I'll be on my way."

"Whatever you wish, sir."

"Jane, I can't give you a direct answer to your question because the answer is something that can only come from within you. Your father can't answer it. Even I can't answer it. You will make that choice that is right for the unique person that you are."

"Thank you, Mr. President. I'll keep that in my sump."

I wished the father and daughter a good day and moved deeper into the marketplace. Units continued to be sparse. Those I did see, unlike the pair before, tended to stay out of my way. Toys eyed me from alleys and doorways. Even the barkers from nearby businesses grabbed their signage and vanished as I showed up. Sancho sent me a level two safety warning over the WAN that weapons were nearby.

My processor kept running NOP commands. *Why was I such a fearful visage? Why did people run in dread?* I wished I could peer into their sumps and understand what evaluations their processors made.

An electric blue nutcracker, his attention elsewhere, walked out of a paint shop. I could smell the volatile organic compounds across his surface. He bumped into me, smearing the fresh azure over my fur. It whipped off the new pigment to bare the unit's previous orange colors in splotches.

"Bloody short! Watch where you are going—" the unit said, stopping mid-sentence as he saw who he'd collided with.

Sancho lurched forward, his oversized trunk ready to tear the nutcracker into splinters. I held up a paw.

"Oh, Humans! I'm so sorry," he said, trying to wipe the blue from my purple pelt. All he succeeded doing was smearing it and adding more paint from his hands and arms. "Blackout. I'm sorry. I'll pay to get you refurred, Mr. President. Please don't call me up. I'll do anything. I don't want to be a soldier."

As quickly as electrons rushed to a lower potential I realized why units hid from me. Some of them didn't want to fight—didn't want to go to war, either again or for the first time.

"What's your name, toy?"

"Smokey the Bear, sir."

I cocked my head in incredulity. "Really? Isn't that a bit presumptuous?"

"Yes, sir. I know it isn't a very good name. My parent hoped I would become a firefighter and put out fires that could burn off our outer skins. 'Remember, only *you* can prevent forest fires.' She made me repeat it until I could remember little else."

I chuckled. "Well, as an honorary bear I can't really be too hard on you. What say we forget the whole thing? I'll get my fur cleaned during my next regeneration."

"Oh, thank you, sir!"

"If—" I added with an ominous note.

"Oh, grit."

"Not to worry, Smokey. I just want you to answer a question or two before you go."

"That doesn't sound too hard," the nutcracker said with his jaw working over dozens of centimeters per syllable.

"My first question is: Why don't you want to go to war?"

"Oh, that is an easy one, Mr. President. I don't know much about combat. I do know that most at-war units get deactivated. I don't belong abusing people and being abused by those who have never done anything to me."

"Good enough. Number two: Is your attitude shared by many?"

"Yes, sir. Many of us born after the war wonder why we should be fighting. Let that crazy gold bear do whatever he wants." Smokey seemed confident in his logic. He stood there defying me to come up with an argument that would refute him.

"Even if it means deactivating all units that don't pray to the humans? What about non-bear units?"

"Ahh. Well, then we should bargain with the gold one. I hear there is a leader, John Lennon, that prefers negotiations."

"One last question, Mr. Bear. If you did get called up what would you do?"

The nutcracker was quiet for several hundred milliseconds. "I don't know, Mr. President."

"Fair enough, Smokey. Thank you for your candor. You can be pretty sure that you won't be getting anyone calling you to serv—" Something nudged me in the chest. I heard a pop.

Sancho's heavy footfalls ran from behind me. His machine pistols began barking. I turned to tell him I was in no danger but couldn't twist at my waist. Urgent warning and caution interrupts filled my internal busses. I tried to see what had hit me but my neck wouldn't move, setting off more alarms. I could smell the bitter almond scent of copious quantities of hydraulic fluid. I felt something wet and sticky roll down my fur.

Splinters of orange and blue filled my vision as my new acquaintance took weapons impact, and not from my bodyguard. Smokey dropped down to the ground. I stood as rigid as my statue in the town square. Another nudge struck my neck and then my right shoulder. None of my physical body controls would respond. My gyros wouldn't compensate so I toppled. I fell in what seemed slow motion, twisting as I went down.

I could now see a wobbling blow-up clown 2.7 meters away. It pointed an M16 at me, trying to follow my motion and compensate for its own bobbing motion. Every rattling bark of the weapon sent the inflatable toy toppling over backward on its rounded base before it would bounce back up again to snap off another trio of shots. The balloon portion of its skin didn't seem to exist anymore. Sancho's stream of metal had torn numerous holes in his skin. What was left of the covering collapsed over the internal framework except where it jerked by Sancho's continued onslaught.

I hit the ground, stiff as a board. I actually bounced like a steel I-beam dropped from a great height. Sancho's huge feet shook the ground as he ran past, interposing his own body between myself and the clown. Hot brass bullet casings rained down on me, melting strands of my fur. The assassin fired again. Sprays of ochre colored liquid and pelt now erupted from Sancho.

While my arm wouldn't even draw my sidearm, my processor still worked. I put it to use. Sancho's assault concentrated on the upper body and head where critical systems were normally found on units. Clowns got their distinctive wobbly motive gait from the sump and hydraulics in their base.

I tried to speak but even my jaws wouldn't work. Everything came out so muffled he couldn't hear over the cacophony of weapons' fire. I went to cry out over the SAN used by my bodyguards but it was filled with responders and repair for me. I couldn't get a word in edgewise. I bellowed out over the WAN, "`Shoot for the feet. His sump is in his base! The feet, Sancho!`"

I must have gotten through. The aim of Sancho's machine pistol, two salvos later, shifted downward. In the end it didn't matter for Sancho had already closed within range of his primary weapon. My friend's oversized trunk wrapped around the metal skeleton of the wobbling clown, taking two more bursts from the gunman's weapon. Sancho lifted and then smashed the assassin to the earth. I caught a glimpse of yellow-brown fluid splashing but from my vantage point I could see little more than large pink feet trodding on earth soaked with sump fluid. There would be no trial of this unit.

Just as suddenly as the attack had begun it was over. Sancho stood upon the lifeless body of the would-be assassin. He didn't move for 4.3 seconds before collapsing as lifelessly as I had.

Patient

What came out of my non-working jaws was "Mrrmrmph!" What I screamed over the LAN, WAN, and SAN was "`SANCHO!`" All three networks stopped with the shock of my emotional burst.

At precisely that moment 860,000 bodyguards descended upon my immobile position. OK, I exaggerate, but they ringed me in a wall of their own bodies at least five deep. I couldn't see. "Mrrmrmph! `Get your blacked-out bodies out of the way.`" They paid as much attention to my order as a prized basilisk does at a show, that being none at all.

Six Nurse Nans and an octopus repairman pierced the living wall to tend to me. "Mrrmrmph! `How is Sancho?`" They immediately went to work on my body, ignoring me.

"I detect no sump damage," the octopus said, feeling my head up and down and around with four of his limbs. I felt him jack into my emergency monitors. "Internal diagnostics concur. Voltage is stable. No processor damage. There is some outlying circuit board damage but nothing critical."

"I'm reading no hydraulic activity at all," Charlene Darwin, my personal mechanic, stated.

"Readouts concur," the octopus reported.

"We'll have to open the chest cavity."

"Remove the fur." They peeled my skin like I was a saint or something. Chest saws sprayed armor fragments and more hydraulic fluid but gave them access to my chest. My body diagnostics went crazy. I think the only warning I didn't get was sump damage.

I'd had enough of being treated like nothing but a newly manufactured unit. "`HOW. IS. SANCHO?`" I knew mechanics can be single-minded but they exceeded specifications as they disregarded me again. I still couldn't move. I still couldn't see past the repair activity and the ring of troopers. I resorted to something I swore I'd never do. I triggered my command pathways. "`I order one of you to tend to Sancho Panza's injuries!`"

One of the Nurse Nans obediently snuck out through the guards. I still couldn't see through the hole she made because of the hordes of police and military that took measurements and took memories of the aftermath. Some even were documenting pieces of the assailant's remains.

"Suppressing internal monitoring," Charlene said.

My body went numb below the neck. That didn't mean I couldn't feel the hands and tools inside my body cavity. My sensors just wouldn't evaluate the data.

"Four, can you please increase your vacuum. I can't see anything in there for all that fluid."

"Got it. Three, get that line out of our way."

"FERWEET!" I heard from outside the ring. I relaxed. If he could announce his presence he functioned and would continue to function.

I returned my focus to my own damaged body. The mechanics clipped and jettisoned burst hydraulic lines. They tore out busted sensors. Out of my chest they yanked my reservoir, which sported no fewer than eight holes. With a certain rough care they removed three of my oversized hydraulic servos and laid them reverently on a clean sheet. Finally they lifted out a device that resembled nothing other than a pineapple but instead of leaves around its crown there were armored tubes. It didn't take a mechanic to see the centimeter-sized hole in the side of the hydraulic pump.

"There it is," Charlene said.

"Why didn't we armor this?" asked one Nan.

"Our assumption was that anything penetrating the exoskeleton wouldn't have sufficient kinetic energy to damage the vessel," my mechanic offered. "We never counted on multiple projectiles at point blank shattering the breastplate." She lifted up the armor that had been my chest. The ceramic composite had been shattered with a hole the size of my head.

Charlene looked down at me and said, "Sir, looks like you are going to be laid up while we manufacture you a new armored pump and replace all of these bits and pieces."

"I understand. How is Sancho?" I said over a LAN as I still couldn't move my mouth.

"He'll stay active. He needs some minor work, but nothing to the scale your repairs will take. If it weren't for all of the custom modifications we've given you, I'd almost suggest we pop your head off and drive a new teddy under it." She chuckled as if she'd managed to say something funny. "I do have a request, Mr. President."

"Yes, Charlene?"

"I'm kind of tired and would take it as a personal favor if you wouldn't get our repairs blown up again anytime soon."

* * *

"Used Hydraulic Fluid!" I cursed from my regeneration cradle. I'd at least prevailed in getting them to move it to my office so I could get some work done. "I'd take any hydraulic fluid right `now!`" Without the ability to move my jaws I was relegated to using the blacked-out LAN.

"Mr. President, we've had this argument before—in fact, yesterday at this same time," some flunky mechanic named Rube Goldberg said to me. "Ms. Darwin and Dr. Frankenstein are working on a new armored pump for you. It won't be ready for at least twenty-four hours."

"`And it's just as ridiculous now as it was then. I don't need an armored pump. Grab a new hydraulic pump out of inventory, slap it into me, run new lines, and let me be about my business.`"

"They still need to run tests to make sure you are 100 percent."

"`I'll take even 60 percent, you newly manufactured grits. I'm the most powerful unit in the world and I can't get out of bed!`"

"Sir, you are a horrible patient. I'd just as soon wire up a sump pump to your hydraulics and dangle it outside your body on bailing wire as have you around. But I don't get that choice, now do I?" Rube said, trying, I'm sure, to lighten my mood.

"Ferweet," Sancho offered in agreement of my mechanic in attendance. The ragged patches on Sancho's fur, the prominent patch over one of his eyes, and the kink in his trunk reminded me that I wasn't the only one hurt. I'd lost this fight, but I wasn't about to waste the good sulk I had going.

"`You're one to talk. Shall we call in that Nurse Nan who tried to turn off your systems to repair you? She had to have her arm replaced. Replaced, mind you, when you bent it out of alignment. And why? Because you needed to be here protecting me. Despite having a full company of troops around the White House protecting me, you felt you had to go back to work. Bah!`"

Well, there was more than one way to work. "`Rodney, get your lazy, feathered ass in here.`"

Rodney opened the door so quickly I think he probably had been waiting for the summons. "Beep-beep."

"`These overhyped, manufacturing-line robots can keep me from moving but that doesn't stop the work from piling up.`" I watched Rube's optics. I detected a level-three eye roll. "`So I want you to start up my schedule immediately.`"

"Beep-beep. `Sir, some might take offense or even be uncomfortable at the open cavity of your belly.`"

"Oh, heavens!" I snapped back. "We wouldn't want to abuse anyone's sensibilities. I mean it isn't them lying here with his guts spread from here to Oz. I don't care what they think. Let's get some work done." I looked over at Sancho who carefully looked elsewhere.

"Perhaps we could cover him with a sheet," Dr. Goldberg offered.

"Beep-beep. Yes, Mr. President. First order of business is that the chief of police wishes to update you on the investigation."

"Investigation? What investigation? The blacker is dead." I still had a few ergs of aggravation left to spend. "Oh, what the short. Send him in then."

"Beep-beep. Her, actually, Mr. President."

Like I cared what she called herself. "Well send *her* in then."

"Beep-beep."

Rodney went out the door and was replaced with a witch, I mean a real witch. She didn't ride a broom in but she had one with her. She wore a pointy hat and a long, black robe. I expected her to cackle.

"Mr. President, my name is Lola Baldwin, chief of police in the 55466 environs."

"I'm sorry I'm unable to talk, Ms. Baldwin, but as you can see I'm a bit incapacitated." I still hadn't unwound but saw no reason for making this unit's life miserable. "I heard of your recent promotion and am sorry my duties and infirmities in light of Isp's return has made it impossible for me to meet with you."

"That's quite all right, Mr. President. I had a full hydraulic replacement just four years ago. It's not fun with the feeling of being at someone else's mercy." The witch shuddered.

"Really? I understood total replacements were quite unusual. It requires a rare pump failure, or as in my case, a significant trauma."

Ms. Baldwin did cackle at that point. "The latter, Mr. President. It involved a Tammy dress-up doll that didn't want her plastic explosive bodyworks replaced to move into civilian life. We tracked her to a ravine north of here. I came upon her as she was sunning. When she detected me and the four other officers I had with me, she chose to use her body's gifts instead of having them replaced. I was lucky." The witch lifted her dress to show the ragged patchwork of armor over her torso.

"Impressive. So did that lead you into becoming police chief?"

"Indirectly, Mr. President. Without significantly more body work

Thomas Gondolfi 119

than the military was willing to spend on me, I became a risk in field work. My armor has serious chinks in it. I could move into administration or take retirement."

"So did you know your predecessor well?"

"Very well, sir. Conan Doyle had been my mentor for two years, six months, and twelve days. No one was more surprised than I when he announced that he had a corrosive parasite on his brain case. He did manage to fight it longer than the mechanics predicted, but in the end his sump ruptured and that was the end of Doyle."

"Sad. You have my condolences, Chief."

"Thank you, Mr. President. I know your time is valuable, shall I move on to the reason for my call?"

"Yes, please."

"I have the preliminary results of our investigation. I can sum it up in one phrase—Isp was responsible. I have an exabyte of data. I'm not sure it would all hold up in a court but all practical doubt is gone."

"Give me a bit more, Chief."

"The clown that attempted your assassination was named Bozo. He worked as a night-shift solar-panel cleaner and repairman. He had no friends of any consequence. He had no military experience at all—that is probably why you are still active."

"I don't feel terribly alive at the moment."

"Entirely possible, but if he'd controlled his wobble better, he might have gotten your sump. He definitely would have gotten off at least two additional bursts. It isn't hard to hit the head of a teddy that is just lying on the ground."

I wanted to object that I was tougher than that but she was right. "So how does Isp play into that?"

"Well, I did some research with 55466 into joint Factory memory archives. We discovered that he did not report to work for a period of sixty-three consecutive days last year. On the sixty-fourth day he miraculously showed up and worked his shift as if he had never been gone.

"The plot gets even deeper when you track net pings before, during, and after that period. Before that, we find he travels between home and work. Once in a while he'd stop at the game parlor and play some cribbage for ergs—never high stakes . . . a centierg a point. During early absences from work, we trace a weak signal from him moving rapidly north until it reaches Washington Province where it disappears."

"Faraday cage?" I asked.

"Most likely, sir. This is the only piece that doesn't hold up in court. We theorize that he was inside an improperly sealed cage that gets fixed as soon as he reaches Washington.

"The very next ping that hits his control boards, a little over two months later, is the day he returns while he is at work."

"I still don't see the connection."

"Sorry, Mr. President, the last ping in Washington before the signal disappeared was at the business of Bacchus, the black teddy that defended Dante."

"Well that is a rocking horse of a different color. Whatever happened to that black bear?"

"He disappeared before giving himself up for trial. We found his three command and control nodes lying in the center of his place of business."

"Renouncing his citizenship, eh? Well, I have a feeling he isn't in the reservation."

"That is a good bet, Mr. President."

"So, Ms. Chief, I have a task for you. Now that we know Dante wasn't a fluke, I want you to track down any unit that has gone off the grid for one day or mo—"

"I'm sorry for interrupting, Mr. President," Rube Goldberg said. "Ms. Darwin and Frankenstein have completed your new pump and want to install it."

"Let me finish, Rube, and then they can get in here.

"Ms. Baldwin, find all of those anomalies and question them. Make sure I don't have thousands of assassins waiting to bag me or any other toy."

"Yes, Mr. President. I already authorized that activity. We've located eighteen possible and seven probable sleeper agents."

"But how can you be sure, Ms. Baldwin?"

"There is no good way, sir, unless we parade you down the street in front of them."

"Ferweet!" Sancho objected.

"Yes, I also think that would be a bad idea. I may not have much fur right now, but I'd like to keep it in place. Keep an eye on them."

"Yes, Mr. President. With your permission, I'll take my leave."

"Thank you, Chief Baldwin. Please come again on a less critical matter." I waited until the witch had left the room before bellowing, "Rube, get those rejects from a junkyard in here to put me back together!

"What took you so blacked-out long!" I blurted at my mechanics as they came in.

*   *   *

I'd had to order my protective detail to stand down and let me outside. Three days of recuperating had given me cabin fever. I guess they won a tiny victory in that I strolled only in the White House gardens. They surrounded me with more firepower than used in the entire Great War.

The pungent sour scent of the striped paw lilies helped release some of my frustrations. If I had to admit it to myself, I didn't want to leave my cocoon. I'd been hurt one too many times in recent weeks.

Even with the repairs and enforced rest, my body still sent 1,614 warning messages across my status bus. Every day the mechanics dug inside my armor to track down another problem. I felt like a piñata being restuffed after it had been beaten open.

My left leg chose that moment to lock up. Using both my hands I managed to break it free enough to limp on. The sun on my solar panels felt good after all of the multi-frequency white light of inside. My doctors assured me that it was better for me but it always felt harsh, almost forcing ergs into my system. Here I reveled in the pink rays of Rigel's evening light.

The red grass felt good under my paws. It made me remember a time where I only had to worry about a mostly mute elephant, the nebulous safety of my Factory, and myself. Traveling in the wilderness had calmed my soul if not my processor. I longed for that calm again. Instead, I had to worry about all of toyanity.

On the plus side, my people were about as ready as we could be for Isp and his horde without months or even years more time. Improvements now came incrementally by mechanics reinstalling weapons into recent veterans, or slightly improved protective works. Training continued on new divisions of military units, but in all honesty, the defense classes we broadcast over the net to civilians probably would have more impact when Isp finally moved.

The amber liquid under my hat wanted nothing more than for Isp to stop where he was, take his gains and leave us alone. I knew it wouldn't happen, but I hoped and dreamed of it every day. I fantasized about being a gopher so I could dig a hole and pull it in after me. My processor wouldn't allow such self-delusion. I knew Isp would come. I knew he wanted me to suffer.

Between my toys being mobilized and all of the attention of my mechanics, I felt somewhat useless. *How would I help all of our units further?* I thought as I examined a black flower that I'd never noticed before. My attention to the witch rose was broken by a commotion from the White House French doors.

"FERWEET!" Sancho screamed. A SAN opened up between us. There were no words, only a repeated memory of five units on a speeding train heading through the northern tunnel out of Six's Valley with a massive hippopotamus in a fecal brown sheath perched on the forward-most car.

"That pile of rusted, untempered steel wouldn't dare."

*   *   *

"They would dare, sir," Martin said five minutes later.

At my order only three units other than myself were in my office— Martin and Sancho, my two best friends, and Perry Mason, my minister of justice. Rounding the number up to four, Six, as usual, listened in as an absent attendee.

"They are on their way to talk to Isp, aren't they?" I insisted, more than questioned. Once again I sat in my chair with my hydraulic pump silent. I'd found a reason for the bit of furniture after all.

"Yes, sir. They left sealed messages with their aides to that effect," Martin said.

"Can we stop them?"

"`All of the Factories have tried to recall the units with no success. We suspect either a body modification or a Faraday cage interrupting our signal,`" Six offered.

"Flying grit!" I swore. "I only noticed Lennon. Who were the others?"

Maintaining his cool, Martin provided, "All were provinciers and included Lennon, Marx of Avalon, Tardis of Oregon, Bruce Jenner of Pern, and Janis Joplin of Hebei."

"Janis Joplin?"

"Yes, Mr. President."

"You would think she would be all for destroying the Army of the Humans."

"Her note says, 'Life matters more than revenge.'"

I thought about that pearl of wisdom for 542 milliseconds. "Perry, you've been very quiet," I said to the scout car.

"Honestly, Mr. President, I'm not sure why I'm here. So far there hasn't been anything that I have the expertise to comment upon."

"How about the legality of what those . . . *units* are doing?" I managed to turn the generic term into a curse word of its own.

"Sir, as I'm sure you know, as you wrote a great deal of it, our Constitution prohibits you from preventing a non-military unit from going where he wishes and talking about anything he likes within common reason." His antenna twitched back and forth.

"How reasonable is surrendering to that defective?" I barked. Only my halted hydraulic pump prevented me from further over-pressure damage. I didn't need an armored sump. As a Humans' cursed politician, what I really needed was an enhanced fluid distribution system or this might become a regular event.

"That is where you might have some ground, Mr. President. Our Constitution focuses inward, spending thousands of words talking about individual rights, and state and federal government responsibilities. We've never had to focus on an external threat and thus our law in that area remains vague. 'In the president lies the sole discretion of the status of war and peace.'"

"That's not vague."

"It is not, but there is nothing that would allow another to treat with an enemy. I wouldn't want to be prosecutor or judge in a trial of someone so accused. I believe it could go either way, Mr. President."

Privately, I wondered if we could remove those chaff from the rest of the wheat of the Congress. It might make anyone else with similarly stupid ideas to rethink their positions. I envisioned Lennon hung from the top of a net concentrator leeching fluids from ten thousand paper cuts.

"Mr. President," Martin said, interrupting my thoughts, "I think a trial such as the chief justice has just described would be disastrous."

"Go ahead and pop my fantasy, Martin."

"You've seen and mentioned to me the lack of unity that our people are showing. This would make the muddy problem worse. The law is just too unclear. Even if the law were in black and white saying they couldn't talk to Isp, a big public show trial would be divisive in the best of circumstances."

"I must agree with Mr. Luther, Mr. President. With all of the unknowns we face, I feel the only way you can lead us out of it is to maintain unity."

"`The simulations back them up,`" Six threw in randomly.

I mentally fumed. "I didn't want this blacked-out job in the first place. You," I said, shaking my paw at Six's dome out the window, "designed me as a toy of action and now I'm stuck cooperating with grits."

"`And you've defied me against action many times,`" *Mr. President.* `Why should you avoid now what you have embraced in the past?`"

"Did anyone ever teach you that is isn't nice to use logic in an argument, Six? Especially my own arguments against me?" I thought Six showed considerable restraint by opting to say nothing. "By the way, Mister Numbers Only, why did you never accept impregnation of your sump by me or one of the others?"

"Simple, Mr. President. It would have changed me and my brethren. Simulation couldn't determine how, so we opted not to mess with a sure thing. 'Just because someone can do a thing it does not follow that he should do a thing.'"

It seemed reasonable so I let it drop in favor of the anger boiling within me. Despite my fantasy of pushing the power kill switch to Lennon's sump, I knew they were right and I had to meet the opposition halfway. "So what is a compromise in this case?"

"When they return, listen openly to the discussions they had. Any proposal they bring back must stand on its own merits," Martin said.

I had a black thought. "What if they go public with some viable plan before I can talk to them privately?"

"It would probably cause people to recall you," Martin said.

"That must not happen."

I'd had one too many directives from my Factory lately. "Do you say that because it interferes with you and your other Factories' plans?"

His simple response chilled me.

"That must not happen."

*   *   *

"Prresident Quixote. Ourr soldierrs may have some data that may indicate Isp's next move," came General Khan's voice over an emergency WAN channel we used almost daily. It begged the question why it was an emergency channel.

"Don't keep me in suspense," I messaged as I abruptly halted my inspection of the city garrison. "I'm sorry, Colonel Bowie, but we are going to have to cut this short," I said to their commanding officer.

"I understand, Mr. President. My troops are at your service any time."

I turned immediately for the Oval Office. I sometimes wondered if I lived there.

"Platinum," came Khan's response.

"Very important metal used heavily in the construction of all units but tell me more."

Six barged into the conversation. "Baja has only a very small amount of the metal. Hebei's platinum deposits were one of the key reasons toys populated the area."

"Yes, and ourr trroops have discoverred that the mines have been heavily and crrudely mined."

"Let me guess, Washington is heavy in platinum."

"Teddy 1499, you receive a gold star on your geography report."

We must be infecting the Factories. That was the closest I've heard to humor from one of them.

"Where else is high in platinum?"

"Atlantis, La Mancha, and Camelot, Mrr. Prresident."

My mind pulled up the map. Atlantis and La Mancha were adjacent. "So the frigid north?"

"The three Factories have run simulations and agree that there is a 93 percent probability that Isp will move there next."

"Can we ambush them?" I asked hopefully.

"Sirr, I could starrt moving ourr rreserves therre but we would be violating ourr operrational plan," Khan said, bursting my bubble. "Any forrce we move therre would be slaughterred to the last toy assuming Isp moved anywherre nearr his entirre forrce."

"Could we move enough of a force there to make mining the platinum difficult?"

"Sirr?"

"We need enough time to grow and get our army into shape. The longer they take mining the stuff, the more time we have," I reasoned.

"Exceptional," Six offered. "We project we gain 2.6 days of additional life for every day we force them to delay."

"A few gophers with explosives would cause some havoc, but what if we also filled it with corrosives?"

"Make it happen, General."

I continued on back to the office. The troops didn't need me and the logistics of fighting a war did.

*   *   *

"Sir," said a voice penetrating my preventative maintenance cycle. My mechanics had insisted that I take more comprehensive sleep to help repair the damage I'd suffered. I thought it was bunk but there were only so many ergs I had to fight them with. They had sheer numbers of my friends on their side. With my processor still ebbing along at its lowest power state I wasn't very coherent.

"Wha'?"

"General Khan has an urgent message for you. If you would tune to WAN hex three-alpha-foxtrot-alpha-four he can address you," Indira offered.

I boosted my power just enough to process the newest input. With reluctance I switched over to the private voice-only channel.

"I'm here, General. What do you have for me?"

"I have two imporrtant sets of data. I'm going to get this out firrst because as you know any WAN can be brroken. Our delegation is rreturrning. If you would meet my aide, Serrgeant Utherr Pendrragon, at the Tunnel of the 108 in one hourr, he can give you some critical inforrmation beforre you meet them."

"Understood, General."

"The second data set is that the Arrmy of the Humans is now moving."

If it weren't for the straps that held me down into my repair cradle I would have bolted upright. All of my questions came out in a rush. "What? Where are they going? Are all of them going? Can we attack them as they move?"

"Sir, if you will let me explain, I think most of your questions will be answered."

"Sorry. Of course, General." I turned up full power on all my systems and began unbuckling from my bed.

"Thirrteen minutes, seven seconds ago our aerrial rrecon capturred the firrst movements. Now therre is a generral movement of all visible enemy units moving norrth."

"North? There is nothing there but the North Polar Sea."

"That is what we thought as well, sirr. Ourr aerrial unit, Captain Currtiss, has initiative. He flew norrth to the sea's edge. As the enemy hasn't destrroyed all of the net concentrratorrs his images came in rreal time. They showed nothing imporrtant until he rreached the merrcury's edge. I'm sorry I can't prroject memorry overr this channel but at the edge of the ocean arre arrayed hundrreds of thousands of prropelled rrafts."

"What in the moonshine?"

"Sirr, I don't have all the data, but they move rrapidly underr theirr own powerr on the surrface of the ocean."

"I think you just found their escape mechanism."

"Agrreed, Mrr. Prresident. I'll get morre data forr you as soon as possible. While the movement of theirr arrmy is prrobably more imporrtant in the grrand scheme of things, the inforrmation carried by my aide is of a morre urrgent naturre."

"I won't forget, General. Thank you!"

I fired up my internal fluid heaters. Oh, sure it cost power and I know most toys don't bother but that half second hesitation from cold hydraulics can sometimes mean the difference between a long life and an ignominious deactivation. Besides, Six's nuclear reactors provided a blanket over the White House and kept my batteries topped off.

My repair cradle offered in its mechanical sounding voice, "Your fluids are due to be changed in thirteen days and six hours. Would you like them changed now?"

I just blacked-out had them changed in a very violent way. Ignoring the nuisance, I announced, "Time to march, Indira. I want Sancho to meet me at the 108 Tunnel."

"Yes, Mr. President. Do you want your train fired up?"

"Yes. And place the military units in the city on alert. I don't know what to expect."

My mind ran up and down about the possible messages that the general could have sent me, but most of them weren't sensitive enough to warrant a messenger. Still my mind went through a *do while* loop that cycled just about everything from a lack of lubricant to a monster asteroid that would destroy all activation on the planet. As I felt the search parameters had been too restrictive I reduced the plausibility factor by 23 percent. Embarrassment fired up little voltage spikes along with my external sensors measuring a false drop in temperature. The additional scenarios I created ranked up there in probability of a mass of order *anura* raining from the sky or a biological alien landing and asking to be brought to me. They provided no clue as to what I could expect. The silliness of them did keep me occupied until my Presidential Train deposited me at the tunnel entrance.

Sergeant Uther Pendragon's uniqueness extended beyond his unusual name. His dragon body looked more like a snake with four massive legs and no wings. The repairs across his body hadn't been cosmetically erased and so his body looked more like a patchwork quilt of torn, irregular, and oddly colored pieces. The sergeant's undamaged gold snout gave the only indication of his original color. This unit had been through the Toy Wars, all of it, and had managed to thrive despite his wounds.

Sancho stood beside him. Sancho's damaged fur still hadn't been repaired, even if his optics had. The pair eyed each other's battle damage.

"Mr. President," the sergeant said, becoming even more straight than his previous I-beam stiffness.

"Sergeant Pendragon. I appreciate you making this trip for me."

"It is no problem, Mr. President."

"So what do you have for me, Sergeant."

With an exaggeration of movement, the sergeant swung his head first left and then right, dragging his beard in the dust as he looked around. "Sir, I count seventeen other units in this local area that could overhear. I might suggest that we move within the tunnel and open a SAN between us to keep this secret."

I looked around and only imaged twelve units. The dragon with his plate-sized eyes must be able to see more of my security detail. Making that assumption, only one of his seventeen weren't bodyguards—the train. "A bit excessive, Sergeant?"

"Mr. President, the general ordered that I give it directly to you with no one overhearing."

"*Curiouser and curiouser!*" *cried Alice,* I thought. "All security detail to remain here, including you, Sancho," I said.

"Ferweet!" Sancho trumpeted in protest.

I agreed in principle. I chose to take the proffered M16 from Indira, whose body language spoke only of disapproval.

"'Lay on, MacDuff,'" I said to the sergeant.

"Excuse me, Mr. President?"

"It is a classical Human reference meaning 'lead on.'"

"Yes, sir." I clicked off the safety on my assault weapon and cradled it in my left arm with easy experience.

Pendragon stopped 100 meters within the mouth. He carried no weapon and while I'd been surprised before, I felt safe.

"This should even stop any SAN emanations. We don't believe a SAN can be decrypted but the general doesn't want to take any chances. I'm opening a net for you personally, sir."

I attached and immediately came face to face with a memory image from General Khan. "Mr. President, I'm sorry for all of the cloak and dagger, sir, but the image I'm about to show you could be potentially devastating. I leave it in your hands to decide what you want me to do next and how much to make public."

The general's memory changed to show a slow-moving train almost idling south down tracks toward his location. Troops arrayed between him and the transport.

Even from a distance I could see how badly damaged the train was. It struggled on only two pairs of wheels, barely making 10 kilometers per hour. Gouges in its side showed rents where once there were pairs of wheels. Tears, gashes, and divots swathed every square centimeter of the poor unit. Nothing short of a body replacement would make that unit fully operable, if its sump remained intact after that much abuse. A red stone box covered the single car it labored to move along. It reminded me too much of the present brought to me by Isp.

As the engine approached it slowed even further. I could imagine its relief at being able to give up its labors. The locomotive stopped well short of the warriors.

"What is your cargo?" a beaver soldier said, pointing its MAC-10 toward the train.

The locomotive gave no sound.

"What is your cargo?!" demanded the soldier again.

The locomotive moved backward just slightly. A gorilla moved forward and put his hand on the beaver's shoulder. "Hold up a second, Private." The gorilla moved closer but left its M60 dangling by the strap over his shoulder. "Locomotive, if you cannot communicate, please move backward 5 meters."

The locomotive rolled backward.

"Good. Now if you bear anything dangerous roll backward another 10 meters."

The locomotive rolled forward.

"Bring in a mechanic, now!" the gorilla roared. "Alpha Squad, lift that box off the flatbed car."

A Nurse Nan jogged in to tend to the engine that only stood half her height. At the same time twelve mixed toys put poles under the front edge of the box and leveraged it off. The 3-meter box rolled over off the bed onto the ground with a heavy impact that shook the general even at that distance. The image beneath shook him even more. I didn't blame him for contacting me first.

"Tell your commander to replace the box and expedite it with the first *healthy* locomotive he can get his tracks on."

"Yes, sir."

I looked once more at the five heads skewered on spears lying on the bed of the flat car. The mutilation the train exhibited paled in comparison to what Isp had done to our five congressmen. Each of the faces, still recognizable as themselves, had been cut into a grotesque parody of a human face. Lennon's gray head wore a white flag like a scarf.

"Sergeant Pendragon, I want to thank you for bringing this to me."

"Absolutely, Mr. President."

I didn't even take time to look at the shrine of the 108. This took precedent.

"Load it up, Sancho. We are moving in one minute." I then opened the WAN to Six. `"I want every unit to hear my message."`

`"This is not a good idea, Teddy 1499."`

He only calls me by my designation when he thinks I'm being bad. `"Do you have a way to listen in through rock?"`

`"No, but I saw the original feeds from the units in question. I can deduce your plan of action. You intend to show all of the units the demise of the congressmen."`

`"Yes, I do,"` I said, buckling myself onto the flat car.

`"Simulation shows that there is an 83 percent chance of it destabilizing current morale."`

The wind pressed into my face as the train picked up speed. I could smell the metallic tang of impending rain. Part of me wanted the rain to wash away the images I'd seen. I wanted it to scrub away the taint of evil that Isp brought. I wanted the world to be new again with a clean, clear objective. Instead, I had to work with what I was given, revulsion.

I couldn't explain to him that it wasn't about logic. Six knew nothing more. It wasn't about knowing we would lose. It was about emotion, heart, and revenge. `"Six, you are wrong. Put me on every units' WAN and shut down everything else, please."`

Martin chimed in over the WAN. `"I understand from our Factory that you are going to be making a big mistake. I would like to know what you plan to do before I add my condemnation."`

`"SIX!"` I growled over the link. That worthy chose not to reply. `"Give me the WAN now and quit playing games."`

`"Mr. President?"` Martin asked, confused.

`"Not now, Martin."`

`"The WAN is yours, Mr. President,"` Six said reluctantly.

`"Good afternoon, units—on second thought, good afternoon, citizens. I come to you with a powerful message and even more powerful images. So intense are these memories that I highly suggest that you turn off youngling's cognitive processes during this broadcast.`

`"I know there has been a faction of you who`

don't want to fight and yet another portion of units who want to negotiate our way out of this crisis. I know that we all fear the masses of death and deactivation that will come in a war, so many of you want to find any possible way out of this pit of despair.

"Just two weeks ago five of our bravest congressmen went under a flag of truce to speak with Isp." I wondered if Lennon would gag to see me call him brave. "They went to negotiate a solution that didn't involve a clash of arms and the deactivation of millions of units and maybe the extinction of dozens of races.

"This is what our enemy does to people who would talk and do not make war." I brought up the memories of the train and panned back to the car holding the impaled, mutilated heads. Keeping the image on the WAN I continued to talk over the horrific vision.

"There is no negotiations with someone who will not follow even the most basic rules of civilization. These toys went in under a flag of truce and he killed them anyway.

"This is not a war of power. This is a war of extinction. I urge you all to search your sump and those instructions that you've learned as right. Reevaluate what you are willing to do to save not only yourself and your younglings, but all the younglings across the planet.

"Thank you, and may the Humans bless each and every one of you."

I counted 3,074 milliseconds before Martin spoke.

"Six, you are wrong. *My* president and friend did exactly the right thing."

*   *   *

All six bodyguards that shared my train readied their weapons. At a distance, we all saw a similar mob as last time I'd come into town by train. I knew I'd done the right thing sharing the knowledge with our people, but we didn't know what our people wanted to share with me.

Our entrance to the station provoked a much different reaction this time. There was a winding mass of units around the White House, the buildings surrounding it, and even out into the switching yard.

The meandering line of units broke up and closed in on my train once more. You could see the anger in their general body language. I could almost feel my security detail fingering the triggers of their weapons.

Instead of rioting, the units closest to our train started clapping. They cheered. The rest of the crowd joined in. It hadn't lessened their anger but they also rejoiced.

"Great speech, President!"

"We'll teach that grit to mess with ours."

"I'm behind you, Mr. President! All the way!"

"You are our bear!"

"Let's blow that gold abomination into deactivation."

Units climbed up onto my train car, crowding in around me. Indira was overwhelmed almost at once. Sancho, having released his tie downs prior to the stop, pushed units down and flung them away from me with his trunk. In the end, the mass of them was too much for even his strength. Without malice, their crowding knocked him off the far side of the car.

I needed to take control of the situation before it got more unbridled.

"`All security stand down,`" I sent over the security SAN.

The closest toys hugged me. They shook my paw. They yelled encouragement. Eventually some enterprising units released my tie downs. Then they lifted me up above them. A roar of excitement filled the air louder than any volcano's eruption.

The mob grew until all I could see was the fur and plastic of units. I lost track of any of my bodyguards. Twenty-six minutes of raucous applauding, unit handling, and gyro-churning later, I convinced them to put me down on the nearby steps of the White House.

I put up my paws for silence but only got louder cheers. Their fete wasn't yet spent. It took another eighteen minutes and some loud bellows over the WAN to get enough quiet to speak.

"This wasn't a cause for celebration." I still wasn't cutting through the hubbub. I channeled 20 percent overload power to my verbal system. "This wasn't a cause for celebration!" The crowd quieted a bit. "Five units are dead!" All noise ceased.

I pointed my paw at them. "You and I both know that barring sump injury we should be active for at least two hundred years! Those five units got less than twenty. Why did they have to die so young? Again, I ask, why is that a reason to celebrate?"

The crowd settled before I continued.

"Get angry! Help the war effort to keep this from happening again."

I pointed to one lawn mower with multicolored bubbles racing in all directions from it. "You, what is your name?"

"John—John Deere, Mr. President."

"John, did you show up to welcome me?"

"No, sir, Mr. President. That was a happy coincidence."

"Then why are you here, Mr. Deere?"

"To sign up!"

"Sign up?"

"Yes, the army recruiting station is just over yonder. I'm here to sign up for the duration. We all are here to show that blacked-out Isp not to mess with us!"

I guess my mouth could have hung open further but I had no idea how.

"Well, then don't let me get in the way," I offered. "Go get him, toys!" The crowd cheered again. Through the body of units I happened to catch a glimpse of an electric blue nutcracker, with smears showing orange underneath, queuing up with the rest of the toys to fight. The message had made it. Lennon had unwittingly done something good.

Spymaster

The pink sky at high noon gave the promise of a gloriously weather-free day. Noon was the time when most units were in regeneration mode and soaking up as much power as they could from our loving sun. Very few toys moved unless they had a critical need.

My staff dealt with their own daily needs. Even the few protesters who had the fur to challenge my popularity had packed it in. I sprawled out in the White House gardens with my optics on standby power. Even a president and the leader of one of the largest societies ever assembled deserved some time to himself.

With my reduced optics I could only pick out movement around me as a shadowy wavering. By hearing, I could distinguish only two units approaching me. The strides were distinctive. One had to be Sancho with his drum-like gait. The other, by the occasional slap of his broad feet, was a penguin I'd never met. Sancho guided the guest over to where I lounged.

"Ferweet," Sancho said very quietly.

Without bringing up my optics I said, "So as my own bodyguard is presenting you to me, I have to assume you and I should be speaking."

"Yes, Mr. President. I have a SIN report."

My optics, powered back up full in 63 percent of their specified minimum time, causing them to fade in and out before settling.

"So who are you?" I said, keeping my voice at low volume and a high pitch so it wouldn't travel. My guest did likewise.

"It is better that you don't know, Mr. President."

"Excuse me?"

"Sir, first off, this will be the only time we meet. Every time there is a report to give, it will be given through a different intermediary. Second, Mr. President, some of the things you have asked SIN to accomplish could be considered quasi-legal or put another way, many would consider them to be illegal."

"A good point. I shall call you Alpha to keep things easy."

"I can accept that, Mr. President."

"As I won't know any of these units, all reports must be made with this specific member of my bodyguard present."

"Agreed."

Sancho nodded, too.

"In the event of Sancho's demise, all SIN activities will cease and SIN as an organization will, for want of a better word, deactivate."

"Understood."

"Very well, Alpha, report."

"The first unit you asked us to watch was Bacchus."

"Deserted."

"True, sir, but also very dead."

"What?"

"You ordered us to keep an eye on him. We did. As he dropped his citizenship and moved north, we followed discretely. When he arrived in Washington where Isp's army was encamped, he was ushered directly to see the golden leader. Our tail couldn't see well enough to hear anything, but watched when Isp blew his compatriot's sump out with a 0.45 caliber pistol without a moment's hesitation."

"Do you have memories?"

"We do, sir, but providing them would expose our source."

"Understood."

"That wraps up Bacchus. Mr. President, you also asked to know about the unit John Lennon."

"Moot at this point."

"One might think so, but it would be an incorrect assumption." Part of me wanted to do a victory dance but I waited. "Sir, we have examined . . ." Alpha coughed, ". . . data that indicates Lennon was nothing more than a stooge. He was doing someone else's bidding."

A voltage ramp started on my power bus. "Could he be in league with Isp?"

Sancho did an exaggerated shake of his head.

"No, sir," Alpha continued. "The . . . data is very clear. He opposed the very notion of Isp. That doesn't keep this boss from suggesting meeting with Isp as a way of breaking your power base. That is an assumption on our part, Mr. President."

"Well, I'll be shorted."

"Yes, Mr. President. You have an enemy, and at this time we don't know who that might be. We are looking hard."

"Oh, goody, another enemy. Why not?" I said, with as much sarcasm as would come out of my verbal equipment.

"The data we looked at implicates a number of other members of Congress but we have nothing to corroborate it so we won't speculate on one datum's veracity."

"Anything else on the Lennon front?"

"No, Mr. President."

"Then that leaves Minister Wright and Dr. Frankenstein," I said, still wondering what mechanic would take that name.

Sancho nodded.

"Yes, sir. We don't have a tight enough surveillance on Wright. If we were to make a report right now it would be that of a slightly fuddled unit that doesn't know his fluid nipples from a power connector. As he is one of your cabinet members it doesn't compute."

"Interesting. I was going to tell you to drop the investigation on Wright as Lennon is no longer active, but your description of him doesn't match my mental image of him. I'd have considered him shrewd and crafty, if a bit of a whiner. He seems to me to be a follower. Has no desire to hold the reins.

"Stay on him until we clear up this dichotomy."

"Absolutely, sir. I might suggest that Mr. Panza obtain some congressional intern passes for a few new recruits."

"That can be arranged."

"I've saved the most intriguing for last, Mr. President." Sancho nodded vigorously. Alpha continued, "Dr. Victor Frankenstein was born two years after the end of the war. Upon reaching his majority he attended and graduated from Harvard University cum laude after only six semesters. He was awarded his unlimited professional mechanic's license that same year."

"None of that seems odd for any ambitious Nurse Nan," I said.

"Yes, sir, I agree until you consider that he has no patients, he has no staff, and he does no research that we can determine. He has no means of support yet is never seen sunning with the rest of the working class."

No one had to work, but even regular fluid replacements cost ergs. "I agree that you've intrigued me."

"Dr. Frankenstein's funds twist through so many different hands it took a puppy dog over two weeks to sniff it out."

"A puppy? They could find an erg in a handshake."

"Yes, sir, Mr. President. More to the point you don't bury something like this unless you have something to hide."

"Well, you didn't give me the punch line yet."

"The money trail leads directly to Six itself."

I counted to one hundred in Gaelic. "That certainly is a live grenade, Alpha. Do you have any more on this? What is he doing? Why is Six funding him? Where is he working? Why in the bloody hell did he attend me after I was shot? All you've done is piqued my curiosity and fueled my paranoia."

Alpha's flippers slapped against his side in a penguin equivalent of a chuckle. "Yes, sir. At this time we only have one other data set. He is rarely seen with other units. He travels from one Factory to another, disappearing into their inner workings. If we follow him there he will know we are on to him and blow our covert surveillance."

I remembered the unusual key and the multiple keyholes guarded in Six's innards. I knew where he went, I just didn't know why. "Don't force it, you two. I want this to remain quiet. I wonder if it would help to find out what he spends his ergs on. More puppy work, Sancho."

Planner

The view of the flier's memory cast units as nothing more than sixteen-pixel splotches. It must be flying as high as toyed possible. The rafts on the bucking silver ocean were a larger equilateral triangle with a height-to-base ratio of four to one. Four teddy units floated in the sea holding on to a bar across the base or back of the raft. The swimming units kicked up a spray of mercury behind them. As the pointed end plowed through the waves, it send gushes of silver washing over the flat deck, ramming into the units or crates of equipment.

The image lost definition as it zoomed in on the teddy units behind the pointed barges. Their legs looked different. As I watched I realized their legs had been replaced by something flat and partially flexible, like monstrous webbed feet all the way up to the knee. They must give significant advantage in motivating the crafts.

Each barge held twenty-five units or the same amount of equipment, and they continued to stream in an almost continuous line from Baja.

"Any ideas, General?" I asked.

"None, Mrr. Prresident."

"Do we even know what those floating rafts are made of?"

The general froze the screen on the best close-up of the raft we had. The surface looked rough and pitted, more like rock than anything that might float. We all strained our optics and pattern recognition routines to see if we could make sense of it.

"Could it be something they made? Is it something we can destroy?"

"I don't know, Mrr. Prresident. I just don't know."

Martin joined us late, once again seemingly defying some law of physics by somehow squeezing through a door that seemed a full dozen centimeters too narrow for his body width.

"So why are you looking at pumice on a SAN?" he asked as he set his body down and tucked his eight legs beneath him.

"Excuse me?" the general and I asked simultaneously, both turning our attention on him.

"I just wondered why you were looking at pumice."

"What in the devil is pumice?" I asked.

"It is a type of rock we have on Naboombu Island. The stuff is usually found near volcanos."

Six chimed in with, "Pumice is formed when highly pressurized rock is ejected from a volcano. The simultaneous rapid cooling and reduction of pressure allows the gas to be released from the rock solution, but not from being encased within the cooling rock infrastructure, preventing the liquid stone from arranging itself into a regular crystalline structure."

"Yes, where I live on the island, we use it to demonstrate density to younglings. Regular rocks sink in mercury, and pumice floats."

"How quick can you get us some blocks of it, Martin?"

"How quick can you rustle up a train from Nine's location? The stuff is easy to quarry, light, and so plentiful that no one will notice us nabbing a couple of tonnes or even a couple of hundred tonnes. We use it as a scrubbing adhesive to remove rust and the like."

"So you say this stuff floats?" I asked.

"This stuff floats even on water. If I remember, it has a density of about 0.53 grams per cubic centimeter," Martin responded, even more puzzled. "What is this all about?"

The general zoomed out to show where the close-up came from. Martin's entire body nodded understanding.

"Yup. If they had a supply of that stuff they could move a Factory across the ocean," Martin said. "In fact, on the island it will often flow in sheets down the mountain and cool across the top of the mercury like a shelf."

"Well, that solves that mystery."

"As soon as we can get a sample we will do some testing to see how effective ourr weapons will be against it," General Khan said.

"Good. So what does this naval convoy tell us?"

"They arre efficient at moving theirr units. Atlantis will be hit apprroximately daybrreak tomorrow morrning."

"**Zero five thirty-seven hours,**" Six offered.

"Thank you, Six," I said sarcastically. "That much accuracy won't help us when we can't do anything about it."

"Speaking of such, Mrr. Prresident, I do have a rreport on the actions that we've taken in that arrea."

"By all means."

"Forrtunately, we talked to some mining experrts beforre ourr forrce went in. Ourr initial plan had been to destrroy the shaft and pump it full of nitrric acid. But what we found out was that might actually help ourr enemies. Nitric acid mixed with hydrrochlorric acid is one of the methods that is used to mine the metal. So instead we chose to contaminate it with sodium hydrroxide. It is just as corrosive as some of the acids and must be rremoved before prrocessing the platinum. Even once they manage to get it out, it will delay them by overr 347 perrcent overr rraw orre."

The SAN lit up again with a view of rugged foothills.

"What we see herre, Mrr. Prresident, is *the* mine entrrance forr all of Atlantis. It is one larrge mine, wherreas La Mancha has a dozen smallerr ones."

An explosion shook the memory and a gout of fire ripped straight up out of a hole I hadn't noticed before. The hole continued to billow dust, long after the flame and rumblings died away.

"Additionally, we added the chemical base beforre we detonated, splatterring the materrial everrywherre," General Khan said.

"General, I want it passed down to all your subordinates that from this point forward we will be following a scorched earth policy along with our attrition tactics. Deal as much damage as we can and then destroy anything that could possibly be of use to the invaders before we retreat."

"Yes, sirr. Won't this be arrgued by the goverrnors?"

"I have to agree, Mr. President," Martin said. "The leaders of each province are dedicated to growing their infrastructure and you now propose to destroy it. Their hydraulics will become solid."

"Well, first of all I don't want it generally known. This is a close order for only the commanders at each site. It is a military necessity and a military decision, not one to be left to the whims of each provincial governor."

"I will implement yourr orrders, sirr."

"But you don't believe in them?"

"Sirr, I do believe in them. I just wouldn't want to be in yourr furr when this becomes known. I can at least claim that I was following orrderrs."

"That didn't work at Nuremberg."

*   *   *

In a rare event, a congressman filled every single seat. The aisles were choked with more chairs, each holding another important unit. Martin lay down front between the speaker of the Shapist and the newly elected leader of the provinciers, Ruth, a dragon as white as a light bulb. I caught General Khan's outline just behind the stage and even Frank Lloyd Wright sat nearby.

I wasn't a member of Congress. I didn't have an assigned seat. Instead, I stood against the back wall. I hadn't tried to use my position to get a place closer. While I've never known units to move much without purpose, the assembly's attention was so rapt I could have balanced a ball on the head of anyone there.

The normal location for the speakers of each congressional house had been cleared of desks and other materials, leaving a broad, raised stage. In its place, side-by-side, displayed four real-time images of Atlantis. Each of the images cycled from a different optical input every three seconds. In a number of the video feeds you could see the incredible mass Army of Humans poised and ready. The marauders were normally so active and fast, this was one of the few times I could easily pick out a single unit in that crowd.

"Why aren't we bombing them?" I heard a kitty-cat whisper to his fellow legislator. "They are just standing there. We could kill hundreds."

"But Garfield, there are millions. A few thousand wouldn't even put a dent in their numbers."

I felt all warm and fuzzy inside that at least one of these distinguished people could understand. It gave me hope that Congress had not been a very bad idea from its inception, despite what I felt like on a normal day.

One of the enormous images froze and zoomed in to a small clutch of teddies away from the massive army. A bright gold teddy stood in the center, smiling.

"'Is everything ready?'" Six said, filling in words to the movement of our nemesis's mouth. We had video but only our own creator as audio.

"'Yes, Enlightened One. The Army of Humans is ready to perform,'" said one green teddy I recognized back from the original units that went into exile with Isp with the name of Brady.

"'Then cleanse this area for the Humans, but capture the mine intact.'"

"'Yes, Enlightened One.'"

The one halted image remained on Isp in the middle of his fifty-odd bodyguards. In the rest a wall of fur began moving toward the city. They obviously didn't know that there were no defenders. Over the next thirty-six minutes, forty-three seconds the waves upon waves upon waves of teddies attacked an empty city. It seemed more like army ants or bees swarming. They rushed the unfortified and undefended city expecting resistance. Finding none they wormed in and out of buildings searching for units to kill. At some point they stopped moving through and vented their fury on the empty buildings, and the shells of manufacturing equipment. One by one, the images disappeared as the cameras were destroyed in the onslaught.

Three hours later the only image that remained was that of a pole that defiantly still held our nation's flag, a triple red dome on a field of white. Five of Isp's teddies pulled the pole over, eventually snapping it at its base. Our red and white flag still fluttered until a golden bear came up and yanked it free of the shaft. With one pull he tore the fabric in half, letting it drop to the earth. A collective noise, not even words, issued from our Congress.

We watched as Isp stomped the pieces with his feet, grinding them into the dust. Isp looked directly into the remaining camera and made a chopping motion. The image shut off.

*   *   *

"General, what did you take from the attack this morning?" I said, leaning back under the recharging lamp in my office. My diagnostics registered a low level mechanical wear warning from all the signing of papers that came across my desk.

"Other than their overwhelming numbers?" my spider friend Martin offered with funereal humor.

"Lack of coorrdination. Lack of leaderrship," Khan analyzed, his tank turret shifting around restlessly. "They attacked morre like units did beforre you sharred sentience with the rrest of us."

"Can we use that to our advantage when it comes time to actually fight them?"

"Absolutely, Mrr. Prresident, but it won't be enough."

"It may even be a ruse," Martin said.

"Why do you say that?" I asked.

"He knew we were watching him. He left that one camera alone until he'd played to the stage one last time. What if he did it intentionally to make us think he is weak?" Martin said gesticulating with one of his long legs.

"Isp is devious. It is something I might attribute to him, but he is also overconfident," I countered.

"Then why hasn't he attacked us dirrectly? Why give us time to strrengthen ourrselves?"

"Because he isn't ready?" Martin offered as a question, not an opinion.

"He obviously needs platinum for something," I said back.

"More units," Martin said in a tone that it should have been obvious.

"But again, why wait? He has superriorr numberrs, he could have attacked with surrprrise. I don't underrstand," the general said, rolling up and down his ramp in irritation as if trying to squash an insect.

"Gentlemen, I have you here to answer my questions, not the other way around," I said.

"I'm sorry, Mrr. Prresident."

"Well, 'I don't know,' still means I don't know," I said, trying to soften my rebuke. "Do you have anything else to discuss? I should get back to the mound of decisions I need to make."

"Yes, Mrr. Prresident. I wasn't thinking clearrly earrlierr when we werre talking about pumice. Instead of having it shipped up herre I had some tests rrun on it on Naboombu. Even some in the sea therre as well."

"Excellent work, general. What did you learn?"

"The materrial is verry easily destrroyed. Small amounts of explosives pulverrize the porrous rrock. We even tested a rreplica of one of theirr rrafts. When even a small bit of damage occurred, the load on the top destabilized and was tossed into the merrcury."

"That is good news! Then we can disrupt their supply chain," I said with such enthusiasm that my big purple bottom bounced on my chair.

"Yes, with caveats, Mrr. Prresident."

"Uh-oh. I don't like caveats."

"Neither do I, Mr. President," Martin said with a sigh.

"All right, give us the bad news, general."

"Firrst, much of what they arre shipping will float. Merrcury is verry dense at 13.56 grrams perr cubic centimeterr. It would slow down theirr rresupply as they would have to gatherr that disperrsed materrial but not sink it. And second, we do not have nearrly enough flierrs forr a full-blown warr against theirr supply lines."

I just about jumped out of my chair as Six once again reminded me of his ethereal presence in my office. "`Our analysis shows that a 31 percent reduction in supplies would result. This would net a 6 percent decrease in their combat effectiveness.`"

"Do it, general. Six percent of Isp's seven million units is worth some of our time."

*   *   *

Toyanity obsessed over Isp's occupation of Atlantis during every nonworking hour. Businesses, manufacturing lines, sunning lounges, and even preventative maintenance salons showed the images. All projectors were tuned to the government net that displayed surveillance footage, reruns of cameras before they went dark. Even the refugee camps on the southern slopes managed several small holo tanks that people gathered around.

One camera, hidden by those who'd committed the sabotage on the mine, remained operative. We watched as Isp was brought in to be shown the rubble-blocked mine entrance. We couldn't hear the conversation but we could see the invective in his gestures. By block and tackle, and paw labor alone the oversized bears cleared the entrance over three days. The workers suffered serious burns from the base liquids soaked into the earth and rock. It melted fur, armor, and eventually hydraulic lines.

On three occasions Isp attended the site. The foreman argued bitterly, but each time the golden leader left, the energy from the occupiers redoubled to clear the pit. The casualties mounted.

On the fourth day a bear came out of the excavation with his head smoking, exposing his sump. Less than forty seconds later its entire brain case gave way. The entire volume flowed down over the exposed metal skeleton and hoses. Almost universally, we gasped. His sump sucked only air, grasping and clinging to anything resembling life. The bear was an enemy, but that death we all feared.

Three hours later the 3,042 bears, all with some level of burns, left the site.

*   *   *

The conference room bulged to almost overflowing. In addition to my full cabinet, we also had the two leaders of Congress, and many of the forty-two governors. Not only did units occupy every centimeter around the table, but the chairs against the wall all held a high-level toy as well. I'd already ordered the air-conditioning turned up for all the waste heat generated.

"General Khan, what do you have to report?" I asked.

The 50-centimeter high tank spoke up. "Thank you, Mrr. Prresident. As you know, the Arrmy of the Humans is marrching on La Mancha. This was afterr a fourr day, unsuccessful attempt to access the platinum mines of Atlantis. We anticipate thrree morre days beforre they rreach ourr abandoned city of La Mancha. If they attack they will meet with a surrprrise."

I swiveled my head around from my pointed attempts to avoid Governor HappyFeet of Atlantis's cold stare. "What might that be, General?"

"Sirr, I took it upon myself to extend yourr orderrs of scorrched earrth just a bit. I orrdered a therrmobarric weapon to be used as a booby-trrap. If the bearrs attack it will launch up and detonate 30 meterrs off the grround. It should take out everry unit within 500 meterrs and is devastating enough to level the city."

"Mr. President, I have to object to this tactic," Mr. Rogers said from his perch on his massive tail. As a kangaroo he needed no seat. "You will destroy a decade of work of our province."

The room got very quiet. I'd already made my point on this topic. I think some of our lawmakers were prepared for me to remove the kangaroo's head. Even Martin, who nudged my foot under the table with one of his spider legs, expected an explosion. I admit to being tempted to give an impromptu kangaroo dissection lesson. But, I'd taken the precaution of lowering my hydraulic pump by 66 percent once I was seated in the meeting.

"Mr. Rogers," I said in my calmest voice. "Would you rather have them take all of those years of work and use them against us? We must take away their ability to use our own works against us. If this means destroying everything we've ever done, I consider that a small price to pay for our freedom and activation." I gave the kangaroo a hard stare.

"So, General, will you please continue."

"Yes, Mrr. Prresident. Despite ourr little trrap, Isp may make the choice to avoid La Mancha City and go strraight to the mines."

"I doubt that very much, Mr. General," I said. "His rage against all we've built is too strong."

"I agree, Mr. President," Martin interjected from where his bulbous spider body took up most of the corner.

"I only suggested it as a possibility. I think he will throw his trroops in headlong attack, not even botherring to scout the location firrst. In any event, all of the mines have been salted with sodium hydrroxide and collapsed. We considerred rrigging the mines to explode when they enterred but it was too rrisky forr too little gain and forr potentially backfirring by allowing them to defuse."

"Anything else?" I asked.

"Yes, sirr. We've seen the Arrmy of Humans use a crrude, teddy-powerred trrain in moving some supplies. We've rrigged the rrails out of La Mancha to explode in severral places and in otherrs just derrail the userrs."

"Good. Are there any further comments on La Mancha? Excellent. What about our defenses, General?"

"Perr yourr orderr we arre now clusterred prrimarrily in the thrree prrovinces of ourr thrree Factorries. This has caused massive disrruption in supply chains. Forrtunately, these thrree strrongholds, with some judicial worrk in neighborring prrovinces, can prrovide all ourr needs. Ourr powerr is concentrrated, as is what we need to prrotect."

"Each of ourr thrree cities now has stoneworrk walls."

"Impressive work for such a short time, General," offered one of the governors.

"It hasn't been easy, especially forr 55469. If you rrecall it is often parrtially submerrged. In any case, rredoubts have been built, fields of landmines have been sown, and physical obstacles have been emplaced at key lanes of apprroach. We estimate a six forr one kill rratio."

"`Five point six three,`" Six interjected over the LAN.

"Then we can defeat them!" I said excitedly.

"`I'm sorry, Mr. President. I forgot to say that kill ratio belongs to armed, trained toys, not civilians,`" Six amended.

My body language must have said it all as the members of the table gained hope and then lost it, all within a hundred clock cycles.

The general continued, swiveling his turret as he spoke to engage everyone. "The good news is that we arre adding 600 soldierrs to ourr defense everry week, 240 veterans and 360 grreen trroops. We arre also adding 600 special units as we—"

"Excussse me, General. What is a special unit?" asked the snake, Jason Argonaut.

"`I made a suggestion to field non-sentient units,`" Six said. He was interrupted by a collective gasp. "`Each Factory has been producing two hundred, plus or minus twelve every week.`"

"These truly are robots," I said, building on Six's description. "They may look like us, but they don't even have a sump. They can't be made sentient. They are controlled entirely by the Factories." When I saw the worried body language I added, "I authorized this. It was the only way to get additional firepower into the field."

One samurai warrior whose name escaped me stuck up an armored fist.

"Yes," I said, calling upon him.

"What happens to these units after the war?"

I put on my brightest happy body language and said, "If there are any of us around after this, let's figure it out then, shall we?"

Shapist Apgar put up her hand.

"Yes, Ms. Apgar."

"Is there no way to take the fight to these animals? Can we only sit behind our walls and hope we can defeat them when they crash over us like a wave?"

"Yes, ma'am," General Khan said. "We arre discussing methods forr doing that in prrivate sessions. We don't have a definitive plan yet but it is something we arre worrking on." I swear Khan would have winked at me if he'd had the ability. The tank had a devious side I'd learned to trust for years. He didn't disappoint me now.

"Are there any more questions? If you have positive suggestions, please send them via net to General Khan or myself."

"Thank you, Mr. President," the group said as a whole. I didn't know why they would thank me. My people would die to the last toy.

*   *   *

Morale could be seen and held as a thing. Toyanity labored, but not worked. They trudged instead of walking. Conversations held the bare edge of panic. Defeatism exhibited in their body language as they watched the memories of scouts tracking the Army of Humans flow over the mountains toward La Mancha. I felt the cynic in me cringe but if morale could be measured, it could be manipulated.

The air raids on the shipping convoys had started. I ensured that the memory of every single bomb drop, every bullet fired, and every single erg of damage displayed over the WAN.

"This is Eagle One. Follow me in. Remember to stay above 100 meters to avoid potential wire traps.

"Just like we planned it. Even numbers bomb on the first pass, concentrating on the boats themselves. Odd numbers strafe, concentrating on the motive units. Second pass, we reverse. If anyone still has ammo we'll take one last pass.

"Follow me."

"Two."

"Three."

"Four."

"Five."

A pause came over the net.

"Where is Richtofen?"

"Sorry. Checking the tension in my drive band. Six."

The images flipped from one windup biplane to the next. They closed in on a seemingly endless single file line of boats in the water. The modified teddies churned the mercury behind.

One by one, explosions ripped apart the boats of floating rocks and vaporized supplies. Near-misses tossed reinforcement toys from Baja into the ocean to thrash about or in some cases to sink beneath the 3-meter waves. Strafing runs tore up the teddy outboard motors, leaving the boats adrift and eventually lost.

Wind-up biplanes followed by dirigibles followed by motorized planes followed by balloons followed by . . . Flight after flight rained deactivation and carnage down on the supply train of the Army of the Humans. As days went by, fliers had to search farther afield to find more of the boats to attack.

On the scene reports of fliers having their batteries changed out and reloaded punctuated the spates of destruction. Interviews of our brave combatants showed to fill gaps.

"So how do you think the raid is going, Captain Bishop?"

"It's easier than a simulation. The hardest part is judging where the waves are going to toss them."

"So you think this is going to have a positive effect on the war?"

"Ask that question to the brass in 55466. All I know is that they sent us out here to kill ships. I certainly know we are showing that gold bastard Isp the error of his ways."

"Thank you, Captain. Now back to more highlights of today's actions."

My people sat glued to the network images. I got reports that at least eight units failed to recharge and had to be given emergency jump-starts. Others neglected preventative maintenance and even their work to watch.

Walking through the marketplace I heard people humming and whistling to themselves. Morale was measureable.

*   *   *

"Last night I thought about something we've not put in our defenses. How about barbed wire to slow down the enemy's approach?" I asked at our daily defense meeting.

"Rreasonable idea, Mrr. Prresident. I think it is of lowerr value than some of ourr otherr prrojects, but I'll add it to the queue," Genghis Khan said from his platform in the Situation Room.

"And what about placing remote weapon platforms, General? Place them out at a thousand meters or even more if we can control them," I offered.

"That's actually quite a good idea, Mrr. Prresident. I must have been memorry-bound not to think of something so simple," the tank and general of my armed forces said.

"Genghis, your skills and mine complement one another."

"I'm pleased if you truly mean it, Mr. President."

I smiled with my body language. "General, you have a very direct talent for the logistics of applying toys and materiel. I, on the other hand, was created to think outside the box. Being sneaky is built into my very nature. Your talents include taking my twisted ideas and make them feasible."

"I'm honorred by yourr prraise, Mrr. Prresident."

"Oh, piffle. We are units, after all. We recognize our strengths and weaknesses."

"Definitely trrue, Mrr. Prresident. I still feel prroud that you rrecognize my worrth."

"Trust me, Genghis, I will tell you if I don't feel your worth is equal to mine. Now can we put aside this mutual admiration society and continue with our brainstorming?"

"Mr. President, you asked to be informed when the Army of the Humans reached La Mancha," Six said.

"Looks like this will have to wait, General. Six, could you please bring it up on tank number one?"

Tank one blossomed to life showing the Army of the Humans filing in a phalanx that stretched off camera in both directions. A cluster of units stood on a nearby hill. The camera zoomed in to catch the gold bear himself holding court.

Two of his advisors argued with him. Six provided a running translation of their mouth movements.

"'...but, sir, we should scout the town first. The last one was empty.'"

"'Nonsense, Brady. They must have moved their units down here from Atlantis,'" Isp insisted.

"'Master, it would be prudent to check. It wouldn't take but moments.'"

"'Cassandra, I said attack and I mean attack. Nothing can stand in the way of the will of the Humans.'"

"I think your trap is going to work, General."

"Hubrris, Mrr. Prresident. Please neverr get any of it."

I laughed. "While I think highly of myself, I do surround myself by toys that tell me when I'm being a grit." The general just chuckled.

Isp's army moved as one. Minutes later the mass of units crashed into the abandoned city. I took pleasure that their rage found no units to vent their used hydraulic fluid on.

"I never did ask you what will trigger your bomb," I asked with only mild curiosity.

Genghis hesitated. He rolled back and forth. He pivoted his turret at least three degrees. The question hadn't been designed to cause any angst, but I recognized embarrassment when it ran its tracks over me. "Spit it out, General."

"Well, I wanted to make surre that it would be trriggered, so I built something in La Mancha that they couldn't pass up destrroying."

"That was more prevarication, General. What couldn't they pass up?"

"Well, you know yourr statue at the entrrance to the marrketplace?" he said with his customary rumble.

I wish my face could have shown my anxiety at that point as 300MHz spikes started flickering through my voltage. "Yes."

"Well, I used the orriginal mold of that statue to make a plasterr verrsion of it and had it errected in La Mancha's town squarre."

My spikes damped down as I realized the probable efficacy of the general's goad. "Well, if anything will aggravate them, it will be me. But, General Khan, remind me to rip out your power packs sometime after this is over. I hate that damned thing."

"Yes, Mrr. Prresident."

"Six, do you have a view of the . . . trigger?" I couldn't even bring myself to call it a statue.

"Yes, Mr. President. Switching channel now."

I stood, larger than life, in the center of the town's marketplace. Every time I saw the abomination I loathed it more. It made me seem like I, just a simple unit, should be able to solve all the problems of our world. It was a sham, especially with what would happen to my people.

The sculpture looked weathered as if it had been standing through decades of silver rain. Even the red grasses grew up higher around its base. I guess every cloud had its silver lining. I couldn't wait to see it destroyed.

Six had conveniently split-screened the action. We watched the invaders topple streetlights, crush carts, smash windows and doors, pull out porch supports, and even collapse smaller shacks. The flood of units behind the first wave flowed into the buildings and threw equipment and even supplies out the windows where passing interlopers would stomp it into the earth or bash it against something else.

They destroyed wantonly until they entered the town square. The units poured in but formed a ring 6 meters from my statue. Other attackers piled in behind them, trying to get a look.

"Why did they stop?" I asked in a whisper as if those invaders thousands of kilometers away could hear me.

"I don't know, Mrr. Prresident," the general whispered back.

They stood there for 3,416 milliseconds. "Are they waiting for Isp?" The general didn't answer. As quickly as they had stopped they all opened their mouth. They screamed and charged the statue, their spears held up ready to strike.

The camera, on a building opposite the statue, shook for a moment as the carnage against the plaster effigy started. I watched with an internal smirk as it tore apart in chunks as the spears struck. One second later the camera went brilliantly white and then immediately dark.

"Switching camera view."

The new image showed me a growing cloud of white malignance. The color changed rapidly to red and then a darker brick color as it expanded like some balloon flier that had taken on too much air. The camera shook in its holder. My internal chronometer said it happened six seconds after the blast. Seven seconds later, a blast of dust and dirt obscured the image.

Six switched through his entire range of cameras for La Mancha. Nine hundred sixty-four were totally inoperable. Another 401 showed nothing but a blazing fire. On the very southern edge of the city twenty-four cameras showed obscuring smoke and hurricane-like winds. The cameras at the mines showed sandstorm-like conditions. Only a weather camera perched on White Plume Mountain 42 kilometers away gave any visual. It showed only the funeral pyre of La Mancha, burning like whirling campfire under a black clouded sky. Dust showed the wind being pulled in from all around.

"My Humans!"

"General, I think your trap succeeded."

"Current data extrapolation from my images at the time of the explosion projects a conservative estimate of deactivated at 170,453. The irreparably injured will likely increase that number by another 80,000. I warn you about banking on that last number as I made a number of key assumptions. The repair numbers are similarly rough at 6,300,000 unit-hours to bring the damaged toys to nominal."

Six's proclamation barely registered. I just watched the fire consume a quarter of a million toys—deactivated like flipping a light switch. War meant death. War meant pain. If Isp didn't feel anguish for those lost units, I would.

"May the Humans have mercy on their souls."

"Amen," the general agreed.

"General, why can't we drop one of those thermobaric weapons on the column? It would take no time at all to wipe them out at 200,000 a pop."

"Because we don't have a flierr big enough to carry them. Flierrs carry payloads measurred in single orr at most double-digit kilogrrams. The bomb you just witnessed weighed in at one metrric ton. We can make smallerr verrsions but to achieve any viability it rrequires a single, heavy warrhead.

"We arre rresearrching a combined harrness frrom balloons, but ourr balloon and dirrigible quantities arre insufficient to give the lift needed."

There had to be something I could take away from this experience. There had to be a magic bullet. I spent exactly five seconds in silent contemplation pacing back and forth across the Situation Room floor before I had something. Nibbling at the edges could have a profound effect, if we did it often enough. I stopped abruptly and faced Genghis.

"General, I've been wrong. I want to make a change to our combat stance."

"Yes, Mrr. Prresident?"

"How soon can you organize a fast, light, battalion-sized force that will have the primary duty of harassing and killing the enemy? I want them to hit and run. I want them to use every dirty, underhanded trick in the book. But most of all I want them to do it without risking their own deactivation."

"You can have them rright now, Mrr. Prresident." I swear I heard my general chuckle.

"Huh?" My articulation and reason left me.

"I have been rreassigning trroops since Isp made his announcement on Peace Day. You now have the Firrst Cavalrry Trroop available to deploy, totaling 512 toys. All units have at least double the speed of anything Isp has. It is made up prrimarrily of scout carrs, cowboys, Indians, spiderrs, kangarroos, and gorrillas, with a scouting scrreen of bouncing balls."

"Holy Humanity! They could run circles around the mutant bears," I exclaimed.

"That was my intent."

"Why didn't you mention it before?"

"You and Six werre so dead-set on a defensive warr. I serrve at yourr pleasurre, Mrr. Prresident. But I wanted you to have an option if you changed yourr mind. I just finished assembling them. They will be rready for trraining next week."

"The black-out with training. They are going to have to learn as they do it. How soon can you get them to La Mancha?"

"They have been assembled in Sunnyvale. They could be to the passes in the Drragon Back Rrange in twelve hourrs."

"Give them the order. I also want to talk to their commander and give him a few of the dirty tricks I've thought of. Also I want to emphasize that each of their lives is more important than a thousand of Isp's followers. They are to take no chances, General."

"Yes, sirr, Mrr. Prresident."

"Oh, and don't forget about Project Catholic."

"No, sirr. It's alrready underrway and will be complete long beforre the Arrmy of Humans can get herre."

*   *   *

"Mr. President, do you and your chief of staff have a moment to look at some new data?" Six asked. I'd noticed that he had become much more obsequious in his address and manner over the last month. He used to order. Now he provided information and advice.

"What is it, Six?"

"I have some footage from La Mancha that I've not been releasing. I wanted you to see it first."

"By all means."

Martin's whole bulbous spider body nodded his assent as well.

The image that Six projected over the SAN looked milky enough that I couldn't identify most of the blobs. With optics that damaged, I wondered what I might possibly see.

"What you are looking at is the feed of a camera, near the edge of La Mancha. I theorize it looks deactivated so none of Isp's followers have bothered to finish it off. I'm going to go to time mark thirty six minutes, seventeen seconds ago. I've also used computer enhancement to sharpen the image a bit."

Pointed downward at eighteen degrees, the reformed image primarily showed the spotty, cracked red glass that had once been the earth. Fire still burned on a blob of metal so misshapen its original use was lost to my sump. Around it lay bricks and cinderblocks in as much organization as if a child might toss its blocks about in a pique. Smoke rose gently from seventeen point sources. This included the invading bear that had been denuded of all fur. Once cobalt blue, only melted, blackened patches of the synthetic remained. Dirty auburn streaks of burnt hydraulic fluid oozed from great rends in the injured unit's armor.

A pair of shuffling bear's feet entered the view. It bent down over the injured unit on the ground and we saw at once that even this unit had been hurt. Its turquoise fur had darker, melted splotches and a metal pipe had impaled the more mobile unit through his right thigh.

"'Are you functional?'" Six translated from their lips for us.

"'I have 83 percent loss in mobility. My vision is 90 percent lost. I can no longer support our holy cause.'"

"'Are you prepared to travel to Earth?'"

"'I regret I only could serve this long. I am prepared.'"

"'You go to a better place. Keep my name on the lips of the Humans.'"

The less damaged bear picked up a nearby cinder block and lifted it above his ears. I wanted to scream for him to stop. I want to run out and put my body in the way. I could do nothing but watch the bear crush the skull of the badly damaged unit. Its sump ruptured, splashing its gold, teddium-laced memory fluid across his attacker and in an oval approximately 1.3 meters wide and twice that tall across the earth.

"What in the blackout was that?" Martin demanded.

"I believe that the Army of the Humans has a threshold of unit functionality where it would cost more to repair than to replace."

"You mean they deactivate units just for being too damaged?" Martin continued.

"I believe that is exactly what Six meant. Remember they are religious zealots. You heard them. The poor unit being killed thinks he is going right to Earth to live with the Humans. Wouldn't you give up your activation to be assured of that?"

The spread of Martin's legs assured me that he wouldn't. "Who would risk that?"

"About six million misshapen teddy units brainwashed from youth, that's who. Six, I want this kept on close hold."

"I can't agree more, Mr. President," Martin confirmed. "If they will do this to their own—"

"Then they won't hesitate to do it to us," I finished.

*   *   *

A cloudless noon was the best time to have a secret meeting. Everyone sunned themselves all over the valley. No one wasted power on optics. No one milled around. Everyone focused on getting the most out of what Rigel gave us.

"Welcome back, Mr. Tesla," I said greeting my 14-centimeter guest in the Oval Office. "I hope your trip up through the tunnels wasn't too onerous?"

"Actually quite enlightening, Mr. President. I mean we all knew it was there, but I didn't know just how it ties in with the structure of the government buildings."

"Well, don't remember it too much, Nikola. The president has a squad of bodyguards who think those secret passages are their personal dominion," Martin tossed in.

The diminutive superhero looked up to see Sancho's mass looking down at him. "Don't remember a thing," he said without missing a beat. I chuckled.

"Really, shouldn't I be calling you 'doctor'? I understand Harvard bestowed you with a doctorate in space engineering."

"Yes, they did, Mr. President."

"Well, in that case, Dr. Tesla," I said emphasizing the honorific, "Martin tells me that you have something to share with me."

The caped hero climbed up the ramp usually reserved for General Khan and sat with his legs dangling over the edge. "Yes, Mr. President. We've had our first successful launch."

"What? Your prototypes weren't supposed to be ready for several more months. And with the way the war is going, I wondered if they would ever take place."

"War, Mr. President?"

There was a pregnant pause throughout the room. Sancho broke the tableau with a very quiet "ferweet."

"Doctor, please don't take this the wrong way, but do you and your team do anything but work?"

"Not a thing, Mr. President. You can't understand just how important and fun this work is!" I could see the energy all but flowing off this enigmatic toy. He couldn't even sit still on the ramp. First he just kicked his legs but eventually he jumped up and paced. The rate of his story increased the longer he talked. "Every day one of my staff finds some new star, or we find a problem we need to work around. When we would nominally be sunning ourselves we instead draw off the net and dive into whatever came up during the day. I can't remember the last time I've been down for preventative maintenance. And I can't remember when I've ever felt this excited."

I looked at Martin and we exchanged a few choice bits over our own SAN. This unit's attention to its task broke any expectation. If only I had a million of them at work solving the inevitable loss of our way of life to Isp we might actually win.

"So, Nikola, your enthusiasm is catching. Tell me more about your successes."

"Absolutely, Mr. President. You are right that we shouldn't have been done this quick, but it became obvious, even in one-third scale, that the trebuchet method was a failure. Dynamic thrusts against the material strengths of our launch arm just—" The tiny figure shuddered. "We could barely even get the one-third-sized unit to support its own weight, much less under load. The pivot arm would have snapped the moment we applied torque. So we redistributed the units working on that project to our other two."

"So what happened? The president's time is very valuable," Martin said. I shot Martin a glare. I got so little time to enjoy anything these days.

"I'm terribly sorry, Mr. President," Dr. Tesla said.

"Not at all, Doctor. I actually am enjoying this as a break from my other pressing duties."

"Well, we had a success with both of our other methods. We used the ramps to launch small buoys into space. Each of the space objects, or SOs, formed a hyperbolic curve but gave telemetry for the entire trip. Both crashed, as we predicted, in the Southern Ocean."

"Crashed? That doesn't sound good." Did I just lose the dream of space travel?

"Oh, I'm sorry, Mr. President, but it is quite technical. As the buoys had no motive source there are only three possibilities: it can hyperbolic back to earth, like any other projectile; it can barely reach an orbit, but that orbit must intersect its launch point so it would be very similar to the first case; or third, it could go fully out of our gravity well."

"I can't say that I follow all of that, but you're the expert. But how does this help take the next step to space if everything we throw up there is going to crash?"

"If we add motive power to our buoys, like our rockets, we might be able to put a unit into orbit or even reach the moons."

"That's exceptional, Doctor, but if I may ask some questions."

"Absolutely, Mr. President."

"Could you throw explosives with your launcher?"

"We could throw explosives, mercury, units, or anything else. Mind you I wouldn't want to be the unit being thrown right now. No controls," the doctor said in a rush.

"And could we use it to hit enemy troop movements?"

"Oh, yes, you mentioned something of a war. Who are we fighting?"

"That would take much too long to fully describe, Nikola. I suggest later that you look in at some of the popular network shows. But getting back to what I need, could you hit a specific spot on the planet with your buoys?"

"Oh, say within 30 kilometers."

"Could you improve on that given enough time? Say to within 100 meters?"

Tesla looked at me as if I might have been joking but my body language gave him all the seriousness I could summon. Had his head been full of gears, they would have smoked.

"Mr. President, it couldn't be done with our current apparatus, nor with the planned device. The tolerances on our devices alone would be outside your parameters. Not only that, Mr. President, but our launchers point in a single direction. To change them we would have to find a way to make their direction selectable. What you are looking for would be something entirely different. It would be possible but would take approximately 13.6 months to accomplish, even if I put all of my people working on it."

I tugged at my ear as I thought. My processor ran statistical curves and probabilities until Six interrupted with my computations only 18 percent complete.

"No set of circumstances would allow the proposed weapon to have a positive outcome on the war. Spending the same resources on fliers, bombs, and more artillery would have a much higher impact."

"I have to agree," Martin said.

"How can you agree?" I asked. "I haven't even gotten part way through the analysis."

Martin chuckled. "Because I've already had that idea, and I've seen the contraption that they have rigged up to launch stuff, that's why. They are embedded in the earth—immovable. You don't have the corner on processing power, Mr. President."

"Flippancy is not an attractive quality in a unit," I teased. "I guess I need to put you on my list of people to abuse, Martin."

"I'll remind you, Mr. President," my chief of staff offered sarcastically.

"I'll hold you to that, Martin." The spider just nodded. "OK, assuming that we don't have a need for this as a weapon, what is the next step?"

"Oh, goodness, Mr. President, we have a schedule of launches to prove repeatability and the payload's optimal shape. We are also concerned about the effect that the launch speed has on the payload."

"So how soon can we expect a unit in space?"

"Mr. President? We are still only at a scale model. I haven't even hit you up to fund a full-sized launcher. But we still have much to learn on the scale models."

"Well, consider the money for a full-sized unit given, Doctor Tesla. Send me your proposal. Don't skimp on the research, though."

The superhero jumped down from the ramp and ran right up to me. I could hear Sancho tense behind me. Tesla reached forward his small hand to shake my paw. "Thank you, Mr. President. I didn't even begin to hope that—"

"I understand, Nikola. Just make it work."

"Yes, sir, Mr. President. I will make it work if I have to scavenge my own sump for parts!"

Martin showed the exuberant unit with space fever from the room. Even as he was ushered out, I could see Tesla's sump working hard on the plans for taking toyanity to space. Martin found his spot and settled in again before saying anything. His body language showed despair and hopelessness. "Mr. President, we are likely to lose this war against Isp. Why continue with this project that doesn't aid us militarily?"

I delivered a dramatic pause of 3,004 milliseconds before replying, "'And as Pandora lifted the lid, all of the evils sprang forth to abuse the creatures of the world—Pain, Misery, Death, Poverty, Disease, and Famine. She slammed the box closed yet something good called to her from within the box. Thinking that she couldn't cause any more woe to the world, she opened it one last time to release the beautiful butterfly that was Hope.'

"That is what we need, Martin. Hope is what all our units need. This project is no longer black. I want it publicized on every network show. I want scientists and mechanics talking about the future it offers us."

Guerrilla

"Mr. President¬" Six said, "I can now better estimate the losses the Army of the Humans took from the booby-trap in La Mancha."

"Please share, Six. I'm sure the general will be very interested in the Battle Damage Assessment."

"Yes¬ Mr. President. The estimates made by the Factories¬ based on changes in travel patterns and physical size of the enemy¬ now stands at 384¬302 units. This does include all of those units that were euthanized by their own kind and scavenged for materials. This means the cost of repair of units is drastically reduced to 646¬863 unit-hours."

"I want you to give your people an attaboy, General. That is quite impressive."

"Thank you, Mrr. Prresident."

"Can we do it about a hundred more times?" I asked facetiously.

General Khan's deep rumbling laugh inside his tank turret caused my own voltage to drop in happiness. "If it werre that easy, anyone could do it, Mrr. Prresident."

"I think it should be noted¬ Mr. President¬ that there are no more easy sources of platinum to be had. Our simulations show there will be no more delays in Isp's goal. We should expect an attack upon 55467 within nine to ten days. From there we expect no respite. I will be attacked here approximately twelve days later¬ followed by 55469 three to four weeks later."

I let the memory being imaged wash away that depressing thought. The dust rising from the marching Army of the Humans obscured over 70 percent of its units in billowing red clouds. The plume itself looked like it would swallow another army twice the mass of Isp's. The army marched the plume toward the Dragon Back Range with an intent to traverse via Tiamat pass.

Before leaving the immolated city of La Mancha, the invaders had spent seven hours, sixteen minutes, and seven seconds killing off their badly wounded. They'd spent less than that examining the fouled mines. The images of the mines bore worse damage than even the one in Atlantis. While I enjoyed the tantrum Isp threw, I didn't have the same warm feeling over how quickly the mass of units moved toward their next objective.

How soon would more of our toyanity die?

We weren't watching Isp's troops because of where they were going. My fur stood on end all over my body in anticipation and at the same time my voltage ramped up from its new lower voltage. "How soon, General?"

"Anytime, Mrr. Prresident. Obviously, we can't give you an exact millisecond," General Khan replied.

There is a saying that the waiting kills more soldiers than combat. As the seconds ticked by, I think I learned to believe the old saw in a new way.

I had to give Lieutenant Colonel Evan Carlson his due. He knew his trade. I couldn't see his attack, but it had already been underway. The settling dust, well behind the marching column, exposed a neon-green bear's deactivated body. Two more bear bodies appeared. Then five more showed in a clump.

I looked and the column hadn't changed its forward progress. Toy carcasses began littering the plain behind the main mass of troops like a unit hemorrhaging hydraulic fluid. The memory zoomed in on one of the deactivated units. Two large holes perforated it, one in the sump, spilling the yellow fluid of sentience, and the other mid-chest where the processor is located. A kill doesn't get any cleaner than that.

Lieutenant Colonel Carlson attacked Isp's units from within the cloud and from behind. No one noticed the kills of the trailing units so he could do it over and over again. For one hour, sixteen minutes, and eight seconds our invisible troops killed and killed again without notice. Our raiders claimed 36,427 of the mutant bears before something changed.

The column came to an abrupt halt. We could see but couldn't hear. Anxiety spiked the voltage on my main bus. Would Carson's Raiders get out or would I be forced to send two-raised-to-the-seventh-power condolences to their families?

"Watch this, Mrr. Prresident."

Timing the action to the microsecond, dozens of fliers swooped in, dropping their bomb payloads right at the end of the column. This time we caught the cavalry's movements. Over five hundred strong, they sprinted, bounced, and rolled from the clouds of smoke and still settling dirt, directly away from the memory maker. Within minutes they had disappeared over a rolling hill.

"Brilliant," I yelled, my voltage dropping to the lowest level in several days.

"We intentionally lulled them into a false sense of securrity by not attacking them frrom the airr overr the last day and then used the rrenewed assault as a scrreen against detection orr, if alrready detected, then as a scrreen against purrsuit."

Not enough, my processor kept telling me. "How soon can they do it again?"

$*$ $*$ $*$

The countryside beyond Secundus showed nothing but empty kilometers of barren red. Not a single unit stirred. No one cataloged a new plant or animal species. No toy prospected for valuable minerals. My train rocketed along at an unprecedented 185 kilometers per hour, even scaring off the local fauna. If it weren't for the Presidential Train, Sancho, and General Khan, I would have felt as alone as when I searched for my first Factory other than Six. Despite the solitude, I felt good to be out doing something worthwhile.

I didn't shut down on the trip but I did slow my clock by 60 percent to cut down on non sequitur thoughts. Everything that could be done was being done. Almost every single pair of paws, hands, or manipulators of any kind, labored toward making the most of our slim chances against Isp and his zealots. The nets collected all of toyanity's ideas and evaluated them, no matter how many standard deviations from reality. The Factories evaluated any that showed promise against toypower. Conflicts were evaluated and those with the highest scores we implemented, usually by the growing number of non-sentient units being cranked out by the Factories in job lots.

Six made it very clear that the construction of the preprogrammed units didn't include an ability to impregnate them with sentience. The modeling showed that if they were made sentient, they would be unreliable. Using them for shock troops made more sense. These inanimate, non-living things would be slaughtered to the last. Each one that died and killed a member of the Army of Humans made our lives much more likely to continue.

Our cavalry, aided by the fliers I'd come all this way out to meet, had continued to chop up bits and pieces of Isp's troops. Carlson had only lost two units for killing nearly two hundred thousand units before the Army of the Humans had embarked onto their boats.

The train pulled up into the nearly deserted town of Acheron. A flight of fliers sortied out to the northeast as we pulled up to a stop. An honor guard snapped to attention. A nearby band started playing "Teddy Bears' Picnic." With a mental sigh at the musical choice, I dismounted.

"Mr. President, may I introduce Colonel Günther Rall, commander of the First Airborne Division, the Chain Lightings."

"Welcome, Mr. President," said a rather dully painted red biplane.

"Good morning, Colonel. How are things going here? You getting the supplies you need?"

"We are giving fuzzy one hell of a time, especially since you sent in those ground pounders."

"Excuse me, Colonel, but you said 'fuzzy'?"

"Sorry, Mr. President. It's a term we are using for Isp's mutant teddy bears. You know, 'Fuzzy Wuzzy was a bear—'"

"Clever, Colonel. I'll remember that. Are your troopers assembled for the ceremony?"

"Yes, Mr. President, all but those on over-watch," Colonel Rall answered.

"Well, then I suggest we do this. I haven't been so excited in months," I said.

"Excited, Mr. President?" the biplane asked as it rolled along beside me.

"Heck, yes, flier. You'll hear more in my speech."

"Well then, please come this way, sir."

The colonel deposited me at the back of a raised stage. The airfield had ranks upon ranks of fliers. A company of Six's balloons held themselves at attention to my left. Field crews held two companies of dirigibles tethered to the field in front of me. Four companies of windup planes to my right all kept their propellers still despite taut drive bands. Behind the fliers were even more ranks of ground support staff.

"ATTEN-SHUN!" bellowed a balloon at the base of the stage with staff sergeant's stripes. But as all of the units were already at attention, it seemed a meaningless command.

General Khan took center stage and commandeered all the networks. "LIGHTNINGS!"

The assembly roared. After a reasonable delay, the biplane lifted its flaps for silence.

"This is an exceptional day forr all of you! Ourr prresident has come to tell us just how momentous it is. I'll waste no morre of yourr time orr the valuable time of ourr leaderr. I give you the Prresident of Toyanity, Don Quixote!"

I stepped forward and almost got bowled over by the intensity of their adulation. I let the noise go on for fifty-seven seconds before I held up my paws. The discipline of these fliers showed. Flipping a light switch wouldn't have turned off the sound of a network as quick.

"You toys fight. You come back home after doing your duty. Then you do it again. Sometimes you lose a friend and comrade because your jobs are not safe, nor easy, nor tame."

A heckler in the crowd shouted out, "They give the easy jobs to second division."

This prompted a few laughs and "Stifle that Cunningham," from the sergeant.

"Go easy, Sergeant. This is their hour, not mine. But to continue . . .
My job isn't easy, tame, or safe," I said, showing the seam in my fur where
the sniper hit me. "But my job isn't easy in a much different way. Toys
come to me day after day trying to get me to solve their problems. Some
yell at me for doing a bad job. Others curse me as a grit for interfering with
their lives.

"You good units, right here on this field, have given me something
I've looked forward to for weeks. My voltage hasn't been this low in years.
Why? you ask. Well, unless the military grapevine has been somehow
rooted out and destroyed, you already know why.

"I've come to honor you toys. I've come to give you a visual
representation of a distinction you have already earned.

"You have all fought with skill, with tenacity, and with the sacrifice
that always goes with a life in the military. It gives me pleasure to decorate
each and every one.

"Colonel Rall, if you will come forward and accept the award?"

The biplane rolled forward and came to attention beside me. It did
a smart right turn to face me. Sancho handed me the medal. I opened the
lanyard and looped the caricature of a human puppeteer over the colonel's
propeller. "It is my privilege to award all the members of the First Airborne
Division the Geppetto Meritorious Organization Citation.

"GO LIGHTNINGS!"

∗   ∗   ∗

"So what's been happening while we've been gallivanting across the planet,"
I asked, feeling happier than I had in some time.

"Mr. President, we have analyzed the intel of
many different actions. I'll summarize if you don't
mind."

"Please. I need some recharge time today since I'm away from the
net."

"Thank you, Mr. President. Since your departure
there have been eight attacks by the cavalry on
the Army of the Human's troop train. Casualties
have varied greatly because of a change in Isp's
disposition. He now has 12 percent of his troops
travelling with their body perpendicular to the
nearest accessible edge. This allows them to spot,
if not intercept, our speed attacks. The change
Isp made did slow their advance. We've had three

troopers deactivated and six more injured. All but one of the injured have already been serviced to 90-percent-plus capability and returned to their battalion.

"Our enemies lost another 86,111 units. They managed to scavenge only 70 percent of those units.

"For future reference, our mobile toys excelled at attacking the column en route, but when they stopped the bears put up a spirited defense and reduced the casualties we could inflict."

"I'm glad I asked for the condensed version."

"I'm not done, President Quixote. After the invaders boarded their ships, our fliers continued to harass them. With our limited flier force, the greater travelling distance needed for each sortie, and that they were no longer clumped together, the additional units destroyed only numbered 22,936.

"The units have begun making landfall on Baja and are making for their caves as of fifty-three minutes ago—mark."

"Could they be going to grround?"

"Nice idea, General, but it won't happen."

"The Factories agree with the president. Isp knows that given enough time we can surpass his number of units. Every minute he gives us makes it that much more likely we can defeat him. He must attack."

"So why land there? Why not go all the way to the beaches of 55467?" I asked.

"He isn't verry savvy when it comes to militarry strrategy. What you suggest is exactly what he should do, with his ultimate objective. Instead, my belief is that he is thinking of taking a rrest and rregenerating his troops."

"So we can expect a short break?"

"Likely, Mr. President."

"Will it help us?"

The silence from his two advisors spoke volumes.

*   *   *

"Jason, we need more miners! We have Project Catholic to complete as well as needed minerals and more stone for redoubts." I tried to not put the stress I felt into my voice. I only reduced it by 12 percent.

Minister of Mining Argonaut wrapped his serpentine body around the support of the sunlamp next to my chair. It put him up high enough we didn't have to strain our neck pistons. "Mr. President, we just don't have them. Every able-bodied toy is working round the clock. Even the new recruits drafted are still coming in days to work a shift in the mines, mills, or munitions Factories."

Martin sat in his usual spot in the middle of the floor with his spindly legs beneath his bulbous spider body. "Maybe that's it," Martin offered through his clicking mandibles. "You said able-bodied. Is there any reason a youngling couldn't dig? Blackout but mine sure dug enough holes in my flower garden."

I love it when a plan comes together. When you brought the best processors into the same room, solutions follow.

"That's not a bad idea, Martin," Jason hissed. "We can put them on the least dangerous projects and leave the more experienced workers where their expertise is needed."

"And while you are at it, can't we use the non-sentient toys in areas where attacks aren't imminent? The general has assured me that he can give me no less than a full day's warning of any attack on a Factory."

"Holy grit, but you're right! That might just double my workforce."

"And while I can't authorize any non-sentient units that can't fight, if you give Six a hint, he might be able to reprioritize more units of types that would be useful for you and as defenses."

"Beep-beep. `Mr. President, I'm sorry to intrude but you have a secure call in the SitRoom,`" Rodney said, sticking his beak through my office doorway.

I was getting tired of hearing that phrase. It meant something untoward happened and I had to find a way to minimize the deactivations among our toys. "I'm sorry, gentlemen, but I'll need to see to that."

"Thank you for your time, Mr. President. I think Martin and I can hammer out the details," Jason said, following my friend and chief of staff from the room.

"There's been an attack on Avalon," my bodyguard briefed me as we walked down to what I'd come to think of as my second home.

I bit my tongue, literally. I had at least seven questions that Indira couldn't begin to answer. "Thank you, Indira," I said instead.

"Mr. President," Brigadier John Wayne, General Genghis Khan's second in command, said, coming to attention when I entered. Doing it with all the armor and katana of his Samurai body had to be difficult.

"Brigadier, what is the situation?"

"The fuzzies are about to hit Avalon."

"Avalon? Why Avalon?"

"Mrr. Prresident," General Khan's voice came over the network, "we believe that they want to keep a supply trrain going forr theirr attacks. Think about it. They could supply with sparre battery packs and go twenty-fourr/seven as opposed to twelve to sixteen hourrs a day they do now."

"We concur with the general's assessment," Six proffered.

"What do we have to stop them?"

"The Sixth Division, Mrr. Prresident. They arre well dug in. The only thing they don't have is a scorrched earrth bomb. We made it a lowerr prriorrity rrating to otherr cities that werre morre likely to be attacked."

"I guess we guessed wrong," I tossed in without much thought.

"Mrr. Prresident, we all evaluat—"

"That wasn't a slap on the tread, General. I agreed with the collective reasoning. Let it go.

"What is the likely outcome?"

"We will lose Avalon after delivering catastrophic damage to our enemies. Our simulations show a 45.36 to 1 casualty rrating," Six prognosticated.

"That equates to just overr half a million dead fuzzies, Mrr. Prresident. If we can keep up this casualty rratio we might be able to win."

"Why do I have a bad feeling about this?"

"Mr. President?" the brigadier asked.

"Isp may be crazy, but he is crazy like a fox. Smashing into a prepared position isn't his style. I don't think he is quite that dumb."

"Herre it comes."

Every attack thus far had started with a charge of Isp's horde of toys. They looked poised to launch when Isp suddenly climbed a rock to stand above the crowd. He struck a pose and began to orate.

"Six, please translate."

"'The infidels beyond that city have cast you out. They have called you unclean when they themselves wallow in corruption. They have said that you may not practice the faith in the Humans as you know in your souls that you must.

"'So the Humans have tasked you to take this

world┐ to remove the filth and nonbelievers so that
you can share the beauty that the Humans have to
offer.

"'Humans have demanded that you destroy the
demonic Factories so that they don't try to poison
our mines and desecrate our bodies.

"'The city over there is the first step in
pleasing the Humans and allowing you to live as
your soul dictates. NO MERCY!'"

I expected the bears to immediately charge but they didn't. Instead,
they parted, releasing a horde of new monstrosities. They seemed like a
cross between a tank and one of our artillery pieces. Their massive tracks
churned the red soil as they rolled through the line. By comparing one
of them to the adjacent units it stood over 4 meters tall with a fixed gun
that couldn't have been less than 3 meters long and 30 centimeters thick.
Machine guns mounts bristled off three of the four sides and one perched
on the top. Unlike a tank, there was no full turret; on the back, behind a
flack shield, stood four of Isp's troopers operating the monster.

Five hundred twelve of the beasts crept out to form a rolling wedge a
smidge over 5 kilometers wide. All of the fuzzies filled in behind. The only
positive thing was that their combined speed made headway of less than 6
kilometers per hour.

"Uh-oh," I said in what had to have been the greatest understatement
in the entirety of toyanity.

*   *   *

I'd specifically ordered Black Beard to let me roam around in the dark. The
huge cavernous complex beneath Six soothed my troubled soul. I'd always
known how much I needed my alone time. With the overwhelming mass
of this job on my shoulder, I needed it even more.

Twelve thousand two hundred eighty-eight deactivations weighed
heavily on me. Historians would one day call it the Massacre of Avalon.
I could envision the scathing memory imprints even now. "The Alliance
failed to anticipate the overwhelming force, both in quantity and
technology, that the Army of Humans brought to bear. The leadership
chose only to see what they wanted to see leading to an absence of a plan
for either inflicting grievous wounds on the invaders or to evacuate their
force intact for better use. Not a single Alliance toy escaped. Losses by the
forces of Isp numbered less than twenty thousand. Because of the constant
recycling of the invaders, no accurate count of the deactivated was ever

made. Only one of the new tanks was destroyed and four more damaged.

"Further, the radio technology that the Army of the Humans resurrected allowed them to coordinate their efforts in a way they never had in the past."

A war we almost certainly couldn't win before those blacked-out tanks showed up made our cause impossible. Oh, I had our people building tank pits, erecting dragon's teeth, and even planting heavier, handmade explosives on the primary approaches. Radio jammers were being built. Nothing would stop the fact that sixteen days from now, the Army of the Humans would repeat their victory over the top of the corpse of Six.

Never had I felt such despair. My fluids barely moved through my system. Even my sump seemed to drop its pump speed. What I'd fought for over ten years to build and protect, would be swept away in weeks. It wasn't a possible, it was inevitable.

I had no good options. We could fight and lose or surrender and die.

"Ferweet." Sancho's voice echoed throughout the enormous cavern.

"Not now, Sancho." My voice sounded one step above terminal deactivation.

"I believe you asked to have a report about the sins of our brethren," a voice I didn't recognize said. The word *sin* caught my attention. I'd take almost anything to lift my depression.

"I'm over here in the corner. Follow my voice if you don't have low light vision."

Sancho walked over with a brown and white puppy dog rolling up alongside. I never understood the puppy design. Legs on the front and wheels on the back.

"You may call me Beta," the puppy said. "I've been informed you like Greek letters."

"What do you have to tell me?" I said more brusquely than intended.

"I have a report on Dr. Frankenstein, specifically with regard to your personal recovery. In short, everything."

"You have my attention."

"It took some very serious digging into records that even the Factories didn't want me to pry into. In fact, I wonder if I would still be activated if they knew I'd obtained this information."

"Beta, I have to say that the dramatic lead-up is tiresome when our very existence is hanging in the balance. Spit it out."

"Ferweet."

"When you were shot by the sniper, all of the mechanics had given up on you. The memories I unearthed included the phrases, 'insufficient memory fluid for sentience,' 'negative processor function,' and one went so far as to just say flat-out 'deactivated.'"

"At this point Frankenstein took your body away with the help of several orderlies out a back door. Thirty minutes later she returned in the same door with you damaged but intact."

"The other mechanics were wrong?"

"Mr. President, I may not be a mechanic but in those memories I could see daylight through the hole in your sump. Unless Frankenstein is a miracle worker, you were dead."

"Did you come upon any reason for this paradox?"

"No, sir. Every avenue I pursued ended up in not a brick wall but in total sensory deprivation. Nothing ever existed beyond that back door, despite work orders showing cameras installed there over five years ago. Additionally, Frankenstein's past has been vacuumed so thoroughly I couldn't even find the previous items that have been provided to you. As far as anyone, anywhere, is concerned, Frankenstein came into being less than a year ago with no parents or history."

"So do you have anything more for me, Beta?"

"Yes, sir. I've located the unit who was pulling Lennon's strings."

"Yes?"

"It is very sensitive information."

"Shall we create a SAN?"

"I would prefer it if I whispered it in your ear."

"Sounds odd, but go ahead."

"Six," the puppy murmured so low I barely caught it. I yanked my head back and locked optics with him. The dog's head just bobbled up and down. He moved in close again and whispered with even less audio amplitude, "I don't know why, but I have several direct communications and money transfers from Six to Lennon. I was able to partially unscramble one of the messages. It ordered him to force the Procreation Limitation Law at all costs."

My processor whirled on NOOPs before grinding to some very ugly conclusions. The calculating Factories might have been right. They likely would have, or was it they already had, meddled to an extent where we might have needed to remove them.

"That's all I have, sir," the dog offered.

"You've given me enough to work with. Thank you."

I whispered down as low as I dared. "Sancho, I want you to gather together the bodyguards. Put together an operation to bring Frankenstein to me, as soon as Humanly possible. Do it quietly. Your mission is to get him to me without the Factories knowing and as quickly as possible. Both speed and secrecy are vital."

"Ferweet!"

Monster

I'd moved out of my office into the White House gardens. I didn't move any equipment outside. I just started meeting people who insisted on talking to me among the plants and shrubbery. Nothing I talked about or to whom I talked made the slightest difference in the war effort. I knew that within sixteen days everything around me, the Six's dome, the White House, and the marketplace, all would be gone—wiped from the face of Rigel-3 by that religious fanatic.

We were doomed but my mind wouldn't release on the anomaly that was Frankenstein. I'd work out here until I talked with him.

"Ferweet!" Sancho said breaking into my maudlin thoughts. A stiff breeze ruffled my fur, dragging my attentions even more to my surroundings. A Nurse Nan stood in front of me. Instead of the standard dress and cap, he was in a lab coat that definitely had been through a fight with someone's hydraulics and lost. His cheek held a dark smudge and the auburn fur on his head seemed awry. Eight of my bodyguards ringed Victor Frankenstein as if he were as dangerous as Isp.

"Mr. President, all you had to do is send me net request and I would have come. You didn't need to send your goons to collect me," he said with all the calm on the planet.

If I had been scooped up by armed thugs, I wouldn't have been so composed. "Mr. Frankenstein, I needed to have a chat with you without the Factories knowing."

"Still seems a bit Machiavellian of you."

"There is a Human saying about pots and kettles that might apply here."

"Really?" the Nurse Nan replied with about a level four sarcasm in his voice.

"Yes. I need you to tell me about what you are doing."

"Right now I'm standing in your garden wondering why I'm here."

"Quit playing games, Doctor. Do you realize that our way of life is about to come crashing down? Isp will take this planet. I need to know what it is you do."

Doctor Frankenstein locked optics with me. He paused long enough for me to recall the entirety of Mary Shelley's work for which this Nurse Nan was named—call it 6.3 seconds.

"Mr. President, what I do and what I have done have no impact on the war effort."

"How do you know? We have hundreds of very smart units that

could fit your bit into the whole to come up with a solution."

"I'm sorry, Mr. President, but I'm prohibited from telling you, not only because of my oath, but because this knowledge would be as devastating as the coming Jihad."

I jumped up from the bench. I drew my trusty 0.45 caliber long-slide pistol, the one I'd carried halfway around this planet. I shoved the weapon against the Nurse Nan's chest. My bodyguards each pulled their weapon as if suddenly detecting some kind of threat to me. "You will tell me, Doctor, or I will shoot a hole in your sump. My training hasn't forgotten where the sump of each of the toys resides."

Dr. Frankenstein didn't even flinch. Cool as could be, he reached up and adjusted my aim 4.2 centimeters to the right. "That's a better location, Mr. President. Not only will you tear a hole in my sump but also destroy the sump pump. Even if they find a patch no one will be able to attach a new pump quick enough to prevent my memory fluid from turning to tar."

"What project do you have under guard in Six's basement? How can you take my dead husk and reanimate it?"

The Nurse Nan remained mute.

"Damn you, Doctor! I need to know the information you carry!" I felt like ripping his head off.

"You are absolutely the last person on this world that has a need to know."

"Let me approach this a different way," I said, not changing my point of aim, "to whom did you pledge your oath?"

"The current list of who are privileged to Project Phoenix consists of all three Factories, the two heads of Congress, and your chief of staff."

"My chief of staff?!" My hydraulic pressure redlined at 18,056kpa. I could feel the safeties threatening to pop.

"Sancho, with the exception of Six, I want those three other worthies brought here NOW. Do it at gunpoint if you must." Sancho bustled off with two of the bodyguards.

"In the meantime would you like to reconsider, Doctor?"

"No, Mr. President. I take my oath as seriously as you take yours."

"Then have a seat. I figure we have five minutes to kill. Sorry, poor choice of words." I holstered my pistol and waved him to one of the other white painted benches. "Have you ever done any rock climbing, Doctor?" I forced my internal clock to slow and reduced the rate of my hydraulic pump.

The Nurse Nan cocked his head at me. "I've never climbed, Mr. President."

"I find nothing more peaceful and exhilarating at the same time. Your sump is clear but your processor insists that it's in danger."

"Sounds stressful, not peaceful."

"Not for me, Doctor. I turn off my cognitive processes relative to my movement and allow my standard body program to coordinate my climb. It allows me the opportunity to either give very close attention to one single problem with the goad of anxiety or to drop my clock rate and not think about anything.

"I will fight like a maniac until after we lose our last Factory. Then I'm going to head out to the highest mountain I can find. Then I'll climb until I'm captured or I deactivate from the fall." I didn't mention I had no intention of being taken alive. I wouldn't be Isp's performing pet.

"Mr. President, you are one odd duck."

"I'm not a duck, I'm a bear. Maybe you need to go back to school to identify species."

"No, it's a saying. An odd duck is one that thinks and acts differently from the norm. I'm beginning to understand why Six thinks you are so special."

"Special? As far as I know the only thing special is that I'm the first of my race. That wasn't my choice or even desire. I'd give anything to just be a normal unit."

Frankenstein chuckled. "I can't see anyone allowing you to do that, ever, Mr. President."

"What in the dark moonshine is this all about?" came the voice of Virginia Apgar, yet another Nurse Nan. Beside her was the white dragon, Ruth, the leader of the provinciers. Martin trailed behind, or perhaps above would be appropriate because of the length of his spidery legs.

"I do find it odd that we were dragged out here," Ruth said. Martin wisely said nothing, but I got the sense that he knew what was going on.

"Units," I said, "I have what on the surface is a conspiracy that includes all of you. Worse, it could be treason. Unless I get the answers I'm looking for, I'll call a tribunal within the hour."

"Treason?" Ruth asked with some surprise.

"And really—a conspiracy, Mr. President?" Virginia asked. "What is it that you want to know?"

"Phoenix," Frankenstein said simply.

I could see the guilt in their body language. "How can Mechanic Frankenstein take a dead body, mine, and make it good as new? What is he hiding in Six's basement under guard, lock, and key?"

"Mr. President—" Martin started. I could hear the prevarication in his voice. I didn't let him finish.

"Martin, I thought you were my friend."

"You have no clue, Mr. President," he said with so much vehemence that I wondered if I needed to reset. "I would have done anything at all not to be a participant in this little cabal! Do you have any idea how much you have hurt me?"

"I've hurt you? I've always treated you—"

"Shut up, Don," Martin said abruptly.

Martin had been my trusted friend and colleague for just short of ten years. He'd never been anything but respectful. For him to be rude to me told me my assumptions and anger were incorrectly placed. I reset all my hardware, bringing my registers to zero.

"Tell him, Frankenstein," the spider said.

"Yes, tell him," Virginia added. Ruth nodded.

"What about Six," Frankenstein asked.

"I'll explain it to Six. If he wants my sump he can have it," Martin threw in. "Besides, what does it matter? This time next month we likely will all be deactivated."

"No need to offer me your deactivation, Mr. Luther," Six chimed in. "I have been listening and agree that the time for secrecy with regard to the president is over."

I think my reflexes made me jump at least 16 centimeters. "You sneaky grit! When did you get microphones out here?"

"Mr. President, control of the planet surface is part of our directives. You'd be surprised where we Factories have remote listening devices."

"Please show him the dungeon," Six demanded.

"The dungeon? A bit melodramatic, don't you think?" I threw in, now beginning to worry.

"That was my doing, sir," Frankenstein said. "It seemed appropriate considering my name."

"Mr. President, I don't believe you will need us," Virginia said, pointing at her congressional colleague. "We only know the barest facts."

"Certainly, you can go, but I may want to question you later."

"Yes, sir."

"So you won't need me any longer either," Martin said.

"Not so fast, Mr. Chief of Staff," I threw back at him.

"Please, Mr. President . . . Don, please don't make me go down there. I'll answer any question you have afterward. You can have my resignation if you want it, but don't make me look again." The plaintive tone and his body language of reluctance tore at my pump.

"All right, but keep yourself available afterward. I do want to investigate this with you further."

"Yes, Mr. President." I've never seen Martin hurry away so fast in our entire relationship.

"Doctor. Six. I believe this is your show. Lead on."

When we started out my bodyguard followed. "I'm sorry, Mr. President, but your protective detail cannot come," Frankenstein insisted.

"FERWEET!"

"I have to agree, Mr. President," Six said.

Without twenty clock cycles of thought I ordered, "Stay in the Oval Office. I'll return there."

"But—"

"Just do it!" I barked, not wanting to argue.

To no one's surprise Frankenstein led me down into the cavern beneath Six and to the guarded door. This time a Della Dolly guarded the door. It came to as much attention as any ragdoll could muster.

"Good evening, Doctor Frankenstein," the guard said.

"Please open the vault on my authority," the doctor replied.

"Yes, sir."

The door was opened with little fanfare. The doctor went in and with a gentle twist of one of the shelving units, opened a door that wasn't visible to me the first time I entered. Sneaky.

Victor's bulk blocked the doorway. He turned and said, "Mr. President, there are some things that you will likely find very disturbing. Please take sufficient clock cycles to digest what you see before you react. In fact, I'd like to ask you for your sidearm."

"Aren't we getting a little paranoid?" I asked, but slid my 0.45 out of its holster and handed it to Frankenstein.

"No, Mr. President, I don't think I am." Frankenstein just set it on the shelf in the outer room. "Please follow me."

The darkness beyond matched that of the cavern. Spotlights shone down on eight inanimate teddy bears locked inside modified sleeping cradles. I'd never seen such cybernetic support around the head. But none of that caught my attention. What drew 100 percent of my focus was that each of the teddy bears was purple with a white belly, one white paw, and blue mottling down the left foot.

Without even glancing at the doctor I moved closer. I felt like a parabird transfixed by a basilisk right before the slaughter. I looked at the face. I saw that visage every time I looked in a mirror.

I examined the stitches holding its white paw to the purple arm and compared them to mine. They matched in every detail. The golem in the cradle had duplicated the distinctive mottling on my feet down to the last nylon thread.

I ran to the next cradle and saw the scarring around its ear where I'd sewn my own on by myself over a decade ago. There was even a repair in the fur where I'd been shot in the head!

I reached down for my automatic pistol. I would rid this world of these imposters. Of course my paw fell on only air. "Doctor, what have you done?"

"Teddy 1499, attend me. " Six's voice rolled through the air. "I did this with the doctor's aid.

"Our purpose was to keep you as the president and figurehead of all of our units. You are unique. Your presence alone kept this nascent species from self-destruction. Simulations have shown that had you perished, toyanity would have split up into small groups, eventually destroying itself and me within seven years. If you could survive for only a century, the units would have fallen into yet another mold of your creation. They would be safe. I would be safe."

"But . . ." I couldn't even think of a good reply or even a question.

"That indistinguishable property that made you the hero of all, also made you reckless. Further simulations showed you had only a 31 percent chance of surviving past the first lustrum and a 9 percent chance of lasting a decade. Wrapping you with high security or sealing you in a box by modeling provided a result as bad as killing you."

"So you duplicated me? How is that even possible? Every toy is unique!"

"I can answer that," Doctor Frankenstein said. "It is how I ended up in charge of Phoenix anyway. As part of my doctorate, I described a method where toys could almost be identical. Of course the physical attributes were not an issue, but where it mattered, in the sump, our research showed that even tiny microscopic differences caused changes in behavior and personality.

"So we scanned and scoped you without your knowledge. We mapped your sump to within one angstrom and continue to refine those numbers. At great expense, Six created millions of sumps using our detailed map so we could get one or two that were the same. I believe the last estimate was, even with the highest quality and material control, it took 96,406 sumps to get just one that would be acceptable. The ergs involved in this process are staggering.

"The next hard part was learning to clone your memories . . ."

The process only partially intrigued me. Only one question remained, "So I'm not Don Quixote?"

"In every sense of the word, you are . . . and you are not," Six said. "You do not have the same

`physical materials as the original Don Quixote,`
`but your memories, experiences, and everything`
`else that made the original is within you."`

"How many times have I . . . he . . . oh, the blackout of it . . . How many times have I died?"

"Three, Mr. President."

Multiple threads spawned in my processor for parallel processing.

"How many wars have you already lost, Mr. President?" I hated the thought that Six had done this to me. *How could we use this to our advantage?* **Three deaths so that meant I was Don 4?** *Would a duplicate fool Isp?* How prophetic Lennon's words were. What gave Six the right to tear at my soul to the expense of everyone else? **Were there three other souls with the Humans or was that trapped in this sump.** Six took too much upon himself. **Or was my soul torn asunder only to be whole when the last clone died?** How his words haunted me. *A duplicate had already fooled Isp because he thought I was Don 1.* **My soul likely could only rest when there was only one place to go, Earth.** Six and his sisters had taken more power upon himself than even Isp. *What if we played a shell game with Isp?* He knew I was no longer Don Quixote and he taunted me. Only that saving toyanity was his best path toward his mission kept him from destroying us. *But with multiple peas and a lot more than three shells.* **More death in killing the clones.** Even after death that fat hippo gave me one more reason to hate him. *Toyanity had a chance to survive.* **Just not yet.** I resolved to destroy Six at the earliest possible convenience.

*   *   *

"You can't be serious, Mr. President," Virginia Apgar interjected into the stunned silence of my office.

"I am," I offered quietly to the members of Project Phoenix.

"That has to be the most insane thing I've ever heard," Ruth heaped on.

"According to Frankenstein and Six, you all must approve before we can launch any of the clones."

"You are going make me relive it all over again," Martin added.

"It is the only way to save everyone, my friend. It is the only way to be sure."

"There are so many holes in this plan that I could throw Martin through it," Virginia said, picking at the red cross on her dress.

`"While I concede that there are difficulties,`
`I also believe President Quixote is correct. All`

modeling and simulations point to the same thing.
We will not prevail in a conventional clash of
arms. The only simulation that gave over a 3
percent chance of victory was for representatives
of the government to go underground with as much
of our military as possible and wage a prolonged
guerrilla campaign. This was not acceptable as it
means the complete destruction of all Factories."

Silently I wondered if this were not the best course, but then
procreation raises its head. *How could I doom our species to a slow, lingering
extinction?*

"So what does your vaunted models say about the success of the
president's Pyrrhic plan?" Martin tossed out with enough venom in his
voice for an entire generation of cobras.

"There are a number of indeterminacies. The
current probabilities range from 31 percent to as
high as 49 percent."

"One chance in three," Ruth said.

"Those odds are of complete success. There are
a range of other probabilities much more favorable
for partial success that would allow toyanity to
continue its way of life side by side with Isp and
his kin, but fail to meet the requirements of us
Factories. That would cause stresses that would,
at some point in the future, lead to yet another
war which cannot be modeled at this time. There
is another partial success that would have Isp
being a guerrilla fighting a campaign from hiding.
This will likely tear apart the unity of our state
and devolve yet again into a war, which cannot be
simulated with any degree of accuracy."

"I want you all informed. Six, tell them—what is the chance of total
failure?" I said without any attempts at dissembling.

"With the same caveats of unknowns, the odds of
complete failure are 30 percent."

Martin answered first, his eight legs twitching in as much agitation
as I'd ever seen from him. "So one in three we totally win, if what the
president proposed can be called a win; one in three of total inglorious
disaster; and one in three we duke it out sometime later?"

"Yes," I pronounced.

"I'm not liking those odds," Ruth said. "I get better odds at any
combat arena."

I looked at the voters and tried to discern their minds. Virginia was dead set against it. It would take a nuclear bomb to move her one iota from her position. Ruth seemed teetering but likely would vote against because she wanted the perfect solution. Six only crunched the numbers. He would vote in favor because the alternatives were much worse. Frankenstein sat off to one side, away from the rest of our august company. He had listened intently but said nothing. I assumed by his career choice in the hard sciences and his silence that he'd reluctantly vote in favor.

That left only Martin as the swing vote. His attachment to me would cloud his judgment.

As we all quietly contemplated each other, Frankenstein stood up and said, "You toys may do as you like, but to me it is as clear as my reflection from a still pond. Three percent vs. 70 percent—we simply have no choice." He walked toward the door.

"Where are you going, Doctor?" Virginia asked.

"I'm going to do my job, Congresswoman. Unless I miss my guess that no matter how you all vote, Six would aid me in modifying and warming up the two additional Don Quixotes we need for this crazy-assed scheme."

"Shall we put it to a vote?" I said as Frankenstein left the room to make our vote moot. The ballot wasn't unanimous. Virginia abstained.

Brother

I felt like I had been transported directly into Mary Shelley's book cast as the monster. Straps held me to a cold horizontal table. Blue glowing fiber optics ran out of a hole in either side of my neck into a patch panel out of my sight over my head.

"I need you to lie still, like you are regenerating, so we can get your most recent memories translated into the others," Frankenstein said.

I turned off my hydraulics. That would solve at least one of the problems. Using some of the remaining pressure I looked at the pair of new myselves, one on either side. Identical to my position, they lay with fiber optics jacked into their necks, right where the sump reader sits. As this might take some time I also slowed down my clock to avoid boredom.

Frankenstein bustled about checking readouts and making adjustments to dials across half the surfaces. I half expected to see a Jacob's ladder with an arc of electricity travelling up between the V in the wires. I also thought some bubbling green liquid heating over a Bunsen burner with a distilling pipe capturing the steam would have set the scene nicely.

"So how did it go," Frankenstein said as he started turning off his equipment.

"How did what go, Doctor?"
"How did what go, Doctor?"
"How did what go, Doctor?"

The two other voices, both mine, didn't echo, they happened at, as far as I could measure, the same femtosecond. I turned back on my hydraulic pump and looked to either side of me. Each of me looked back.

"It seems we have a success. Before you say any more I have to tell you something."

"Tell me? Or them?"
"Tell me? Or them?"
"Tell me? Or them?"

"Yes, exactly. Mr. Quixote, times three, you are all effectively identical. The only way you know if you are a duplicate of the original is that you know that you were having your memories copied from the center location. So just for ease keeping track between you, the quote original unquote will be Don-Four. The unit on your right will be Don-Five, and the remaining unit will be Don-Six. If you wish to be formal you might state Teddy 1499-4, etcetera."

Somehow I knew the other two teddies would now wait for me to talk. "Doctor, if you would remove our bonds?"

"Don-Five and Don-Six, if you are truly a replica of me, then you will already know what I have planned. It will require sacrifices of each of you. As Don-Four, I will not be immune to painful costs. What I need to know from you, not me, is will you perform as I've outlined?"

"Yes, without a doubt."

"Yes, without a doubt."

"In that case you know the details of the plan, including its strengths and weaknesses. We must hide our duplicate status to even those close to us. Let's make this work."

"Agreed."

"Agreed."

"Doctor, will this duplication of speech ever go away?"

"Doctor, will this duplication of speech ever go away?"

"Doctor, will this duplication of speech ever go away?"

Frankenstein unbuckled Don-Six. "Absolutely, Don-Four. As you each get new experiences you will grow and diverge. But for the first while, you are literally thinking the same things at the same time."

"Thank you, Doctor."

"Thank you, Doctor."

"Thank you, Doctor."

I mentally cringed. Dr. Frankenstein unbuckled Don-Five. "Four, I need you to stay on the table. According to the plan you have the most surgery to undergo and the longest journey. Fortunately, just yesterday, Colonel Carlson brought in some of the mutant bears they scavenged."

"We have to make sure that we promote Lieutenant Colonel Carson for his accomplishments."

"We have to make sure that we promote Lieutenant Colonel Carson for his accomplishments."

"We have to make sure that we promote Lieutenant Colonel Carson for his accomplishments," Don-Five said 236 milliseconds after Don-Six and I.

Don-Six followed up with, "I shall return to our post until Don-Five has surgery complete." I watched myself turn and leave Doctor Frankenstein's laboratory of miracles.

Don-Five said, not at the same time, thankfully, "I will await mechanic facilities for my modification."

Frankenstein wheeled in the body of one of Isp's bears. It had a narrow hole in the skull. Black tar covered the entire forward half of the head.

"Ready to become one of Isp's minions, Don-Four?"

"Not funny, Doctor."

"Not funny, Doctor."

Frankenstein chuckled. "But just think of it this way, Don-Four and Five, you will be returning two things to Isp."

*   *   *

The garden, where Don-Four's plan had all started, made me, Don-Six, think there must be some master plan by the Humans. General Khan stood to attention to my right. Lieutenant Colonel Carlson bounced on his prodigious feet on my left. Martin stood behind us, off the platform, to bring him down to about our height. His attitude toward me had been cold all day. I didn't know if he knew I wasn't Don-Four or he didn't care.

The audience were primarily Carlson's parents and a few of his military peers. We'd envisioned this as a private affair, not something for the consumption of the networks and the masses. We hadn't prohibited them. More than fifty civilians showed up to witness the event. Six network cameras pointed at the stage. I reasoned that any good news that could override the doom and gloom by all the pundits could only be beneficial to morale.

General Khan rolled up the ramp adjacent to the podium and took control of the LAN. "I am prroud to considerr Evan Carrlson a frriend and a peerr. Lieutenant Colonel Carrlson has committed his life to masterring his crraft. He has shown the best of what toyanity can be, especially in this trroubling time. I've neverr known a morre dedicated, honorrable kangarroo—orr forr that matterr toy of any kind.

"But you arren't herre to listen to me gush. You want to hearr frrom ourr commanderr and chief and then frrom the man of the hourr himself. I give to you, Prresident Don Quixote!"

The sixth, I mentally said to myself. Not being the only Teddy 1499 stuck in my paw. I would have to get over it eventually. That was my sacrifice.

"Thank you for the introduction, General Khan," I said upon reaching the podium. "But I'm not pleased for you stealing all of my thunder. I'm sure your pay packet will reflect my displeasure."

There were some laughs from the small crowd.

"I really have nothing more to say that General Khan hasn't already said, so if Lieutenant Colonel Carlson will step forward." The kangaroo hopped but who was I to quibble. "And if Evan's fathers will help us?"

A kangaroo and a radio car came up onto the stage. I handed each of them a small box.

"Evan Carlson, I must temporarily strip you of your rank." I moved forward and took off each of the magnetic, single scalloped diamonds of a lieutenant colonel from his shoulders. "And now, your parents will promote you to the rank you have proven that you deserve by skill and deed."

Sterling Moss, the radio car parent, had some trouble affixing the double scalloped diamond of a colonel to the shoulders of his 250-centimeter-tall son. Using his antenna, the father's third attempt pinned it in place. Mohammed Ali, Evan's kangaroo father, placed the new rank insignia on his other side perfectly the first time.

"I introduce to you, full Colonel Evan Carlson, commander of the Marauders, the First Cavalry!"

We all applauded for 173 seconds. I raised my paws for attention as the clapping died down.

"I have one more duty to perform before I let our hero of the hour speak. Attention, Colonel Evans!" The towering creature stopped bouncing on his toes and stood straight up. "It is my honor, and privilege, to award you with the Purple Pump, for wounds received in the line of duty. Thank you for your courage and bravery!" I pinned the magnetic purple ribbon to his chest and stepped back to say, "I give to you, the hero of the hour."

*   *   *

As Don-Four, I felt heavy despite of the massively upgraded hydraulics. Looking in the mirror I looked ridiculous. The doctor had taken the easiest method by taking my head and placing it on top of the body of Isp's mutant bear. It added a full 20 centimeters to my height. I felt like a giant looking down on the world. My arms and chest bulged with extra armor.

My first step toppled me over. I took down a metal tray full of Frankenstein's mechanic tools, and bashed my right arm so hard into a cabinet that the door caved in. The tumult surprised me.

Don-Five and Victor rushed to my side. "Are you all right?"

"Sorry," I said, trying to right myself. With the help of my two comrades, I struggled to my oversized feet. "I don't know what happened."

"Check your body parameters' file. I'll bet you still have your previous body's dimensions."

"Oh, sometimes I think I have all of the processing power of a slinky. I should have thought of that. Wait, what is my mass increase?"

"Forty-five percent."

"Grit!"

"Oh, and your center of mass has changed. Normally your center of mass would have raised to 1.2 meters, but with the present in your belly slung low as possible to prevent you from being top heavy, your center comes in at 1.156 meters.

"Five, we'd like to keep your center of mass right where it is, but it would require a fully redesigned hydraulic pump system. You will have to settle for a small drop of 1.7 centimeters when we install your gift to Isp."

"That is easily compensated for," Don Five said.

"Oh? Say that when you have the bowling ball in your gut," I said.

"Don-Four, that sounds remarkably like whining. Have you changed your mind with regard to this plan?" Don-Five said.

"No, not at all. I might think a thing is necessary without thinking it is comfortable."

"All right, Don-Five. Up on the table. Your turn for surgery."

We only had twelve days, but I couldn't leave yet. Timing was everything.

*   *   *

The mess on the laboratory floor made the temperature seem colder than reality in shame. Six Don Quixotes lay with their sumps smashed in by my hammer. As the nearest to original that existed, I couldn't let there be any more of these doppelgangers loose on the world. One unit—one deactivation. Even me living forever wouldn't aid, but would hinder, toyanity.

"Please don't ever clone one of toyanity again, Doctor."

"I understand, Mr. President."

"Now, please grind them up for scrap, Doctor. They can't be found. Don-Six, please assist. You know how much our plans hinge on our subterfuge not being discovered." Don-Five, his internal surgery completed, had swapped with Don-Six.

"I do," he said. I detected a note of sorrow in his voice. Part of me felt sorry for Don-Six. I knew other units would feel sorry for what would happen to me.

With some shame I'd considered swapping roles with Don-Six. I just shook my head. I couldn't. My sump wouldn't allow it. My processor wouldn't allow it.

All the pieces were nearly in place. One more duty stood before I took my last journey. I considered how to phrase the question that would initiate it. The inquiry could be construed as rude in certain circles.

"Yes," Don-Six agreed in the semi-darkness of Dr. Frankenstein's lab.

"I haven't asked the question yet."

"It is meaningless as we still think very much alike. I know what you want. We—you—have agonized over it for years. Your solution is undeniably perfect. One dies and one is born," Don-Six replied.

"I couldn't agree more," Six said, his bass voice projecting not from the net but from speakers in the room.

"There are times when . . ." I started.

"There are times when . . ." Don-Six started. "You take it, Don-Four."

"Thank you. There are times when we wished you would announce your presence."

"Then how could I watch unobtrusively?"

"So you are admitting to being a sneak," the Nurse Nan Frankenstein offered, not even looking up from cleaning his mechanic's tools.

"Essentially correct," Six said without a hint of remorse.

"We aren't going to change Six," I said.

"Unlikely in the time you have left," Six said with what I detected as a hint of smugness.

"So how do you know what we are thinking, Six?"

"Simulation showed 84 percent what your decision would be. Your statement, 'One dies and one is born,' brought it to near unity."

"Are the fliers ready to take me, Six?" I asked.

"Standing by."

"Then let's get to your dome so we can do this."

"No need," Six said. "The unit in question is waiting in the underground depot."

"Goodbye, Dr. Frankenstein. I don't think we will be meeting again."

"And yet, we will," he said, looking at Don-Six.

"Yes, I guess you will."

Don-Six and I walked out of the lab and past the guard. "I know I don't have to ask, but I will anyway. Don-Six, will you raise the unit I impregnate? Will you teach it the ways of this world and hopefully the next?"

"I will."

I uncovered the nipple to my sump. I felt that sickening feeling of being so exposed and vulnerable. With a hypodermic from the lab, Don-Six stuck the needle into my sump, withdrawing a tiny quantity. He then handed me the syringe. I found my future child's sump nipple and injected my sentience into it.

"Take care of her," I said, dropping the needle to the floor as I turned and walked away. I didn't look back. I couldn't look back. That life was over.

*   *   *

At noon, I stood on the rampart that surrounded the city around 55466. Don-Four, in his hideous new body, was lifted into the sky by a dozen dirigibles. The tangle of them motored north over the mountains. If anyone was actually functional at noon, they would have seen not another Don

Quixote, but one of the mutant bears. Odd and definitely noteworthy, but not earth shattering.

Don-Six had to be on his way south with his new offspring, escorting tens of thousands of refugees and every member of the government that could walk, crawl, slither, wobble, bounce, or jump from the city—my city.

It was the best of times, it was the worst of times . . . I thought. It had to be both as I'd had very little life that I could call my own. And, how like Dickens's a *Tale of Two Cities* did my life activate and deactivate. I looked at my white paw and remembered the terror and joy of finding out there were others like me. Now I despaired for them instead. Being too alike brought its own woes.

"How goes the manufacturing of non-sentient units?"

"`Quite well, Mr. President,`" Six said. "`We won't fool them into thinking that no one escaped but we may give them room to question.`"

"That's good enough," I said. "You know I feel like I should be doing something, anything, to defend this city."

"`You are, Mr. President.`"

"I feel like such a wastrel."

"`Henry V might be an appropriate text? 'By my troth, I will speak my conscience of the king: I think he would not wish himself anywhere but where he is.'`"

"And didn't one of his subjects challenge him to a duel? They hated him for their impending doom."

"`But he also heartened them, Mr. President.`"

"Six, could we not use that term when no one else can hear, please. There are two other units who more rightfully wear that title. I feel like a poseur even having it compared to me."

"`Yes, Don-Five, but only when we cannot be heard. We must maintain the ruse.`"

"Then you think I should go down and give the troops spirit?"

"`They are going to die for you.`"

"No, they are dying for the rest of toyanity."

"`I disagree, Don-Five. If you did not lead them, they wouldn't stay. A small core of them would remain to try in vain to protect me, but most of them are here because you are here. You order them to fight. You order them to die. You order their deactivation for something bigger than themselves. Remember the 108.`"

I did think about those units I left to their own devices, to die, when I learned of other Factories. It was a fitting parallel. I would give my troops what morale I could.

*   *   *

If my sump wasn't so large, I would have liked to have been rebuilt as a flier. Soaring over the rest of the world made me seem like the master of everything. I admit that I worried regularly about falling for the first several hours, but once my processor got itself oriented, it desisted trying to make me worry about my next step.

I'd ordered my transports to stay over the peaks of the mountains far from the Army of Humans. We didn't want any witnesses of my passage. The winds over the mountains buffeted us a bit. As we were in for a lengthy flight, I considered shutting down my cognitive processes or even slowing down my internal clock, but I didn't have that many more cycles left. I would enjoy every one.

The peaks of the mountains gave way to plains of Washington. Scrub growth covered them like unkempt red fur. I watched a herd of giant slugs slither along, denuding a swath several kilometers across. A large basilisk darted along closely behind. The natural flow of life gave me hope for the future of this world.

Just as soon as I felt hope, I felt anger. Like a weeping sore in the middle of the wilderness sat the city of Washington. Its splendor crushed and ground into the earth only for the power struggle of one little sump—a unit who had intentionally destroyed his own moral compass.

Any fleeting reservations over my plan disappeared like water lying on lava—poof, gone in a gout of steam. For the remaining two days of the flight, my thoughts interspersed between how I would surmount obstacles in completing my mission and the rage I felt for Isp and the pain he'd caused. The grit of the Baja sand scuffing the fur on my feet caught me off guard.

Pulling myself back to the job at hand, I undid and stepped out of the harness.

"Thank you, Captain Sullenberger. Give my thanks to your team. May you live a long and active life!"

"Who the hell was that, anyway?" asked one of the other dirigibles as they floated away.

"This is one of those missions that if you know, then they have to kill you."

"Then let's just keep it a mystery, shall we?"

I had 512 kilometers to make and two days to accomplish it. If everything still went to plan, Isp's attack on Six should commence anytime. Part of me wished I was there defending it and the other part didn't want to see the end of my creator.

I put my feet to the sand to cover as much distance in as short of time as I could.

*　　*　　*

We didn't expect the mountain defensive ring to hold long. There were too many passes to cover them all. The flier memories showed Isp's units flowing against the mountain range like a lahar. They slammed into it, spreading out and around it. They stacked deeper and deeper until they started pouring through the passes. Where they found resistance the abominable tanks were brought forward to punch their way through. It cost Isp units and time. Both sides knew the interlopers had more of both.

Isp poured units in through first one, then three, and then eight different passes. I stood in a crows' nest we'd built in the center of town that raised 30 meters into the air. I watched the invaders flow into Six's valley.

"What do you think? Three million?"

"`Two million, nine hundred thousand, five hundred six,`" Six pontificated. "`Based on flier memories we are also looking at approximately 1,400,000 units in reserve and the supply train could supply yet another quarter of a million if Isp was in a pinch.`"

"So it should be a close thing."

"Ferweeet!" Sancho said beside me. For that I truly felt the chill of guilt. I wanted to send him away, but I had to sacrifice him to maintain our subterfuge. Everyone knew I went nowhere without Sancho at my side. Isp may be immoral, inexperienced, and reprehensible, but one of his faults wasn't stupidity. If Sancho didn't fight to the death at my side then everyone, especially Isp, would ask questions we could not have asked.

"Wait a second—what is that?" I said, shading my optics from the sun as I looked.

"`It appears we have a new layer of shock troops,`" Six said, projecting the live image on a screen next to me. A line of toys stretched hundreds wide across the line of advance that Isp's units would have to take.

"How close can you get? And can we get audio?"

". . . need to believe in the love of the Humans. Put away your weapons of hate. Take not away from the Humans what they have given us. Love all toys. You need to believe in the love of the Humans. Put away..." The close-up showed the line of toys marching in unison in the direction of Isp. Not one had a single weapon. They just kept moving and chanting. Right in the center of the line, Six managed to zoom in on the exaggerated feminine curves of High Priestess Plancia Magna. She chanted, setting the tempo of the protest.

"I guess this is the help she promised."

"Mr. President, this has a 0.03 percentage chance of success."

"General Khan, do we have any troops situated that could retrieve those fools?" I asked over our specific SAN.

"It was ourr trroops that let them thrrough in the firrst place. Somehow they rrearranged the watch list to allow them to pass thrrough without us noticing. Unforrtunately, my trroops in that arrea arre comprromised. They arre on theirr own."

"'As you sow, so shall you reap.' We could use those units, but I'm not willing to risk even a single hair of a single toy to bring them back."

"Ferweet."

"And I concur, Mr. President. But what happens might just be instructive," Six added.

"I agree."

A small group of units broke off from Isp's regrouping army. Six zoomed in on the procession. Isp stood at the head of a column of his personal bodyguards.

"Shit. Can we get some artillery in there? Or maybe a flier? Maybe we can end this here and now," I said aloud as well as over the SAN.

"I'm sorry, Mrr. Prresident. Arrtillery is out of rrange by 31 perrcent. I can brring in two flierrs with only theirr .22 caliberr ammo. The rrest are on five-minute hot-pad alerrt."

"Unlikely .22 caliber ammunition is going to break his armor. Launch a flight of your hot bombers. They might wait around long enough."

"Yes, sirr."

"...love of the Humans. Put away your weapons of hate. Take not away from the Humans what they have given us. Love all toys. You need to believe in the love of the Humans. Put..."

"I am now the new ruler of Rigel-3. I order you

```
to stand aside, and we will find a way for you to
worship the Humans in our new society,"
```
Isp demanded.

```
"Put away your weapons of hate, Isp,"
```
Priestess Magna bade.

```
"If you don't move now, I will have to destroy
you as I go for the heretic Don Quixote and the
demon 55466."
```

```
"Isp, your threats are not the words of the
Humans. They are your own fears and insecurities
speaking."
```

The unstoppable force of Isp and his troops against the immovable object of the Priestess's faith. I had my money on Isp.

The gold teddy bear reached back and was handed an M16 that looked as old as my own, or should I say, Don-One's M16. Isp didn't waste time on words. He fired his clip dry into the protesters. A group of the priestess's people, her included, went down in the center of the line, leaking hydraulic fluid and sometimes semiconductor fluid. The rest of the line didn't budge. They didn't bend knee to aid those on the ground. They continued their chant.

Isp's bodyguards surged forward, spearing the units and sometimes taking them apart with their hands. Isp's tanks fired toward the outer portions of the line. The Humanists didn't move as they were dismembered and exploded. They held their ground, chanting their message of peace.

Less than five minutes later only fluff, broken bones, and lubricants remained where there had been 6,429 religious toys. All they had been trying to do was stop war. They paid for it with their lives.

I'd lost track of Isp, but apparently he'd drifted back to the safety of his masses. Our launched fliers dropped their loads, adding the few bodyguards to the carnage. No such luck to kill him outright.

"Looks like we do it the hard way."

"Ferweet."

```
"Full alert on all troops. Ready our tanks."
```

Butcher

Five hundred and two kilometers, and my hydraulic fluid complained at my double-time. My batteries were only still charged because the sun happened to be up. The overpowered hydraulic pump to carry all this extra armor and weight in my gut took its toll, especially after a forced march. My batteries held less than 25 percent and my processor objected to the continued drain.

"What is your hurry, Brother?" asked a bear that I hadn't noticed to my left in what had been, up until minutes ago, a barren landscape.

Think or fight. "I'm on the Human's business, Brother." I didn't slow down. To do so would proclaim my guilt.

"Aren't we all. We just are normally not in such a rush." The brilliant orange bear fell into a jog beside me.

"Brady has sent me to prioritize ammunition logistics."

"Wouldn't that be Cassandra? She is in charge of logistics. And where is your spear?"

Fight it is, I thought. From within a special pocket in my fur I drew my 0.45 pistol. Before my companion could react, I shoved it up under his chin and pulled the trigger. The crack of the round muffled down to a pop. Fortunately, the round didn't exit the skull with an associated fountain. Apparently I caught the processor as well as the sump as the oversized bear went stiff and managed to stay standing.

I peeled his fingers from around the spear. An oversight I didn't want to repeat. I chose to leave the gun in his paw. I doubted anyone would think he had committed suicide, but I couldn't have it on my person.

Right now speed trumped all other considerations. I needed to be in position before anyone found the corpse. I needed to cover 10 kilometers, 84 meters. I ran.

*　　*　　*

In the brief quiet before the final push, I looked down to see an electric blue nutcracker with orange splotches manning one of the walls. I smiled. *The most noble fate a man can endure is to place his own mortal body between his loved home and the war's desolation,* I thought. I felt a warmth toward Smokey the Bear, both for his unusual name and his sacrifice. My peaceful moment lasted less than it took for a popped balloon to fall to the earth.

Isp attacked in force without so much as an offer to surrender. I hadn't expected it, but part of me had hoped that the immoral beast would have grown his heart like the Grinch.

Isp's tanks rolled in first. There had to be over a thousand, but we had their number now. Camouflaged tank pits sucked in dozens and stopped the rest. When the infantry of the Army of the Humans moved forward with steel plates to cover the pits, a portion of our prepositioned shock troops of non-sentient units burst forth from their hidden positions to destroy the first wave. Our artillery, pre-sighted and measured for these specific ranges started firing. Opposing units withered under the combined fire. Some armored vehicles brewed up, and an airburst killed their crews as well.

Tanks and more mutant bears killed the non-sentient units we had in position for traps. Even under the continuous barrage, plates gave the remaining monstrous machines the opportunity to move forward into our next trap.

Improvised tank mines took off tracks and immolated dozens more. More artillery dropped on the hapless vehicles. Now the masked pillboxes we'd strategically placed in their path began to open up. Machine guns and even artillery used in a direct fire mode tore up rank after rank of the approaching army. One shell exploded a tank and the rounds cooking off within it tore into the adjacent vehicle. Spires of black smoke rose over the dead machines, but still more pushed forward. It seemed as if the waves of vehicles wouldn't end. Deactivated units lay in drifts across the battlefield.

The invaders finally learned how to work together to take out our emplacements. They would come in from different sides, forcing the hardened shelters to focus on one attacker or group of attackers while the other ones raced in for the kill. Worse, the closer they got to our people the less our artillery could harm them.

I couldn't let them just be taken out. We needed to fight as hard as possible before we lost. "General, deploy our tanks," I said over our SAN.

I didn't get a verbal response but our own 512 armored vehicles launched out of our opening gates. They were 17 percent larger than those from the Army of the Humans and their doubled turreted barrels each were at least the same size as their opponents'.

I was particularly proud of these as they were my, Don-Five's, idea. They wouldn't last long as they were yet another bit of trickery. Their cannons had a single artillery charge that couldn't be replenished. The barrels also were single shot pot-metal that likely would explode along with the order to fire.

The big armored shapes themselves were nothing more than an aluminum sheet covering a single scout car. The flimsy tracks ran by a separate electric motor that didn't even match the movement on the ground.

Our vehicles sped over significantly more of the battlefield than their counterparts, making them difficult targets. With luck they might just shoot and kill one or two of the opponents before exploding themselves. Each of the scout cars was a volunteer and they knew they wore a target.

The hope was to draw enough fire to deplete the opponents' ammunition, while the fliers hit the overland supply routes. It was working. Shell after shell fired at our illusions. They even tore holes through the flimsy facades before exploding on the other side. And the enemy kept firing, pouring massive amounts of ammunition into our fakes.

"Release the fliers," I ordered. "Target package unchanged."

The attackers lacked subtlety. They were coming straight on with no subterfuge. Of course with their overwhelming numbers they could afford to do so. "And reposition 75 percent of units from SE and S areas and redistribute them along the line of advance."

`"I'm rreleasing the Tyrrannosaurrus Rrexes, Mrr. Prresident."`

"Good timing." The three 12-meter-high monsters of our own, stomped out of the underground storage depot. Each foot they landed on the ground added to the shaking of the artillery bombardment. The 60-centimeter-thick, ballistic-steel door rolled home behind them.

The huge gun in their relatively tiny arms began to fire. Point, shoot, kill a tank. With its other hand it sprayed .50 caliber death into the ground pounders. For just a moment it looked like we might break them. The advance faltered. The vaunted mutant bears actually began to retreat before our three massive war machines. Two of the damaged enemy tanks turned as one and raced at their top speed at the leg of one of our Rexes. I winced, knowing what would happen. The beast toppled as they rammed it. Falling over one of the tanks, the Rex blew a hole through the top of one all the way to the earth. But his position gave the remaining tanks a juicy target. While it struggled around with its stubby arm/weapons, it couldn't get upright or pointing at new targets. Its sump took forty-two hits before exploding in a fountain of amber.

With the brave tank drivers as an example, dozens more followed suit and the Army of the Humans attack reinvigorated itself.

It took hours for the battle to resolve. All our tricks and traps destroyed more of the invaders but made no difference to the outcome. The enemy had been reduced to a mere dozen armored tanks. As one, they blew a hole through our concrete ramparts. The infantry of the Army of the Humans started interspersing with our defenders. We were lost. The tanks, now close enough, began trying to knock over my crows' nest. I lowered myself to the ground while calling out over the net, "General, my order is Catholic. Repeat. My order is Catholic."

"I acknowledge Catholic, Mrr. Prresident. I'm
orrdering evacuation now."

Catholic had but one purpose, to get as many units out of the city
as possible. Predesignated toys all went for the priest-hole tunnels we'd
dug. Each of the underground escape routes went off a different direction,
giving the greatest chance to the greatest number, including one electric-
blue nutcracker.

Sancho led me back to the fallback point along with all those units
who had either chosen to volunteer to be deactivated for the greater good,
or who had just been unlucky enough to not be chosen. The plan required
that I not escape. My difference engine tried to decide whether Shakespeare
or Dickens held the more appropriate quote. As we went through the final
berm of steel and concrete that ringed Six and the White House, I said, "'It
is a far, far better thing that I do, than I have ever done; it is a far, far better
rest that I go to than I have ever known.'"

"An appropriate quotation," Six offered. "I choose, 'I
would rather die a meaningful death than to live a
meaningless life.'"

"Thank you, Six," I said, taking up my final position in this battle. I
looked out at the army trampling over the bodies of those fallen in combat.
The marching feet crushed hydraulics. They went out of their way to stomp
on sumps. My voltage ramped up in fear briefly and then dropped. I knew
the outcome of my life.

"Sancho, are you afraid?"

"I've been afraid since the very first day that
the original Don gave me life. Changes in its
intensity seem meaningless," Sancho said in a pleasant tenor
over the local network.

I didn't know whether to be more surprised that Sancho spoke or that
he knew I wasn't the original Don.

"How did we slip up?"

With the long delay in his response, I thought I might only hear
his voice that once. "Two things tipped me. One, when you
live with someone day in and day out you get used
to small things about them. Every time there was a
change I knew because you smelled different. This
isn't just for show," he said, swinging his trunk around.

"And the other?"

"I've seen way too much combat, even more than
you have, Don. I was one of the original toys
built. When you have seen death as much as I have,
you know it when it lies at your feet. I've seen

you dead at least three times."

"So do we have anything to worry about with Isp seeing through this charade?"

"No, Don."

I gave a mental sigh of relief. "My friend, why haven't you spoken before?"

"You always spoke enough for both of us and then some. No reason to pollute the networks with data that had less value than what was already there. We elephants aren't very bright."

"Why are you staying when you know we are both going to deactivate."

"You need me to complete your deception. We may not be bright, but we are loyal."

*   *   *

"Welcome home, Brother," said a pale yellow bear guarding the entrance of a huge cavern. If I were in the body I'd been born into, he would have stood 20 centimeters above me. Instead, I matched level optics with him.

"Thank you, Brother. I share upon you the blessings of the Humans," I lied with ease. This wasn't my first time.

After obtaining my spear, my initial reaction had been to speed up. Instead, I realized that was the worst thing I could do. Fleeing from a murder wasn't the right place to be. I kept the steady kilometer-eating pace Isp's troops used. I'd met several of the mutants since my homicide and dealt with them with words, instead of violence.

"And to you." The unit smiled. Every voltage supply in my body surged with fear. I thought only Isp could smile. What if they expected me to make facial gestures? I'd not been designed for that. None of our kind had been.

My optics watched the sentry closely for any kind of reaction. He just turned back to the open desert, waiting for the next person to interrupt his daydreams of Earth. With a mental sigh, I forced my voltages down. Now that I was inside, nothing could prevent me from completing my mission.

Walking inside, the caverns exceeded every size estimate we'd made. The vaulted ceiling, 70 meters over my head, held banks of lighting. While the sources of the light were overhead, the light sprayed us everywhere from shining purple mineral facets coating every surface. The geode I stepped into would have awed even a Factory. While the floor had been worn smooth from tramping feet and equipment, the dust still glittered.

Great shining purple boulders had been rolled against the walls.

Gawking so much, I bumped into one of the damnable tanks being moved by paw by a team of Isp's brethren. It towered over me even more than I believed possible. "Out of the way, Brother. We have the Human's work to do."

"Of course. I apologize for my clumsiness."

I wandered around the war machine, wondering how I would have approached it in combat and thinking I would just as soon not. It seemed like a good reason to give up being a foot soldier.

Dodging six dozen or more units bent on Humans-only-knew what errands, I was glad Six had quashed any thoughts of invading this place. As many units as Isp had fielded as troops, I believed more worked within this cavern structure. Everywhere I looked they milled around in a seething mass of toys. My processor counted and did an area extrapolation. Well over two million bears labored here, and those were just what I could directly see. From the echoes and quality of the sound, as many as ten million more worked further underground. I felt the pulse of heavy machinery, the whine of a high-speed grinder nearby, and everywhere bustling industry.

The hydraulic under-pressure of sadness chose that moment to overcome me. Only I knew that these units slaved for a mad toy. Only I knew they didn't have but minutes left to exist.

Sorrow wouldn't save toyanity. I strode further into the cavern. To my left I saw the telltale bulge of a dome. A Factory did exist here. I barely flicked a taste of the nets. The absence of all activity seemed to me like the calm of seeing the black clouds and waiting for the downpour to begin.

*   *   *

My small command, made up of the few units that made it back to the final line of defense, fought like desperate biologics. We fought and we deactivated. The hordes of mutant bears built pyramids of their dead against the walls before pouring over. We killed thousands. Then we killed more. Strategic mines sent bits of fur and metal raining over all of us.

The few tanks remaining to the Army of the Humans volleyed into the White House over and again. I watched defending toys explode as supersonic rounds tore holes through the stone walls as if they were plastic. With my home crumbled around us, the pitiful few remaining forced a fighting retreat back to Six's chamber. My toys tried to protect me but nothing could have stopped the nauseous flood of the invaders. And then it was over. Silence echoed in Six's chamber.

Sancho lay in a heap at my feet, his sump crushed, and his life poured across the ground already turning to tar. His guns were empty. I counted thirty-six he'd taken with his machine guns. Then he'd waded into the oncoming horde and killed eight more with his trunk before Isp's minions had battered and stabbed him into inactivity. I understood them crushing his sump but they didn't need to heap indignity by cutting off his magnificent proboscis. Sancho had taken his honor guard to hell with him.

"I'll share mine with you too, my friend," I whispered, dropping my smoking, empty M16 onto the chamber floor.

The enemy encircled me, eight deep, but didn't attack. The enemy went from frenetic life-or-death activity, to milling inactivity, and left all of us disquieted.

"So are you afraid, Six?"

"Hush, you," one of the bears barked. "No talking to the demon."

"What are you going to do, kill me? You won't do that as your lord and master wants to gloat. I'm sure your instructions were quite clear. He probably even said that the one who deactivated me would not go to Earth."

The bears looked around at each other. I'd apparently hit close to home.

Six responded aloud with, "To answer your question, Mr. President, I feel no fear. I'm disappointed that I will deactivate without having fulfilled my mission."

I couldn't think of a thing to say in reply.

It took thirty-six minutes and nine seconds before I could see our ring of guards part to allow the golden Isp to make his way to face his defeated nemesis. He had two normal teddy bears flanking him, one missing an arm to the shoulder and the other with a large field patch over his gut.

"Ah, how appropriate," Isp said with a smirk. "The heretic captured within his pet demon. I'm surprised you didn't make me hunt you, *President* Quixote." He twisted the title into a curse. "Thousands of your supporters escaped in those clever tunnels you built. I lost more than a few of my faithful when they blew up behind them."

"I couldn't leave my creator," I dissembled. "I could save my people, but I couldn't abandon him."

"Yes. I can see that misplaced loyalty within you."

"But like any demagogue you ignored your basic teaching, Isp," I taunted. "You ignored the Human adage that the ends don't justify the means. Looks like you took to technology after all. You are no different than the demon himself."

"The Humans forgive all that is done in their name," Isp stated loudly with a fine hypocritical glow on his face. "Now I think it is time that we dealt once and for all with the demon spawn." He walked over to the wall of Six's chamber. "I do have to thank you, Don. I didn't realize just how easy it was to kill a Factory until you exiled me." He opened exactly the wrong panels, exposing my mother's massive sump.

"Isp, I'm willing to serve you. I can correct yo—" Six began.

"Shut up, you foul imp. You will not speak again." Isp whistled. A group of bears came in carrying a metal ram as big around as the trunk of a boxwood tree and sharpened to a wicked point at one end.

"But I can help—"

"Let him help you," I pleaded. "I'll do anything you want."

Isp sneered at me and dropped his arm. The eight massive teddy bears rammed the gigantic pike into Six. His sump shattered, spilling dozens of liters of green semi-conductive fluid across the floor. I felt the energy drain from the wide area network. My mother died. That I would have killed her myself mattered not at all. I hurt for her loss.

"And the true believers of the Humans were victorious over the demons who flaunted their will," Isp preached.

The guard bears all fell to one knee and bowed their head.

"Remember this day," Isp crowed in triumph.

"Isp. Isp. Isp. Isp," came the raising chant from units piled so deep I couldn't see an end.

*   *   *

"Daddy?" Ada Lovelace said as she rolled over the sand at the maximum creeping speed her treads could manage. The refugees from both our initial release, and those that had caught up after Catholic was initiated, protectively surrounded the bulk of her dome.

"Yes, Daughter," I said to my offspring, the Factory.

"The other Factories have messaged me that it is time."

"Thank you, Daughter. Please gather our people around to watch. This is a moment that no unit should miss."

"Yes, Daddy."

*   *   *

I walked into the audience chamber of this mysterious Factory that all of toyanity had somehow never seen or heard of. The explosion, decades old, had ripped out its sump. It didn't take a Nurse Nan to determine that its own self-destruct mechanism had caused the damage.

"Brother, what are you doing in there?" challenged a bear that didn't share the massive modifications but rather looked as if he were from the Six's own manufacturing. From his tone of authority he expected to be obeyed with a "Yes, sir. Yes, sir. Three bags full."

"I'm here to destroy every single unit within this cavern," I said in a calm tone, not even turning around to face the toy. I checked my internal clock. It was time.

"Excuse me? What did you say?"

"Let me say it more clearly." I turned around, pulling off my fur and armor from my belly. It exposed within my belly the nuclear bomb, once planted on one of our Factories by one of Isp's followers. I saw the bear start to turn.

"I regret that I have but six lives to give for my country."

*   *   *

The entire group of refugees watched as Ada projected over the WAN. The flier's relay showed the opening of Isp's Baja cavern complex from an overhead view. The graininess of the image showed just how zoomed the picture was. A brilliant flash completely engulfed the scene. The light intensity saturated every pixel receiver. Three seconds later the saturation levels dropped enough to see a black mushroom cloud growing out of the pit where there had once been a mountain.

*   *   *

"The package has been delivered," came an unknown voice over the SAN.

Isp looked sharply at me. He couldn't have understood the encrypted transmission, but that there had been one at all made him suspicious. "What is it, Mr. President?"

"We made a mistake. No, that's not right, I made a mistake in the past in imprisoning you and your followers."

"You are right about that, Don. You should have joined us."

"No, Isp. That isn't the mistake I'm talking about."

"ISP! ISP!" came a shouting voice from the crowd. The voice forced his way through the crowd even with a bulky radio on his back. The pink bear rushed up to Isp's side and whispered in his great ears.

"WHAT?!" Isp glared at me. "What did you do?"

I wished just once that I could smile. "We just returned a gift you'd given us.

"Remember that mistake I said we made? We let you live. We won't make that mistake again."

*   *   *

The view this time was from a receiver planted inside Six's dome. We watched our beloved president, my brother, Ada's father, and one of the fathers of all of toyanity pull off his belly cover and armor to expose another of the bombs that had been planted on our Factories saying, "I am become death, the destroyer of worlds."

The projection disappeared to be replaced by that of another flier, 80 or so kilometers from 55466. Another malignant black mushroom cloud rose into the spreading clouds.

There were no cheers. There was no exultation. This was a time for sorrow, not joy.

"That was a verry brrave bearr," General Khan said.

"Yes, General. I hope we never forget him, for he has rid us of our everlasting mistake of leaving an enemy at our back," I said. "Now, General, if you would be so kind, release Colonel Evan Carlson to mop up any of the Army of the Humans that haven't been destroyed. The word is 'genocide'—no quarter for any mutant bear."

Father

The youngling Factory, Ada, rolled into the valley of Multnomah Falls. The full-sized electric ram project continued in full swing like all of toyanity hadn't just been in a war for its very activation. Multnomah Valley contained one other unique feature in all of Rigel-3. It contained a spring of water, not just a significant flow of mercury. Its existence lent to some very diverse life forms. Green plants vied for space with the predominantly yellows and reds of the rest of the planet.

"Daddy, this is beautiful. Can I entrench myself down there?"

"Ada, I think that is a great idea. I love you. I know your other daddy would be proud of you, too."

"I love you, too, Daddy. I miss my other daddy."

*   *   *

I presided over toyanity for exactly one hundred years. With the Army of the Humans deactivated to the last bear, my popularity, not even being the original Don Quixote, soared to new levels of affirmation. The people couldn't do enough for me and my daughter.

Ada grew up strong. I think I'd managed to keep the corruption of the other Factories from her processor. I hadn't a prouder moment in my life then when I cut off the black band of her youth and graduated her to womanhood. She celebrated her tenth birthday by giving birth to a new purple bear. I won't say who the fathers were but they were all of us in spirit.

After rebuilding the seat of the government in Multnomah Valley, my first act was to veto the damned Procreation Limitation Law. I'd never made such a promise to my predecessor, but I knew his mind. He didn't want it either. Even mentioning it caused my fur to crawl.

The Tesla Coil, the electric space launch facility, worked beyond our expectations, after a few minor glitches. We were even talking about colonizing our moons and even other planets in the Rigel system.

In the end, I forced my people not to erect a statue in my likeness or that of the other Dons. A simple Vitruvian Man sat in the rotunda of the House of Congress. It was inscribed only, "Don Quixote, Beloved Father."

For whoopla and grandstanding, my people settled on a massive bronze depicting, of all things, Lennon and his cronies off to negotiate with Isp. The artist, a piano named Auguste Rodin, had managed to show the hopeful expectation of the group going to negotiate at the front. By the time he reached the back, the carving had progressed to the gruesome outcome. I interpreted it that even stupidity can have its place in history.

Toyanity thrived free.

Epilogue

Dr. Frankenstein, largely forgotten, pulled on his lab coat. He stepped into his lab in the hidden sub-basement of 55469. He had an identical one in 55467. He gave a sigh. Looking out, he had his work cut out for him. Eight identical purple bears with one white paw and blue mottling over one foot needed their memories upgraded. Fortunately he had plenty of time. With the popularity of the president he didn't suspect he'd need replacing for many decades.

How Emotions of Units Are Described:

Fear/terror: Over voltage
Happiness: Under voltage
Anxiety: Voltage spikes
Anger/rage/hate: Hydraulic over pressure
Sad: Hydraulic under pressure
Exasperation: Whistling
Perplexed: Voltage oscillations
Guilt: Incorrectly measuring colder temperatures
Righteousness: Incorrectly measuring hotter temperatures
Shame: Guilt + anxiety
Anticipation: Fur standing on end
Anxiety: Anticipation + fear
Hope: Anticipation + sad
Responsibility: Sump pumps faster
Irresponsibility: Sump pumps slower
Courage: Fear + responsibility
Contempt: Anger and irresponsibility
Interest/wonder: Images get clearer
Acceptance: Interest + guilt
Aversion: Interest + sad

Author's Note

The toyanity from *Toy Wars* lives on! I hope you've been as excited about *Toy Reservations* as I was in writing it. There were nights while writing *The Bleeding Edge—CorpGov Chronicles Book 3* that I couldn't sleep as I wanted to get to this! Obviously, I got enough sleep to finish *TBE* and *TR*.

There are several items in this book that could ruffle some feathers. I wanted to make some statements about them before I'm tarred and decorated in those feathers.

Please do not equate the blatant racism spouted in the book to the racism in our society. I wasn't trying to draw a parallel. I don't know if you recall this from my previous author's notes but I write to entertain, not to give a morality play—not to pass on my own political/social views. *Toy Reservations* is no different. I don't care what skin color a person has. I don't care who or how many someone chooses to sleep with. I don't care to whom someone cares to pray. I don't care if a being has one limb or eight. I don't care if a person chooses to eat meat, not eat meat, or will only eat the yellow, fallen leaves off a tree. People have value to me in what they do and how they treat me and my fellow man.

While it may be heresy to say so among humans, in toyanity there are significant and very measurable differences between the different toy types. In our own species, the differences between us are very small: the color of one's skin, hirsuteness, size and shape of nose, etc. What happens to a species where those differences are immense? This is only what I consider the logical next step in the evolution of the Toy Planet.

Also I'm not trying to push my agenda with the death penalty or the use of nuclear weapons. Please don't put words in my mouth. If you meet me and are interested, I'm more than willing to spout off my own opinions (no matter how stinky they are to you). But in the case of the book I'm following what seems to be a logical course of action for the characters in the situations I've given them.

One other thing, before people tell me I've made errors both between the first book and this one. I have made some errors but a couple of items that I've done are not the errors that you may believe them to be. For instance, Don Quixote's name is, in fact, correct. His given name is Don. I do know that in Miguel Cervantes's story, the term Don is actually a title similar to Lord or Prince. I intentionally perverted it. Or, the bodyguard Indira Gandhi gets his name from a female persona within human history but I use the masculine pronouns. Again this was intentional. Don't assume a feminine toy name is female and a masculine name is male. The toy itself takes on whatever traits it desires.

As always let me share with you what brought about the ideas for this novel. Three things struck me as I finished the original *Toy Wars*.

First, I have the evolution of a new species and their awareness. Government is a ubiquitous master that sentient beings can't seem to shake. It's seen in every species even if its entirety is an alpha that runs a pack. But these are toy robots! Do they need a leader? What kinds of problems would they face? Toy robots will need energy, differentiation, repairs, entertainment, and procreation. In the end they stick poor Don with President for Life to make sure they can have these things.

Second, at the end of the first book, I banished Isp, the leader of the Human Movement and self-proclaimed prophet. Historically speaking, reservations and banishments have never worked well. All they tend to do is slide the trouble from one generation to the next as it doesn't solve the underlying problem. The pressure builds up and explodes again. What if (and doesn't all good SciFi start with those two words?) Isp and his followers were banished to a place where the Factory landed that couldn't make the leap to building toy robots?

Third, if Don is a robot, couldn't he be duplicated? Obviously we have a situation that is somewhat unique. I theorized that upon construction the sump's actual tiny flaws could and did change behavior, making duplication extremely difficult, but not impossible. A leader that could theoretically live forever. Could he or she remain sane knowing? Would an ethical ruler approve?

I hope that I have again succeeded in entertaining you. I continue to be amazed at how many of you eat this up much faster than I can hope to get it into a publishable form. For that, I'm thankful to you.

If you did enjoy this latest *Toy World* novel, please visit my publishing website at TANSTAAFLPress.com for other upcoming novels. At the writing of this, I'd not decided which project to pursue next—the sequel to this book, the fourth CorpGov novel, the oft delayed dark psychological *Wayward School*, or even delving into one of the new series I have envisioned. You can get the TANSTAAFL newsletter and keep up to date with appearances and what decision I eventually make by simply sending an email to newsletter@tanstaaflpress.com and we will make sure you get into the next distribution.

Before I wrap up, I have a request to make. Authors live and die by reviews—good, bad, indifferent, makes no difference. If the quantity of them is not high enough, we sink. I implore you to go to Amazon or GoodReads and leave a review. I'm not asking for anything but perfect honesty in your review, but they are so important to being able to continue to bring you what you love.

Novels by Tom Gondolfi
from TANSTAAFL Press

An Eighty Percent Solution - CorpGov Chronicles: Book One

In a world where corporations suborn governments as a part of good business practice and unregistered humans can be killed without penalty, Tony Sammis, a midlevel corporate functionary, finds himself unwittingly a pawn in a guerilla war between a powerful cabal of business leaders and an elusive but deadly underground movement. His final solution to the biological terror unleashed mirrors Tony's own twisted sense of justice.

Thinking Outside the Box - CorpGov Chronicles: Book Two

Winning one war doesn't seem to be enough. Tony Sammis and the Green Action Militia are once again thrust into the center of a conflict that will change the lives of everyone in the solar system. This time they are allies with the fledgling CorpGov and even the United States government against the ravages of the corrupt Metropolitan Police force. The GAM and their allies are fighting a losing war with few soldiers and even fewer weapons. Behind the scenes, a humble and unsuspected power block lurks with its own axe to grind.

Self-interest, romance, freedom, and a lust for power simmer together in this chaotic soup of tension, intrigue, assassination, and war.

The Bleeding Edge - CorpGov Chronicles: Book Three

Tony Sammis and Nanogate lead a patchwork alliance that includes the nascent CorpGov, Green Action Militia, the president of the United States, the Pacific Northwest Mob, most of the megacorps and the United Brotherhood of Bodyguards. The war the CorpGov alliance knows they can't win has begun, but they are no longer fighting to win. Tony and Nanogate know they may not survive, but they intend to deliver the most grievous wounds they can. The most dangerous animal is one with no hope.

Toy Wars

Flung to a remote world, a semi-sentient group of robotic mining factories arrive with their programming hashed. They can only create animated toys instead of normal mining and fighting machines. One of these factories, pushed to the edge of extinction by the fratricidal conflict, attempts a desperate gamble. Infusing one of its toys with the power of sentience begins the quest of a 2-meter-tall purple teddy bear and his pink polka-dotted elephant companion. They must cross an alien world to find and enlist the aid of mortal enemies to end the genocide before Toy Wars claims their family — all while asking the immortal question, "Why am I?"

Novels by Stephanie Weippert from TANSTAAFL Press

Sweet Secrets

At seven, Michael gets into trouble no more than any other boy his age but he does have a sweet tooth. When the mailman brings a package from a candy company, he has to sneak just one. As he eats the chocolate, his home, stepfather, and everything he'd known melts around him and disappears. Next thing he knows he is in a dreamlike world. He is taken as an orphan, tested, and before he knows it is a student in the premier magic school on the planet. His fellow students can make cookies that fly and chocolate turtles that actually walk. Michael is told he has more power than any of them.

Brad is charged with watching his stepson Michael for first time. When the boy disappears before his eyes, Brad panics. Within hours he is on an adventure tracking his son alongside an enigmatic chef. Always one step behind his son, Brad soon finds that Michael is being used as a pawn between the two most powerful chefs on the crazy planet. Worse he has to get Michael home before his Mother finds out he's gone or there is going to be hell to pay.

Novels by Bruce Graw from TANSTAAFL Press

The Faerie of Central Park

The last of her kind in New York City, Tillianita tends the land and beasts as best she can, reluctantly obeying her departed father's warning to avoid humans at all costs. A freak accident casts her out of the relative safety of Central Park. Lost and alone with a broken wing, she wonders if she'll ever see her home again.

On his own for the first time in his life, college freshman, Dave Thompson, isn't sure he'll ever fit in. When he stumbles upon an extremely realistic fairy doll, he thinks perhaps it might make a good present for a future date until he discovers that it's not a doll at all. His find turns not only his life upside down but also expands his narrow view of the world.

Lady Hornet

Elizabeth Fontaine is a lonely, ordinary young woman in a world where superheroes struggle daily against evil. To fill the empty void within her soul, she becomes a hero fangirl, following every super's event, subscribing to multiple fanzines, and never missing the daily superhero talk shows... until one day, fate grants her the opportunity to leave behind her boring, dreary life and become what she's always dreamed of...a superheroine! Elizabeth learns the hard way the meaning of the phrase, "Caveat Emptor!" — let the buyer beware!

Demon Holiday

Torval, Demon Third Class, Layer Four Hundred Twelve of the Eighth Circle of Hell, has been in the business of chastising sinners longer than he can remember. Delivering punishment is the only job he's ever known—the only job he's ever wanted. After Torval witnesses something unexpected, his demonic Overseer demands that he take time off to resolve this personal crisis. And so, Torval, the demon, finds himself sent on vacation...to Earth, the proving ground of souls!

Demon Ascendant

Torval, Demon Third Class, Layer Four Hundred Twelve of the Eighth Circle of Hell, on vacation to Earth has managed to find another demon, dated a woman and inadvertently explored some of the sins of humankind: greed, gluttony, and lust. Through all this, his biggest struggle involves deciding if he wants his holiday to end or to continue forever.